UNTIL FOREVER ENDS

BEAUTY IN LIES BOOK TWO

ADELAIDE FORREST

D1738339

Proofreading by Light Hand Proofreading

❀ Created with Vellum

ABOUT THE AUTHOR

Adelaide lives in her tiny house with her husband and two rambunctious kids. When she's not chasing all three of them and her dog around the house, she spends all her free time writing and adding to the hoard of plots stored on her bookshelf and hard-drive.

She always wanted to write, and did from the time she was ten and wrote her first full-length fantasy novel. The subject matter has changed over the years, but that passion for writing never went away.

She has a background in Psychology and working with horses, but Adelaide began her publishing journey in February 2020 and never looked back.

For more information, please visit Adelaide's website or subscribe to her newsletter.

CONTENT & TRIGGER WARNINGS

Beauty in Lies is a DARK mafia romance series dealing with topics that some readers may find offensive or triggering. Readers of Adelaide Forrest's Bellandi Crime Syndicate series should note that this series is much darker.

Please keep in mind the following list WILL contain specifics about the ENTIRE series and may spoil certain plot elements. Please avoid the next page if you don't wish to know specifics.

The following scenarios are all present in the Beauty in Lies series. This list may be added to over time.

• Situations involving dubious, questionable, or nonconsent
  • 13 Year Age gap, with both characters being of legal age at the time a physical relationship forms.
  • Forced Pregnancy
  • Branding
  • Forced Marriage under threat of death & violence
  • VERY graphic violence, torture, and murder
  • Drug use, attempted date rape, and dubious situations while under the influence
  • Kidnapping/Captive Scenarios

*S*he'd left me.

Nothing in our lives would ever change the fact that she'd tried to leave. That she'd chosen her mundane life over the passionate embrace I offered her. I couldn't remember a time something had affected me powerfully enough that rage blazed inside me so fiercely it tempted me to set the world on fire.

If I couldn't have her, no one would. I'd kill us both before I ever let her walk away.

I ignored the nervous chatter of the three brothers at my heels, hefting Isa higher into my arms and carrying her down the stairs to the lower level of my yacht where the McLaren waited for us. I didn't dare to look down at her as I went. The sight of her deceptively innocent face would only torture me if I did.

Joaquin hurried around me and hauled the passenger side door open as I neared it. Despite my best intentions, I caught sight of Isa's beautiful face as I gently rested her in the seat. Even with anger simmering in my veins, I took the moment to study her relaxed and peaceful features.

When she woke up, she'd hate me. When she woke up, everything would change for her.

I stroked a thumb over her cheekbone, wishing I could feel her eyes on mine one more time before they hardened with the truth of her new reality.

I didn't know what was coming. I had no way of predicting how Isa would react when she awoke as my prisoner. But the murky waters ahead of us would probably more closely resemble the Chicago River than the Mediterranean where Isa had fallen in love with me.

Stepping back with a heavy sigh, I drew my shoulders tight and closed the door to seal her inside. Over an hour had passed since we'd left Ibiza in the early morning. Over an hour where she'd slept next to me, and I was forced to wonder if she dreamt of me.

If I was still the handsome man she'd met in Ibiza, or if she finally saw the nightmare who would consume her.

I made my way to the driver's side. My stare was stern on the man who took too long to open the hatch and give me a surface to drive on over the gap between the yacht and the marina dock. As I lowered myself inside, he finally gave me a nervous nod that it was safe to make my exit.

My home island loomed in front of me, the hilly terrain in the background beckoning me forward. In the distance, the rooftop edges of the main house could be seen. The terracotta Mediterranean style was vastly different from the pine trees that covered the hillside and offered the compound where my people lived in privacy.

The McLaren started up with a purr; the sound vibrating off the inside of the yacht as I navigated my way onto the dock and took the winding road up the hill to the house. The drive was short, punctuated only by my anger and the knowledge of what came next.

Of the start of showing Isa exactly what her new life would be.

A sense of relief lurked beneath my rage, knowing that I wouldn't need to disguise my impulses in the interest of making Isa love me. She'd see the real monster, not just hints of him, and know she'd made the wrong choice.

She should have loved the man; instead, she would be possessed by her worst nightmare.

Pulling up in front of the main house, I threw the car into park and hurried out the driver's side. Alejandro and Regina stood on the front step with their faces drawn into tight smiles. I hadn't bothered to inform them of the circumstances of our arrival, beyond ordering Regina to have Dr. Garcia ready with the items he and I had discussed before my departure.

It'd been meant to be a worst-case scenario, a contingency, but I hadn't known just how much the failure would hurt.

"*Mi hijo*," Regina said, stepping forward as if to hug me. I ignored her, opening the passenger side and watching as her eyes dropped to Isa's unconscious form. The smile dropped off her face as I pulled Isa from the vehicle, cradling her limp body in my arms and striding past Regina and Alejandro's gaping faces to carry her to our bedroom.

To put her exactly where she belonged.

"*Joder*," Alejandro cursed at my back.

"*Mi hijo*, is she alright?" Regina asked, the concern in her voice making me falter in my steps. "She's bleeding." I glanced down at Isa's torn knees, a moment of something akin to regret filling me before I spun to level Regina with a glare.

"She made her choice. And I made mine."

Regina touched a hand to her mouth as her bottom lip

trembled, but I couldn't be bothered to spare a moment for her delicate sensibilities. They'd both always known what would come to Isa if she didn't choose me.

They'd just hoped it wouldn't become necessary.

Turning, I made my way down the hall to the bedroom where Dr. Garcia waited. He took one look at Isa and heaved a disappointed sigh. He'd made himself very clear in our conversations that what I asked of him went against his purpose, that it was unethical in a way he wasn't comfortable with. He'd do it anyway, if he valued having a head on his shoulders.

I found most men did.

Moving inside the open door, I gently laid Isa on the bed. Her chocolate hair spread over the white bedding as her head tilted to the side on the pillow.

"Señor Ibarra, perhaps there's another way," Dr. Garcia said.

"There's not," I snapped, taking my eyes off Isa's peaceful face to carefully turn her to lie on her stomach. Grabbing the knife from my nightstand, I slit the fabric of the back of her dress to her waist, revealing her smooth skin to the eyes of another man even though I hated every moment of it. I suppressed the urge to murder him for laying eyes on skin that should have been for me, even knowing it was no more than a man would see when *mi princesa* went for a swim in the pool. The fact that she was unconscious and finally in my bed worsened the natural instinct I felt to lock her away from everyone else.

But his involvement was a necessary evil that I wouldn't regret should Isa decide to do something stupid when she woke up naked in my bed and remembered who I was.

When she remembered what I'd done.

He sighed, nodding his head as he fiddled with the

syringe to prepare Isa's first tracker. I unclasped her bra, baring the space between her shoulder blades for him to find the perfect position.

Somewhere she couldn't cut it out without help.

She didn't move as he inserted the first tracker. Didn't so much as twitch as he inserted another one into her arm, just above her right elbow.

"I can convince myself that the trackers might save her life," he said, grabbing the other syringe from his bag. I turned Isa from her stomach to her back, deliberately attempting to ignore the advice that was coming. "But not this, Señor Ibarra. I beg you to reconsider making this choice for her. Señora Adamik is young. She may come around to the idea of children in her own time."

"I don't know what I ever said to make you think I gave a single fuck about your opinion, Doctor," I said mockingly.

He bit his lower lip, watching as I carefully cut the fabric away from Isa's stomach. Her dress was nothing but a pile of scraps covering the most intimate parts of her body, but I couldn't force myself to reveal her to another man more than absolutely necessary. If I'd felt comfortable handling the trackers and her fertility shot on my own, I would have.

He delivered the injection with cool professionalism, then stepped back and gathered his things. A glance to his face showed all the confliction there, the evidence of his horror at being involved in my plans for Isa. Leaving without another word, he closed the door behind him and left me to my privacy with *mi princesa*.

I sighed, standing from the bed and making my way into the master bathroom to run a warm bath. I stripped off my clothes while I waited, glancing back at the bed where Isa hadn't moved since I'd left her. Turning off the water, I went back to the bedroom and stripped off her dress with gentler motions than felt natural. In spite of the rage simmering in my blood as though I stood in the pits of Hell itself, my touch on Isa remained gentle. I couldn't bring myself to hurt her while she slept.

All I wanted was to mark her. To claim her as mine. But she'd be awake when that time came. She'd be aware of everything I did to her and know where she'd gone so terribly wrong.

Once she was naked, I drew her into my arms again and carefully maneuvered the two of us into the tub. Her back pressed against my chest, her head resting on my shoulder as she slept. I let the water do most of the work for me, cleaning her body of the dirt that she'd collected in her scuffles along the streets of Ibiza as she fled. The water turned a light pink as it washed away the dried blood from her skin, making it so the very essence of her surrounded me in a halo of pain.

I lost track of how long I sat there with her in my arms, gently working a washcloth over her wounds to finish cleaning them. I thought back to the night when I'd told her I knew how many freckles she had and held her in a similar way. I tormented myself, wondering if all the while she'd rested in my arms, she'd been thinking of the time after she left me.

If she'd been imagining her life back home, when all I could think about was the fact that she *was* my home.

When I finally felt like she'd soaked long enough, I pulled her from the tub and dried the both of us off to the best of my ability. Laying her out on the bed, I examined the wounds on her hands and knees to ensure they'd come clean and would heal properly.

Her body was pliant beneath me as I crawled into the bed beside her, stroking a hand over her stomach where the fertility shot had pierced her skin. The muscles twitched in reaction, signaling her pending return to reality.

I nudged her legs apart with my hand, staring down at the pink flesh between her thighs in a moment where her insecurity with her body couldn't hinder my observations of her body. I touched a finger to the freckle just below her belly button, gliding my hand lower slowly and watching her face for any reaction.

She didn't stir, her eyelashes remaining fully closed as my finger slid through her lips and bumped against her clit. I cupped her sex in my hand, staring down at her in awe and wondering how she ever took me inside her.

A glance back to her face confirmed she still hadn't awoken from the last clinging embrace of the sedative, slumbering peacefully as I violated her in a way I knew she would condemn when she discovered the truth.

And I had every intention of making sure she knew I'd touched her while she slept.

That she was mine to do with as I pleased, and the boundaries that would have existed in a normal relationship would never apply to us.

I maneuvered my body over her leg, placing my face at eye level with her pussy and lifting her knees up to spread her open wider. Running my tongue between her folds, I licked her from her entrance to her clit and back again.

Compelled with the need to ensure she dreamt of me, my fingers dug into her hip bones. Even in sleep, Isa wouldn't be free of me. Not ever again.

My touch turned bruising as my rage consumed me. With the reminder that *mi princesa* tried to leave me. That she'd tried to walk away from me.

Never again to know my mouth on her. Never again to know what it was to have my cock inside her.

I dragged my lips over her pussy and to her thigh, sinking my teeth into the flesh of her leg and reveling in the tiny whimper she released in her sleep. The sight of my bite mark on her skin appeased me slightly. I stared at it and blew a breath against her clit as I watched her, leaning forward to press the flat of my tongue to her firmly. I worked her over without mercy in a way that would have made her scream had she been awake.

Her leg twitched beside my head, the sensation working to draw her from the haze. Sealing my mouth around her clit, I sucked gently until her stomach trembled with her need to come.

Her eyelashes fluttered, her lids remaining closed despite the pull of my mouth on her pussy, trying to draw her from her slumber. I pulled her clit into my mouth, sucking on it with steady and rhythmic pulses until her stomach caved in.

The breath caught in her lungs and her legs tried to tighten around my head involuntarily as she came on my tongue. I watched as her lashes fluttered one last time and her legs relaxed around me, positioning myself to kneel between her legs as I took my cock in hand.

Staring at the wet and swollen flesh between her legs, I stroked myself furiously. Anger that she hadn't woken up yet consumed me, driving me forward with the need to be inside her.

But I wanted to look her in the eyes the first time her nightmare fucked her. I wanted her to know exactly who owned her for the first time. The thought of the shock in her pretty multicolored eyes drove me over the edge, and I shot my release all over her pussy and lower stomach with a ragged groan.

I bit my lip as I looked down at the cum staining her

skin, glistening on her and marking me as hers. I wanted to stare at it while I waited for her to wake up, but the goosebumps on her arms compelled me to pull the sheet over her and hide her body from my view.

I grabbed a pair of shorts from the closet, tugging them on and settling into the chair beside the bed to watch her until she woke up and remembered where she was.

My cock throbbed with the need to be inside her, uncaring about the release I'd just painted on her skin.

I'd waited sixteen months to have her. I could wait another hour to truly make her mine.

2

*M*y head throbbed, a dull ache that pulled me from the depths of a vague memory. The feel of a man's hand in mine, the rough skin of his palm wrapped around me, tugged at me from the past. It tried to pull me under, tried to take me back to the last place I ever wanted to remember.

But the pain in my head pushed the demons back, forcing me to open my eyes with a quiet groan that rattled in my dry throat. I touched a hand to my forehead as I blinked up at the white linen fabric hanging like a canopy from the bed frame above me. Forcing myself to sit up slowly, I licked my lips as I tried to remember where I'd fallen asleep.

Disorientation hit me when I didn't recognize the room, but the shimmering Mediterranean off the side of the balcony was unmistakable. The room around me just wasn't the suite I'd shared with Rafe.

Memories of the night before tormented me in a sudden flash, my bones aching with the fear that pulsed through me. I gasped as my lungs filled with a sudden shock of air, my hand flying up to my neck to touch the sore spot where the needle had pierced my skin. My heartbeat thudded relentlessly, making it hard to breathe past the panic that seized me as I glanced down at where the sheet had fallen to my waist. I grabbed it, pulling it back up to cover my bare breasts. The space between my thighs felt wet as I shifted my legs, reaching under the blanket to touch myself in horror.

My hand touched a dried substance on my stomach, my entire body freezing solid as I realized the implication of what it must be. A wet dream, even a drug-induced one, wouldn't paint my stomach with my own release.

My other hand covered my mouth as I swallowed back the urge to be sick, pushing past the violation to take in my other injuries. The reality of what had happened to me while I slept could consume me later, after I found a way to safety.

After I was away from the man who I'd thought I'd known but could never have suspected the truth of his deception. Of who he really was and what he might be capable.

Everything hurt—the consequences of my flight through Ibiza Town in the middle of the night. I looked to my left as I swung my legs over the edge of the bed as slowly as I could, determined not to make a sound.

Rafael's shocking eyes met mine, cold fury in them as he leaned his elbows on his knees and watched me like the predator he was. Silent and deadly, studying me as I froze in place. I bit my bottom lip as I considered my options, unable to take my eyes off his. I didn't dare to turn my back on him after what he'd done. Licking my lips again, I fought to find the words to speak to him.

To find a way to communicate with the man I'd loved, and not the monster he'd become when I left him.

"Rafe," I murmured, my voice trembling with a quiet plea. He lifted his elbows off his knees, sitting back in his chair and staring at me in the bed with that cruel tilt to his head.

"Princesa," he returned. Shoving off the arms of his chair, he stood and stepped toward me until he was directly in front of me. He towered over me, suddenly seeming even taller than he'd ever been before. He held out a hand, watching me to see if I accepted it.

It felt like a test, like one last chance to appease the nightmare simmering beneath his skin. One last chance to survive with the pieces of me intact, but I couldn't take it.

I couldn't force myself to take that hand. Not after what he'd done and not knowing the answers to all the questions I had.

"Why am I naked?" I asked instead, ignoring what I knew would probably be the last kindness he showed me. The cold fury on his face faded as he dropped the hand to his side, replaced by the burning infernos of Hell as his nostrils flared and he ground his teeth.

His intense eyes burned into mine, a quiet warning in the silence before he growled his answer. "Because you're mine."

"Did you touch me?" I whispered, my bottom lip trembling as I watched the cold smirk transform his face into something crafted from my most beautiful nightmares.

"I think we both know the answer to that," he said, stretching up a hand to catch a lock of my hair in his grip and twirl it thoughtfully. "Or was my cum on your body not enough of a clue for you?"

"Why are you doing this?" I asked, a sob catching in my throat as I looked around the room in fear. "Where are we?"

"We're home," he said, releasing my hair but refusing to

back away from where he stood. It was too close for a conversation, as he practically breathed on top of me and I had to tip my head back at an unnatural angle to look up at him. I shifted back in the bed, desperately needing to put space between us.

I moved slowly, sensing that fast movements would be provoking to the predator watching me like he would devour me at any moment. Fear skittered down my spine when his hand twitched at his side as I moved, looking like he wanted nothing more than to reach out and grab me so that I couldn't have that desperately needed space. He refrained, but somehow I knew it was a temporary reprieve.

"This isn't my home," I whispered, staring up at him as I fought to swallow around my parched throat.

"It is now." He reached over to the nightstand, grabbing a water bottle and twisting off the cap. It was half empty already, and I stared at it for a moment before shaking my head.

As much as I wanted that water, I didn't trust it.

"If I wanted you drugged, you'd be drugged, Isa," he said, jabbing the water in my direction. "I don't need to hide it in your water like a coward when I can just inject it straight into your pretty little neck."

I swallowed, taking the water with a muffled whimper and tossing back the entirety of it.

"I just want to go home. I don't know anything, and I promise I won't tell anyone about you. I swear it, Rafe. Please," I begged. His right knee touched the very edge of the bed as he took the empty bottle from my hands and tossed it to the side. Drawing my knees up into my chest, I tried to make myself as small as possible as I looked away from him and fought back the trembling in my body.

As I pushed back the tears burning my throat and stinging my eyes.

"I know what Chloe told you," he said as his second knee touched the mattress. He put a palm to either side of my feet, leaning forward like he prowled toward his dinner as he came closer and closer in my peripheral vision.

"Are Chloe and Hugo okay?" I asked, daring a look at him. If me knowing even the barest of details about the things he'd done had led to my abduction when he'd spent days with me, what would happen to the virtual strangers who actually spoke of his crimes?

"They're fine. For now," he said, drawing a distressed gasp from my lips. "Whether they remain that way depends entirely upon you." I didn't dare to ask what I'd have to do to keep them safe. What would he expect of me in return for sparing my friends' lives?

"Is it true?" I asked instead. "What Chloe said?" Darkness swirled in his bright gaze, like a monster from the depths coming to claim the victim who'd gotten away.

"You asked me a question," he murmured, his cruel smirk tipping his lips up at the edge as he stared back at me in challenge. "Are you finally ready for the answer?"

I drew in a pained gasp, knowing that I would never be ready. But waking up naked in his bed after being kidnapped off the streets of Ibiza meant that I was out of time. I couldn't bury my head in the sand when the reality of the kind of man he was stared me right in the face.

"Yes," I answered, ignoring the pit in my stomach that warned me to pull the covers over my head. The part of me that wanted nothing more than to pretend my nightmare wasn't happening.

That I hadn't fallen in love with an irredeemable monster.

"She told you I'm a murderer," he said, stretching out one of those hands to tuck a stray lock of bed head behind my ear. The callous of his thumb touched my face, trailing from my ear down to my lips to tug the flesh of it to the side as he stared at my mouth. "It isn't untrue," he said. The odd wording made a moment of hope bloom in my chest—foolishly, because whether it was true or not, the way he'd terrified me and abducted me would never be acceptable. "But your friend has no idea what I've done. Murderer only scratches the surface of the man I am, Princesa. I've lost count of the number of lives I've claimed." If there'd been food in my stomach, I might have been sick.

"I let you inside me," I whimpered.

He smiled at me. "You did. You even let me inside you when I came back last night after killing a man at *Lotus*," he said, his voice dropping lower as he spoke the words. Even in the horrifying circumstances, the cadence of his voice was like the sweetest torment, drawing me deeper into his web.

I wanted to run away. I should have tried. But something in him kept me rooted to the spot and desperate to keep his eyes on mine. Like a deer stuck in the headlights, I couldn't look away from the devastating beauty that was Rafael Ibarra.

He was the worst of me, the worst of humanity, and he called to the demons hiding within my soul. But I couldn't let him have me, no matter how much I wanted to love the monster like I loved the man.

He stood in the way of me going home, of me getting back to the family that needed me and doing what was expected of me. He'd be the reason they worried about me, and potentially, never knew what happened to me.

He'd terrified me, *hurt* me, and stolen me off the streets.

All I wanted was to go home.

He dropped his hand from my mouth, waiting for me to make a move or say something in response to his dark confession. He'd touched me with the blood of a murder on his hands, even if it hadn't been there literally. He'd sullied me with his touch, tormented me with his darkness.

I didn't move for a moment, staring back at him. Then, with the sudden ferocity of a woman fighting for her life, I kicked my legs out at him. One caught him in the thigh, the other in the stomach, and I propelled myself across the bed as I twisted my limbs and fought to get away. He grunted and rocked back, nearly faltering off the side of the bed with the force of my kick.

He moved faster than should have been possible, recovering quickly as a hand came down in a hard slap to my ass while I dove for the edge of the bed. I didn't care that I'd tumble off it face first, only that the other side of the bed was farther away from him.

Away from the arms that wanted to lure me back into his possession and trap me there forever. I screamed, the shrill sound echoing through the bedroom as he grabbed a fistful of hair and pulled me back with it.

My scalp exploded in pain, his grip threatening to rip it from my head as I brought both hands up to try to pry his fingers off. He focused on dragging my body back across the bed, laying his weight across mine to trap me while I whimpered in pain. Only when he had me pinned did he loosen his grip, letting me breathe as the burning in my scalp began to fade.

"That—" He paused, using the more relaxed grip on my hair to turn my head to the side. He kissed my cheekbone, holding me still for his assault as his lips formed words against my skin. "Was very foolish, Princesa."

"Get off of me," I ordered, the steel to my voice surprising even me. The trembling I'd expected faded, erased by the potential violence about to come for me.

For us.

I knew if he did what the hard erection pressed against the flesh of my ass promised, I'd never be the same. I knew that even though my brain knew I should hate it and him, my body would feel differently.

He called to the darkest perversions inside of me, taking and claiming them as his. He knew the hints of my desires, the secrets I wanted to hide from everyone. There was no one, aside from Rafael, who knew even the barest concept that they existed, and he would use them to his advantage. Even the knowledge that he'd touched me while I slept, that he'd painted my skin with his cum, didn't horrify me in the way it should have. The darkest part of me liked that he'd marked me in such a primal way.

If it had been anyone else, I'd have been too traumatized to function. But with Rafael, it somehow just made sense.

"I don't think that's what you want," Rafael said with a chuckle as his breath touched my cheek. His voice was a soft murmur, a tone that should have been sweet. Instead, all it did was promise to corrupt me with his evil.

To taint me and make me his.

He wrapped his free hand around, sliding it between the mattress and my body to touch my lower belly. I jolted in his grip, struggling to get away from the touch that I knew would become invading if I didn't get away.

A tear fell free, making a lone path down my face that he leaned forward and licked off my cheek. "Please don't do this," I begged, trying to shake my head no. He ignored the plea and slid his hand further down my belly. Over the line where my underwear should have been if he hadn't stripped me naked while I slept. Over the very center of my woman-hood, until he slid a finger between my lips and bumped it against my clit. With my legs spread around his hips, he moved through me smoothly until his finger brushed up against my entrance.

"I don't think my pussy wants me to stop, Princesa," he murmured, gliding his finger inside of me. Like the trai-torous thing it was, he met no resistance as he pressed all the way inside me. Not even as he added a second finger, pumping them in and out of me slowly because of the restriction of my weight on top of his hand. "Look me in the eye and tell me you don't want me," he said. "If you can do that without lying, I'll give you clothes."

The arrogance in his voice infuriated me to no end, driving me mad with the need to prove him wrong. Glaring at him from the one eye where I could see him, I forced my lips to form the words. As he leaned further into my space, his lips touched the corner of my mouth, feeling mine move as I spoke. "I don't want you," I spat. "Not like this."

"Hmm," he hummed. "That tasted like a lie. I think you don't *want* to want me, but you damn well know that you're mine, regardless."

"I hate you," I hissed, jerking my head back from his as he shoved a third finger inside me and pumped them furiously.

"That one was true," he chuckled. "Such a shame that I do not fucking care. I gave you the chance to love me. I'll take your hate instead." Pulling his fingers out, he shifted his weight behind me as he shoved the shorts down his thighs, tightening his grip on my hair as I struggled beneath him. "Last chance to convince me, Isa."

"Fuck you! You'll just take what you want no matter what

I say," I said, snarling at him as he leaned forward and bit my bottom lip.

"My world, my rules," he chuckled, sliding his cock between my folds as I squirmed beneath him. The worst torment of it was how good it felt, how much Rafael made me want him.

It made no sense, but it was true, no matter what I tried to tell myself. I had to force down the moan that threatened to climb up my throat, trying to tear itself free from my deepest shame. "I don't want to be in your world!"

"Well, that's just too fucking bad, because you are *never* leaving it, Princesa." He growled the words, notching himself and thrusting inside me with one smooth glide that struck against the end of me so harshly I jolted forward on the bed. His hand still held my hair, pulling me back as he withdrew and pulling tighter so I couldn't move with the next punishing thrust of him inside me. "You will never leave me again, do you fucking understand me, Isa?" he asked, holding me still as I struggled to get a grip on the sheets. I felt desperate with the need to claw something to deal with the mix of pain and pleasure threatening to tear me in two. I couldn't handle the dichotomy of sensations, the turmoil of my emotions exploding inside me.

I wanted him. I wanted to kill him. I wanted to watch him bleed out, and he brought out that worst part of me. The forbidden desires and the violent impulses. The rages that I'd shoved down deep so I wouldn't become like Odina.

He pounded himself into me with aggressive strokes, claiming the deepest part of me for himself as if he could fuck through me. His own anger was potent in the air, matching my own as he took it out on my body. He withdrew as suddenly as he'd entered me, grabbing a leg in his grip and turning me to my back. His hand came down on my throat, a solid weight as he pressed me into the bed and shoved back inside me violently. His beautiful face was twisted with malice, the pure hatred he felt for me now written in every line of his expression. I wanted to be free of him and wanted to comfort him all at once.

I wanted to tell him that it had broken something inside of me to walk away, but I'd done it because he'd left me no choice.

I couldn't abandon my life back home for a murderer.

His grip tightened as he lifted my ass off the mattress with his other hand, resting it on his thighs so he could get deeper. I couldn't hold back the moan that caught in my throat. With my ass higher than my head, blood slowly trickled into my skull past the hand he pressed against the front of my throat. My breathing was restricted as he leaned forward and bent his body over mine.

His lips touched mine in the first kiss he'd given me since I'd woken up, the gentleness of it feeling like a mockery of everything I'd thought we shared before I'd fled in the night. I cried, tears building in my eyes as I held his gaze. As I realized that everything I'd loved had been destroyed by our choices.

Gone and replaced by nothing but a simmering rage that pulsed between us, threatening to burn us both alive. He kissed the spot where my tear fell, sighing when I lifted a hand to touch his face gently. He leaned into the touch, seeming to crave the affection we were missing as much as I was. "I will fucking kill you the next time you try to leave me. Do you understand me?" he asked, making my eyes go round as I stared up at him. "There is no place on this Earth that you can hide from me, Princesa. *Eres mia.*" My bottom lip trembled as my hand fell away, and I stared up at him in shock. He'd terrified me, but some part of me clung to the hope that he would never truly hurt me.

That he loved me, beneath all the dark edges of his soul.

"I understand," I whispered as his grip eased up slightly on my throat, still pinning me in place but almost with the gentle caress of a lover. His thrusts inside me still jolted my body on the bed. He still fucked me like he wanted to live inside me.

As if he thought the way to reconnect with me was through sex, when sex had never been our problem. Our problem was that our lives were shrouded in mystery, in secrets that kept us separate and meant we could never truly know each other. He might have been ready to lower his walls and reveal the truth to me, but I would never be ready to tell him my sins.

I'd take them to my grave, whether it was Rafael Ibarra who put me there or something else.

He reached down to stroke my clit as he fucked me, the wet sounds of our coupling echoing through the room proof of the fact that I might have been more turned on by his violence than I'd ever been when he was gentle with me.

The conflict I felt over that wasn't enough to force down the orgasm building in me, not even when his thrusts lost their rhythm and he approached his own climax. I whimpered my release, clenching around him as I came and digging my nails into the side of his arm where I grabbed him. He groaned, following me over the edge as he thrust into me a few more times and then stilled, dropping his weight on top of me as I fought to catch my breath.

The reality of what we'd done, of what I'd let him do, came crashing over me as I fought for breath, but I tried to push it away.

It was done. I couldn't change it, and all I could do was

try to find a way to make Rafael understand why I couldn't stay. He shifted his weight back to his knees as he pulled out of me, and I stared down at him in horror as I clenched my eyes closed.

I huffed out an irritated breath, opening my eyes to stare at him in disbelief. I supposed protecting us against pregnancy when he was pissed off was too much to ask. I sat up, trying to ignore the liquid that leaked free when I went more vertical. "I need another morning-after pill," I said.

His cold stare held mine for a moment before it fell to the space between my legs. He touched a finger to my entrance, coating it in his release before he shoved it back inside me.

"No," he said, wiping the moisture on his finger on my thigh before standing from the bed. I gaped after him, scrambling to stand up and wobbling on fuzzy legs. Whether it was from the drugs or the sex, I didn't think I'd ever know.

I certainly didn't want to have a repeat of being drugged ever again just to find out. "What do you mean no?" I asked as he reached out a hand to steady me.

He sat me back down on the bed, trying to force me to lay down. "You need to rest," he said, but there was no warmth to the statement. No concern for me, just a dismissal.

"What do you mean no?!" I repeated, my voice going shrill as he glared at me.

"There will be no more morning-after pills, and there will be no condoms between us," he said as he grabbed his shorts off the floor and pulled them up his legs.

"Am I going to be on birth control?" I asked, my voice dropping to a whisper. He couldn't honestly mean to make that kind of decision for me.

Could he?

"No."

"You can't just decide that for me!" I yelled, watching in horror as he made his way for the bedroom door.

"Watch me," he growled, tugging it open and then disappearing through it. The lock latched from the outside, trapping me in the bedroom alone as I stared after him and wrapped my hands around my stomach in anguish.

He could not be serious.

I stared at the door after it closed, my entire frame flinching with the sound of the lock as it echoed through the cavernous room. Glancing around the empty space, I jolted into action when I realized he really intended to leave me locked in the bedroom. My legs got tangled in the bedding as I fought to get to the door, sending me sprawling to the floor with a pained grunt as my scraped knees crashed against the hardwood.

"Rafe!" I yelled, forcing myself to my feet in a hurry. His steps receded away from the bedroom door despite my call, ignoring me as my fists pounded against the wood. *"Rafael!"* I screamed, hitting it with all my might as I tried to turn the knob. My back pressed against the door as I spun, looking around the room for something that I could potentially use to pick the lock.

There was no sign of anything small enough, even if that had been a skill I possessed. I gasped for breath as his release tickled against my flesh, sending me racing for the bathroom to scrub him off me.

Pregnancy wasn't something that was at the front of my

mind. It wasn't something I'd ever really considered possible for me, since I'd spent so much of my life catering to Odina. Our lives were a mess financially, and I'd seen far too many girls I went to school with deal with an unplanned pregnancy and the vicious cycle it created for keeping them in poverty. I used the bathroom, moving to the sink to wash my hands and use the water there to scrub myself clean.

My hand brushed against a sore spot on my inner thigh, drawing my gaze down to it as I spread my legs and stared at it in confusion. The bite mark was red, the early bruising in the distinctive shape of Rafael's perfect teeth marking my flesh clearly and leaving little doubt to what he'd done to me while I slept.

I heaved an angry sigh, turning my gaze up to the mirror. My reflection stared back at me, making me halt my motions as I studied the mess of hair around my face. The light hint of a bruise showed on the side of my neck, the injection site of his drugs a light purple to contrast the tan of my skin. I swallowed, turning my gaze back to my face as I gripped the edge of the counter in both hands.

If I wasn't the poor girl from Chicago who had to help her family, who would I be? Would I be a mother? A wife one day? I hated that when I tried to imagine the picture, the only face at the front of my mind was Rafael's.

I leaned forward, hanging my head momentarily as I tried to force the image away. I couldn't marry the man who'd kidnapped me off the streets.

That was the pinnacle of fucked up. The definition of all the darkness I'd barely escaped as a girl, and the opposite of the responsible thing to do. I touched a hand to my stomach, running my fingers over the flat surface as I bit my lip and willed myself to focus on what mattered in the moment.

Getting away was the only thing that mattered. Escaping was all that I could focus on.

I pushed away from the bathroom counter, striding back into the bedroom and searching for the closet door on the opposite end of the room. I needed clothes if I wanted to attempt an escape. I slid the barn style door to the side, stepping into the closet and staring around in dismay. One side was filled with Rafael's suits, his clothes as meticulously kept as they'd been when I snooped in his hotel room.

It felt like a lifetime ago that the prospect of him being married had been the worst of my concerns.

My eyes drifted to the brightly colored clothes on the other side, to the feminine lines of designer dresses and skirts. To the jeans and tops and shoes. All were in colors similar to what I wore regularly; all were the same kind of styles and cuts I preferred, if not just slightly more provocative. But the fabrics flowed over my skin as I touched them, the luxurious quality of wealth I'd never thought I'd know feeling so dramatically different than all the cheap clothes I'd been comfortable in.

I forced down the questions rising, wondering if the clothing had been intended for me or if it belonged to someone else. Grabbing a pair of shorts off one of the shelves, I tugged the elastic waisted bottoms up my legs and found a tag hanging from my side. I tore it off ruthlessly, dropping it to the floor and studying the rest of the clothes. All still had tags, and that at least reassured me that I wasn't putting on another woman's belongings.

Even if it begged the question of how he knew my personal style so well to purchase it all in such a short time frame. The amount of clothing here was far greater than anything my sister and I had owned combined, and wouldn't have been a quick process to accumulate.

I tugged a bra on and then a cotton shirt over to cover my chest. Whatever the reasoning, whatever the time frame, he was clearly deranged.

It was as if he truly believed we'd live some happily ever after despite the man he was and the things he'd done to me.

My anger rose once again with his clear dismissal of my will to escape him. The windows at the back of the room led to a private terrace and infinity pool, with walls to either side of the space. I wasn't hopeful that I would be able to escape through there, but the rage boiling in my blood compelled me to fucking try anyway.

The asshole deserved to have a floor to ceiling window that needed replacing after what he'd done to me. I grabbed one of the small end tables next to the little breakfast nook, hefting it up despite the way my arm muscles protested the action and my hands throbbed with the feel of something in their grip. Swinging it back with all my might, I threw it at the window.

It bounced off the glass, sending me reeling back with a startled shriek to avoid getting hit. My lungs heaved as I stared at it, irritated with myself for not foreseeing the possibility.

I moved back toward the bed slowly, glancing around as I looked for a weapon. I might not be able to pick a lock or break a window, but I could damn well hit him in the face when he stepped into the room, and run. I'd been afraid to run from him before because being chased would mean awakening the darkest part of my soul.

The unfortunate reality was that he'd made flight an inevitability when he'd drugged me. He'd taken away my choice, and I'd do anything to get it back. I didn't want to think of what I'd be capable of doing in order to get home to my grandmother and my parents.

I ignored the voice in my head that questioned my ability to hurt him. I shoved down the part of me that didn't want to and still clung to the foolish hope that maybe all of this came from some twisted place of love. Because there was no doubt in my mind that I loved Rafe. That the man I'd known had been everything to me in a way that terrified me, but the phantom that threatened me now wasn't him.

I just wanted the man, not the monster.

I stood on the bed, grabbing one of the lantern-style lamps that hung beside it. Hefting it in my hands as I stepped down to the floor, I glanced toward the door.

Then I moved into position behind it and waited for the moment it would open, and I'd find out if I was capable of hurting Rafael to be free.

4

*I*sa screamed my name in the room behind me as I made my way through the house to approach the kitchen. Regina stood behind the island, preparing ensaimada in a misguided attempt to soothe my anger.

If the fact that my cock was still wet with Isa's orgasm wasn't enough to soothe my anger, then Regina stood no chance of doing anything to quell the nightmare within me. The one that begged for release, that needed violence and penance for the failure that had resulted in all my carefully laid plans being decimated.

There was one man who deserved my wrath, but since he'd tucked himself safely away in Russia after our altercation in Ibiza, he was unfortunately out of my reach for the moment.

"No one goes near that bedroom," I ordered Regina. She gave me her best innocent eyes, deception hiding in her dark gaze. I knew her well enough to know she'd go to Isa and give her food and comfort if I didn't lay down the rules quickly and harshly.

Isa would have no comfort but me. She wouldn't take

solace in anyone that I didn't give to her. Everything she had now was an extension of me, each person in her life a bond I allowed her to have.

She was mine, and until the day came when I felt less inclined to keep her locked away in my bedroom with no one to speak to but me, I would be her entire world.

I hoped for both our sakes that my rage would quieten to a less all-consuming irritation quickly, because I couldn't think of anything but the stabbing reality of her betrayal. Of what it would mean for her and the penance she would need to pay.

"I understand," Regina said.

"I mean it," I ordered. "Anyone who disobeys me on this will find themselves no longer welcome in my home." Regina swallowed, nodding solemnly as she turned and left the kitchen without another word. The casual dismissal of everything she thought we meant to each other never sat well with her, but she didn't understand the depths of my obsession just yet.

There was nothing I wouldn't sacrifice to have Isa. Nothing I wouldn't give to make her feel the same pain she'd caused me, even if I already regretted the wounds she'd suffered at my hands. The scrapes to her knees and palms were extensive, an unintended consequence of the terror that had been necessary.

I didn't regret scaring her, not when her fear had tasted so addictive the moment I'd caught her in my arms. But I regretted the fact that her flawless skin had been marked, all the while loving the sight of my mark on her.

Loving the knowledge that she may bear the scars of her mistake for the rest of her life. I had a feeling they were only the first of many, as penance had to be paid. Fleeing through the streets of Ibiza Town was only the beginning for mi princesa.

The worst had yet to come.

"Perhaps it would be good for Isa to see a kind face. I can't imagine she was very happy to see you," Joaquin said as he stepped in at the back of the kitchen. I moved to the bar against the wall next to the dining table, pouring myself a drink despite the fact that it was the middle of the day. I'd been so anxious for Isa to wake up that I'd never gone to sleep.

Now with her wide awake and no doubt raging in my room, I knew bed was a long way off. Sleep beckoned to me, and the part of me that was nothing but a man who craved his woman wanted to curl up with her in my arms and forgive her for the choice she'd made.

The other part of me wanted to make her hurt, wanted to break her and make her into the woman I knew she could become if given the chance, but she'd have to let me do that.

No matter what I said, no matter what I did to Isa, I would never push her past her limits. I'd never take what wasn't mine to take, and if she'd been able to tell me in all honesty that she didn't want me?

I wouldn't have taken her. I wouldn't have forced the issue, but I knew without a doubt that Isa still wanted me. Her panic after sex hadn't been for the fact that we'd fucked in the first place.

But purely for the potential of a pregnancy.

That alone told me everything I needed to know about her mental state. She'd fight me. She'd rail against me, but in the end, she'd understand that she was exactly who she was always meant to be.

Mine.

"She didn't seem too opposed to me," I said, tossing back

my drink with barely a glance in his direction. His brothers followed him into the kitchen, Alejandro trailing at his heels as they waited for instructions. "She needs time to adjust. The three of you need to stay away from the house for a few days until she's ready to know the truth."

"Don't you think it's better to just rip off the bandage now? Get it all out in the open so she can come to terms with it all at once?" Alejandro asked, stepping toward the kitchen. I met him at the island, grabbing one of Regina's knives in my hand and twirling it thoughtfully.

"I think she's stronger than you can imagine, and she's holding up under the pressure of everything I've thrown at her so far, but there's only so much she can take. Knowing that one of her best friends betrayed her and the entire friendship was a ruse will push her over that edge," I explained. "She needs to be more stable in her under-standing of what she and I are before we throw that at her."

"He's right," Hugo agreed. "She can take a lot from strangers. She always expects people to disappoint her, so when they do, it's just another day for her. No matter what he wants to think, Rafael is a virtual stranger to her. She's spent a week with him, and that's a drop in the bucket for Isa. To know that she never knew him, she can recover from that, but our betrayal will trip her up more," he said as he looked at Gabriel and Joaquin. "She trusted us in a way she's never had the opportunity to trust him." My fists clenched at my sides, the truth to his words unsettling the part of me that wanted blood.

Nobody should have been capable of hurting Isa more than me. I should have been her entire world.

Joaquin nodded his agreement, ushering his brothers out of the house as he gave me a meaningful stare. "Don't fucking hurt her," he warned. "She deserves better than that, and what you expected of her was never a fair demand. She was always going to disappoint you."

Alejandro nodded his agreement as Joaquin disappeared out the side door after his brothers, leaving us in silence. "Maybe that's true," I agreed, pursing my lips thoughtfully as I stretched out a hand to grasp Alejandro's wrist in my grip. He swallowed, but didn't fight the contact as I touched the tip of the knife to the edge of his palm and sank it in a line to carve through his flesh. "But your failure to handle Pavel certainly didn't improve our chances."

He swallowed, his eyes blinking rapidly as he tried to force the pain down. I cut into his left hand with deep crisscrossing slices that left his hand a bloody, tattered mess. "I know." He held my stare the entire time, knowing that while the penance might have taken a different form, this was the punishment he'd earned no less.

"If it weren't for you, Isa wouldn't be in my bed with bloody knees and torn palms. She'd be exploring *Atlantis* with me, still in Ibiza. Still falling in love with me and completely unaware of the truth. Because of your failure, she bled," I growled, dropping the knife to the counter when I'd finished with his hand. I left his right unscathed as a kindness, knowing that it would make it easier for him to function as my second if he had at least one working hand.

"I admit that my handling of Pavel caused problems, and I accept my penance willingly," Alejandro said, his voice dropping low as he ended the statement. He always trailed off as he considered the best way to phrase messages he knew I wouldn't want to hear, but he was my second because he always said it despite his fear.

He was honest, regardless of the consequences for himself.

"I think you need to consider the possibility that Isa was

never going to choose to stay in Ibiza. Her life in Chicago holds some sway over her that she can't seem to let go of, no matter how she feels for you. If that's the case, she might not ever be yours in the way you want. What will you do if that's true?"

"I don't know," I admitted, taking his gun from the holster at the side of his pants. Touching my finger to the trigger, I aimed it at his knee as he flinched but didn't try to move away from my aim. "But for now, if she bleeds, so do you."

He groaned when I fired the gun and caught him in the thigh just above the knee. Another kindness, at least in my world, to not have to suffer through the recovery of a shattered kneecap. The bang reverberated through the space, a sound that the walls of my home were all too familiar with.

It wasn't uncommon for me to shoot people, though I tried to keep that kind of activity out of the house for Regina's sake.

Summoned by the noise, she hurried into the kitchen and ranted at me. "*Mi hijo*!" she yelled. "Now I have to throw out the ensaimada dough and disinfect the counter. You couldn't have taken your games outside?" She tutted, stepping around the counter to clean as Isa's scream echoed from the bedroom.

I dropped the gun to the counter, racing for the bedroom faster than I thought my bare feet could carry me. Regina followed at my heels, knowing there had been something different in that scream.

That one had been a scream of pain, of pure terror, and not one of frustration.

5

I dropped the lantern as I screamed, ducking down to cover my head as horror filled me. The potential of being shot, of everything ending so suddenly, seemed like such a ridiculous concept. I wanted nothing more than to be home.

I wanted the comfort of my mundane life as I curled my body in on itself and wished it all away. Rafael had said he'd kill me if I left him.

I hadn't believed him.

Silence followed the sound of the gunshot and the woman's scolding shout, leaving me with nothing but my imagination to fill in the gaps of what may or may not be coming for me. I couldn't imagine the reality that the shot had been meant for someone else, not when it *felt* like it had been in the room with me. But a glance around confirmed that there was no shattered glass aside from what lay on the ground from the lantern. There was nothing but my own panic as I sat huddled on the floor in the room alone.

I heaved a sigh, putting a hand to the wall and carefully maneuvering myself to my feet. The sound of footsteps echoed in the hall as they came closer, pounding against the floors, and then the doorknob rattled.

"Isa!" Rafe yelled, the panic in his voice making me feel like, for a moment, maybe he gave a fuck what happened to me. I questioned myself, and the determination to hurt him to escape, but the vivid memory of that gunshot drove me to pick up the shattered lantern. Glass cut through the bandages on my hands, making me wince as the wounds beneath reopened.

The lock turned, and then the door flung open. I jumped to the side to avoid it as it came flying at me, my feet catching all the tiny pieces of glass that stayed on the floor as I moved hastily. When Rafael stepped through the door, I ignored the pain in my feet and pushed forward. Lunging for him, I swung my arm through the air and tried to hit him in the side of the head with the lantern.

He caught it in his grip, his face twisting with fury as he growled down at me. There was no trace of kindness in his face as he snatched it from my hand and flung it to the side of the room. A woman stood behind him as he snapped out a palm, catching me by the throat. His grip slipped, and I glanced down at the other hand fisted at his side to find it stained red.

I swallowed against the hand at my throat as he leaned into my space and used that grip to lift me up off my feet. His hold restricted my breathing, my blood-soaked fingers grasping his hand in protest. Ignoring me, he walked over the shards of glass at our feet, not so much as flinching when the pieces undoubtedly lodged themselves in his flesh. "Shit," the woman at his back said as her eyes met mine.

"Get the fucking first aid kit," Rafe growled at her. She turned, fleeing the room as Rafe brought me back to the bed. He set me on the edge of it, releasing his grip on my throat as I pulled my legs up and tried to crawl for the other side of the mattress. The blood from our hands stained the white bedding, the blood from my feet only adding to it in my struggle as he placed a hand down on top of my thigh and sat next to me.

"The gunshot," I protested, glancing toward the door. I hadn't seen any sign of a gun since he'd stepped in, but Rafe clearly didn't need a weapon to subdue me. He'd managed that all on his own, with nothing but a hand to cease my fighting.

My throat ached, feeling abused from his grip when he'd fucked me and when he'd lifted me over the glass. But the unmistakable reality was that he hadn't hurt me since he'd set me down. He'd used a brutal hold to carry me over the glass, but nothing more.

"You're hurt," he said, his voice a low murmur as he compelled me to sit still. It wasn't quite affection that I saw staring back at me, more the vague sense of ownership. I'd harmed what he thought of as his property, and he'd do what he could to fix it.

The woman stepped back into the room, her warm brown eyes meeting mine as she stepped around the glass carefully to hand him the first aid kit. "Clean up the glass while I deal with her," he ordered. She nodded, retreating from the room once again.

"Wait, please!" I called, my shoulders dropping in dejection when she ignored my plea and went about her business. Rafael opened the first aid kit and lifted my legs into his lap. With an odd gentleness that betrayed the fierce expression on his face, he carefully tugged each piece of glass from my feet and focused intently as he dropped them on the nightstand.

The fury on his face kept me quiet as I studied him, not daring to tempt him to violence as he worked. I winced as he pulled a particularly large shard free, making him turn that stunning multicolored stare up to me as his fury melted away in concern. He ran his free hand over the top of my foot, a gesture that would have been sweet had it not been for the mix of blood on his skin. Mine and whoever he'd hurt.

"Whose blood is that?" I asked, studying the motion. He glanced down, shrugging as if the answer was inconsequential. As if he hurt people every day and there was nothing that could be done for it.

"One of my men disappointed me, so penance was due. I told you, being a murderer barely scratches the surface of what I am, mi princesa," he murmured softly, setting the foot to the side as he started on the other one.

"And the gunshot?" I asked, studying him carefully.

"I shot him in the leg," he answered. The breath caught in my lungs. The reality of his violence and the fact that he could speak about it so calmly was an entire world away from the life I lived.

"You shot him in the leg," I repeated as the woman returned to the bedroom with a broom and started to furiously sweep up the glass the best she could. Another man wheeled in a mop bucket after her, working to clean up the blood behind her. Still, Rafael worked to get the glass out of my feet without ever motioning for his own. "And you're okay with that?" I asked him.

He turned his stare back up to me again. "I know who I am, Isa. I kept it from you to give you a chance to fall in love with me without the violence hanging over your conscience. That phase in our relationship is over now, and I won't keep secrets from you any longer."

"What if I want you to keep secrets?" I asked. I didn't want to know the details of Rafael's life of crime. Not when I wanted to go back home to my daily life and forget any of this had ever happened.

He finished pulling glass from my feet, setting aside the tweezers and grabbing a bottle of rubbing alcohol and a cloth. He wiped them down while I winced. "If you do not want to be injured, then don't try foolish escapes like that again," he said, his voice going cold once again.

When he was satisfied that my wounds were clean, he wrapped my feet in the same bandages that covered my hands and knees. If I'd had any doubt who had cared for my injuries while I'd been unconscious, that was all the proof I needed.

"What am I supposed to do?" I asked, letting him turn my body to take my hands in his. My body vibrated where he touched me, that electrical current of attraction that always ran between us pulsing under my skin. As if I really couldn't deny him anything, despite my best intentions.

"You're supposed to accept that this is your new life," he said, unwinding the ruined bandages and setting them in the dust pan the woman held up for him. He inspected my hands carefully, checking for glass that might have gotten under the bandage. When he found none, he rewrapped them gently.

"I want my old life," I whispered.

His nostrils flared in his anger. "Get out," he snapped to the woman and the man who were finishing up cleaning. I whimpered, following them with my eyes as the woman shook her head sadly. "Do you think it pleases me to know that you miss your mundane life? Look around you and see all that I have to offer you, Princesa."

"I want my family," I said. "All the money in the world

can't replace them, and you *forced* this on me, Rafe. I want to choose where my life takes me, not have a man I hardly know decide for me." His hand caught my chin, the blood covering him feeling warm on my skin as he turned my face to his and crashed his lips onto mine. He devoured my mouth, building that desire inside me with just the furious strokes of his tongue against mine even though I wanted to bite his off. So I bit down in warning, hating the chuckle he released as he pulled back and tugged his tongue from my mouth.

"I am your family now. If you behave, perhaps there is a way that you can have a relationship with the family you left behind. But that cannot happen if I can't trust you."

I gasped, staring up at him with ever growing hatred. To use my family to control me was cruel, even for him.

He swung his feet up onto my lap, the shards of glass protruding from his flesh as he handed me the tweezers. "You've already bled me once today, little demon."

I glared at him, torn between wanting to shove the shards of glass further into his foot and wanting to help him in the same way he had me. He could have left me to deal with it on my own and let me bleed. Instead he'd shown me a moment of kindness that I might not have deserved considering I'd tried to bash his skull in.

I pulled the first shard free, dropping it into his open palm so he could place it with the others on the nightstand. "My mother was fond of those lanterns," he said, drawing my attention up to his face. "I don't remember much of her, but I remember that."

Hearing him say that made me instantly feel guilty. "I'm sorry," I said, the apology feeling genuine despite the circumstances. I knew what it was to miss a loved one, to treasure the things they left behind for fear of losing the last connection we had with them. I still had both my parents, but my grandfather's loss was something I felt every time I looked at the fossil he'd given me as a girl.

The one that I'd likely never see again.

"It's just a lantern," he said, leaning forward to touch his lips to my forehead. "You're far more important to me. I won't have you hurting yourself."

"Then let me go," I argued, holding his gaze as he chuckled and shook his head.

"No."

"Rafael!" I snapped, dropping his leg to the floor as I moved onto the next one. "You cannot be so hard up for sex that you have to abduct an unwilling girl. Please. Just let me go home."

His eyes darkened as the traces of amusement fled from his face. "Do not reduce what we have to sex," he warned as he pulled his foot from my hand and stood from the bed. There was still glass in one of them, but he didn't so much as flinch as he put his weight on it. "We both know that there is far more emotion between us than that."

I swallowed, wanting to deny the words. I would if he made me, but instead I just said nothing. I watched him in silence as he leaned into my space and touched his lips to mine gently. "I wouldn't abduct just anyone. I wouldn't put in the slightest bit of effort for anyone but you. Just as we both know you would jump off a cliff before you ever let yourself be taken by a man you didn't want. But you know as well as I do, you belong to me." He trailed his lips over my cheek, dragging the wetness of the tears I didn't want to cry as he moved to my ear. "You're mine to hurt. Mine to break. Mine to fuck, and mine to keep, Princesa."

He pulled away, holding my eyes as he made for the

door. "Please, don't lock me in here again," I begged, shaking my head.

"I can't trust you in the main house just yet," he said, pulling the door open as I jolted to my feet.

"Please," I repeated. "I can't not *do* anything, Rafael." Boredom was my worst enemy. In my boredom, I thought of all the things I shouldn't. I remembered all the details of the moments in my life that I regretted.

He closed the door behind him as he left. My hands touched the surface as I dropped to my knees and willed him to change his mind. "Get some rest," he said on the other side as he turned the lock.

I turned to sit, looking at the bloodstained bedding with disgust. I moved to the bathroom to clean the blood from my skin, and then I curled up in the chair he'd sat in as I slept. The cruelty I'd seen etched into the lines of his face since waking up in his bedroom stared back at me every time I tried to close my eyes.

Prying them open, I forced myself to focus on my breathing, and not the panic seeping into my veins with every moment that passed.

He had to let me out eventually. I just needed to wait for the right moment.

I tossed back another whiskey, lifting my leg into my lap so that I could continue pulling the glass from my foot. If Isa hadn't pissed me off so much with her refusal to admit she knew our relationship was more than just a physical connection, I would have gladly let her finish.

Her delicate fingers touching my ankle to hold me still as she worked diligently had been greatly preferable to doing it myself. I wanted her to take care of me in the way I cared for her, but that seemed to be too much to ask of *mi princesa.*

I knew it was unfair of me to even expect it. The logical part of my brain knew I was being too demanding of her, that I pushed her too far and would risk breaking everything we had building between us. The knowledge of that did nothing to stop me from the reality of wanting to push her farther. Of wanting to get to the bottom of her resistance and understand the fundamentals of it.

Just like the day I'd pushed her in the waterfall, I knew the truth would come out when Isa met her limit. She was only ever truly honest when I didn't give her a choice. In the same way she wasn't ready to know the truth about my occupation, I had to wonder if I was ready to know how she felt about me.

"Oh, would you stop it?" Regina said as she wrapped up Alejandro's leg. She'd gotten quite skilled at bullet removal over her years of being married to my father. Fixing the consequences of his raging anger in the men who'd done no wrong to him and suffered for their loyalty.

Some might compare us, but I used my anger and my penance to rule over my men with order, while his had been nothing but chaos.

She moved from her place next to Alejandro on one of the chairs in the back patio. There were no cushions, making it far too simple to hose the blood away and into the earth, never to be seen again. Kneeling on the stone, she took the tweezers from my hand and worked to remove the smaller shards that were impossible for me to see. "You should have let Isa finish," she scolded me. "If she's to be your wife, you must be able to let her do these things for you."

"She was doing it just fine. That wasn't the problem," I grunted, pouring myself another drink and downing it. The pain in my foot was barely an irritation compared to some of the injuries I'd suffered, but knowing that it came from Isa and that it should have been her soothing the pain she'd caused somehow made it worse.

"Then what was the problem, exactly?" Regina asked.

"She was dismissive about our bond," I said, shrugging my shoulders. I knew she would disapprove of the words, and so did Alejandro as he chuckled in the chair across from me.

"Excuse me? Did that poor girl not wake up in a strange bed just a few hours ago, after being brought here while she was unconscious?" she asked, pinching me with the sharp ends of the tweezers.

I narrowed my eyes at her. "I don't recall asking for your opinion."

"Well, you're getting it anyway. You must find a way to forget your anger. She left you. She doesn't understand what's at stake. She is young, and she's scared. You set her up to think that your relationship would never be anything more than a fling on her vacation, and then you ripped the rug out from under her and changed the rules. Give her time."

"I don't have time. I already know what it was to have her as mine. I can't just forget that," I grunted, watching as she set the tweezers on the table beside me.

"Of course you can't. You love her, *mi hijo*. This too shall pass, but not if you abuse her in your anger," Regina said, standing and moving to drop into one of the empty chairs across from me.

"I don't love her," I grunted. Men like me weren't capable of love. Obsession wasn't love, and as mad as it drove me, I would never be able to return the emotion I demanded from her.

She was my everything, but to love was to lose. I couldn't risk that, and I wouldn't even if I could. I still remembered the sensation of my heart being torn from my body, of watching the only person who had ever truly loved me burn on the pyre for her husband's insanity. The boy my mother loved had died with her.

Any traces of goodness she'd managed to instill in me as a child had been lost as I listened to her screams and my father forced me to watch her body turn to ash in the wind. He'd succeeded in making me a monster. *La criatura,* a man with no heart beating in my chest.

There was nothing that could love Isa as she loved me.

"I can't," I said, staring at Regina's mischievous smile and reiterating the point as if she had any say in what my body and soul determined was impossible. Of all the people on *El Infierno*, she would be the one who interacted with Isa more than all the rest.

She needed to understand her place in my life just as much as Isa did.

"You keep telling yourself that, *mi hijo*," Regina laughed, raising an eyebrow at me mockingly as I pulled my phone out of my pocket and strode back toward the house.

I might not be ready to know if my obsession loved me in the way I needed her to, but that didn't mean I wasn't ready for other answers.

"Rafael!" Regina called. I turned back to her, watching as she considered her next words. "You are not your father. Show her how you feel about her. You're the only one besides her who doesn't know that you are absolutely head over heels in love with that girl."

I ignored her, storming my way through the house to get to my office. I was grateful for the fact that it was on the other side of the house, as far away from Isa as I could get. I needed the clarity that distance brought, and yet as I sat at my desk, I brought up the camera feed from our bedroom.

Isa wasn't in bed but curled up in the chair. Her head leaned on her shoulder as she slept. I'd need to remember to change the bedding when I brought her food in a little while. The blood clearly made her uncomfortable, and I could imagine it would take some time for her to get as used to it as I'd become at a young age.

I wouldn't flinch at the sight of blood, but even I wouldn't want to sleep in a bed stained with it.

I picked my cell phone up off the desktop, dialing

Ryker's number and waiting for Matteo's famed executioner to answer the phone. It was early evening in Spain, meaning that Ryker wouldn't want to kill me for calling since it wasn't as early as it would have been had I called when I first wanted to.

"How's Isa?" he asked in lieu of a greeting.

"Distressed," I admitted.

"I take it your plan didn't work out so well?" he asked, a low whistle as he followed the line of thought. "She'll come around if she's really meant to be yours. Just treat her right and give her some time."

"Like you gave Calla?" I asked, pursing my lips as he chuckled.

"Fair enough. Just treat her right and everything else will follow. You're a sick bastard, Rafael. Don't take it out on her that she never stood a chance," he said. "If you want her to love you, you can't treat her like she's one of your marks and torture her into it."

"I didn't call you for relationship advice," I growled. "I'll treat her well enough that my agreement with Matteo will be met. I've no interest in abusing her."

"If you didn't call for advice, then what the fuck do you want?"

"I want you to find the cop who filed the accident report when Isa fell in the river. She's hiding something, and I want to know what."

"And if he's not on Matteo's payroll and doesn't want to talk? What would you like me to do?"

"I don't give a fuck who you have to kill, but I want answers. I want to know what really happened and not the bullshit cover story of a girl falling into the river."

He paused. "Matteo won't like that. I'll see what I can find out and go from there," he said, trying to appease the monster clawing at the surface. Over sixteen months had passed, and I was still no closer to understanding why Isa felt so obligated to her family or why her sister hated her so much.

"Fine," I snapped, hanging up the phone. I should have worked. I had shit to catch up on if I wanted to be able to spend quality time with Isa when she was ready to get more acclimated to her new life.

Instead, I snuck into the bedroom and changed the bedding while she slept. Then I tucked her into bed while she protested my touch on her in her sleep.

Like being stabbed in the chest, I fled the room before she became fully lucid. Leaving her to sleep alone for a few hours before I joined her.

I had a feeling she'd need the rest with the days coming our way.

*M*y eyes fluttered open as the weight at my back shifted and Rafael's arm drifted off my waist. Feeling like I'd slept forever, I rolled to my back as slowly as possible. As my head turned to look at him, I half expected to find the shock of his eyes meeting mine.

Instead his remained closed, his breathing even as he slept. The shards of glass he'd left on the nightstand still remained, and I wondered at the level of trust he placed in me by sleeping soundly with a weapon so close by.

The smart choice would be to stab him while he slept. To rid the world of a monster and escape him once and for all.

But I proved I'd never been smart when I turned my gaze away from the glass, unable to even consider the reality of killing him. As horrible as he was, a world without Rafael in it seemed...

Empty.

Even if we weren't together, I didn't want to exist in a world where his overwhelming presence didn't exist. Where

I didn't think back to Ibiza and wonder if I'd see him if I returned.

He'd made doing that impossible. But that didn't mean I could kill him and the fantasy of it all at once.

Instead, I sat up in bed slowly. Swinging my legs over the side, I stood on the hardwood floor and ignored the pain making my feet throb. Keeping my eyes on him as I backed away from the bed, I didn't make the same mistake I'd made the first time I tried to sneak out in the night. I didn't waste time grabbing shoes, just moved straight for the door and turned the knob slowly. Keeping my body as relaxed as I could, I pulled it open and stepped into the doorway just as the bed creaked behind me and I froze solid.

"Are you going somewhere, Princesa?" he asked, echoing the same words he'd spoken what felt like a lifetime ago. With my heart in my chest, I turned my head to look back at him. Sitting on the bed with his feet on the floor, with his hands curled around the edges of the mattress violently as he studied me. With his face tilted down in the shadows of the night, all I saw was the vividness of his eyes as he watched me.

Like a panther staring out from the darkness, daring his prey to play a game with him.

I turned and ran down the hallway, nearly stumbling over my own feet in my panic to escape him. The house was enormous, a maze of hallways that I had to navigate.

City blocks with chess pieces flashed in my mind, driving me forward. Rafael followed me, his hands tucked into the pockets of his black silk pajama bottoms as he walked quickly to keep up. But there was no stress on his face.

Only confidence, and the realization made me stumble as I emerged from the labyrinth of back hallways to a main room. There was a kitchen and a dining room, and an enormous living area. The door loomed at the front of the house, calling to me as I sprinted across the open space. My bare feet slapped against the wood floors, sounding too loud in the silence of the night. When I grabbed the doorknob in my hand and turned it frantically, I dared a glance back at Rafael as he walked toward me.

He stopped in the middle of the room, tilting his head to the side as I fumbled with the locks.

"Remember what happens when I catch you, Princesa," he murmured, the words striking me across the distance between us. When the lock finally turned, I pulled the door open and sprinted into the night, despite the terror that built in my body from his words.

His warning that day at the waterfall echoed in my head, the question of what he would do loud and clear as I ran through the pavilion at the front of the house. There wasn't a person in sight as I raced down the hill, the pavement tearing open the wounds on my feet as the bandages slipped free. The driveway took me down a hill, making me stumble as I tried to slow my pace and not land on my face.

Still, he followed behind me at his brisk walk. His features stayed calm, his arrogance making me feel more panicked.

He knew something I didn't know, and whatever it was, I was left with the distinct impression I'd walked right into a trap.

"Somebody help me!" I screamed, the sound fading into the night when nobody returned my plea. I kept running, turning right on the road at the bottom of the driveway.

I ran, and I ran, and then I ran some more, until fatigue threatened to overtake me.

Until Rafael's presence at my back became a certainty

that he would catch me, whereas before I'd had a distant hope. Just as my body sagged and desolation threatened to claim me, I stumbled into a village where people lurked outside despite the late hour. They drank in groups, celebrating among themselves as I burst into the streets between their houses. "Help," I gasped, laying my hands on my knees as I tried to breathe. "He's chasing me. Please," I begged.

Hope bloomed in my chest even as I struggled not to collapse to the ground in the middle of the street. People meant safety, but a glance back at Rafael confirmed he just stared at me intently. Never breaking his fixation on me or bothering to hide his presence for fear of the repercussions.

"*El Diablo*," the people around us murmured oddly, bowing their heads with a glance at Rafael. I knew I'd heard the words before, but as I pressed onward to find someone who would help me, I couldn't stop to think about them. Nobody moved to help me, only turning their attention to where Rafael hovered at my back, his face menacing and cruel as he watched me beg for help. One woman stepped up to him, turning her eyes to me worriedly as she spoke to him in Spanish.

He shook his head, and she ducked into her home and left me to my fate. I choked back a sob as true helplessness claimed me, turning and sprinting up the hill that the town street climbed up. *"Please!"* I screamed with a broken sob, waiting for someone to help me.

But as I reached the end of the town, everyone disappeared inside their homes and abandoned me to Rafael's fate. I stumbled, my bloodied feet slipping along the stone. I pushed myself up and continued up the hill, until the little town was lost to the darkness behind me and there was only the night and trees to either side of the road. It turned to dirt, fading into a space with nothing surrounding it as I climbed as quickly as I could. When I reached the top of the hill, I stopped, staring around in horror.

From the tallest vantage point, I remembered what Rafael had told me about living on a remote island. I'd thought the words a lie, assumed it was just another one of many he'd told me in our time together. Instead, I stared out at the darkness of the Mediterranean as I spun.

There was nothing. Just nothing but the water to surround us. The small town below was lit with lights and Rafael's home illuminated another part of the island just below where I stood. I could make out the pool in the back and realized I'd have saved myself a lot of time and running if I'd just gone out the back door.

There was just nothing, and the people who lived here weren't inclined to help me. They were determined to obey Rafael and leave me to my fate.

I turned to face him as he strolled up and over the crest of the hilltop, his cold face appearing as his eyes landed on mine.

My heart stalled in my chest, because I knew what came next.

And there was nowhere left to run.

RAFAEL

*H*er chest sunk, her body dropping as if she
might fall where she stood. She caught herself,
her bottom lip trembling as tears trailed down her flushed
cheeks. I'd known the moment I went to bed that I'd taken
my life in my hands by leaving the shards there.

I needed to know what Isa would do, given a choice, and
the fact that, despite all I'd done, she couldn't bring herself
to truly hurt me spoke volumes about the feelings that still
consumed her.

They were just hidden beneath the surface of her anger.
Of her fear.

She'd chosen to run instead, proving something I
wanted to show her. Something she needed to discover for
herself.

No matter what she did, or where she tried to go, there
would be no getting off *El Infierno* without my knowledge. If
I wanted it that way, she would never leave the fucking
island again.

"Do you understand now, mi princesa?" I asked, slowly
closing the distance between us. She backed up a step, as

though she might try to flee again. Stopping herself at the last possible moment, a ragged moan tore from her lips as she forced her body to be still despite the fear waging war on her body.

"Why wouldn't they help me?" she asked. The innocence in the question tugged at whatever remained of my heart. My poor Isa was so naïve to the ways of the world, so lost with the wide eyes of her youth, that she didn't realize the simple truth that drove our world to spin.

People were selfish. She'd spoken the words to me once, but now she would fully understand the truth of it. "Because I put food on their table. Because I am *El Diablo,* and they worship me as their King."

Her legs shook as she fought to remain upright, pushing through her fear of what was coming as I closed the distance between us. She jolted when I reached up a hand to cup her cheek, running my thumb through the tears on her cheekbones as she turned stunning eyes to mine.

They were always vibrant, but they intensified when she cried, turning a bottled green that women everywhere would envy.

"I own this island. I own the people. If I wanted, they would watch me slaughter you and not so much as move a muscle to help you. There is *nobody* who can save you from me, Princesa. It is time to come to terms with your new life." She didn't move as I touched my other hand to her hip, sliding my fingers inside the hem of her t-shirt.

Her eyes danced with movement as her brain tried to find an escape. As she frantically fought against the truth she now knew.

She'd be mine until her dying breath, and then I would chase her into the afterlife.

"Why are you doing this?" she murmured, her voice

quivering as she asked the question. I slid my hands down to her thighs, grasping her around the backs of them and lifting her into my arms. "I don't understand what I did."

She was so close to breaking, so close to the point of no return where I needed to put her in order to rebuild her the way she'd always been meant to be. Anger pulsed in my body, uncontrollable and all consuming, but with her hollow eyes on mine and the sight of her lips quivering in my face, I lowered her to the ground more gently than I might have.

I wanted to shove her body into the tree and ravage her, to show her everything I would take and all that she would give me willingly. Instead, I placed her on the ground carefully and sealed my weight over hers.

The lights of the village twinkled out slowly as my people went to bed for the night, forced into their homes earlier than they might have planned because of Isa's moonlit run.

She couldn't possibly know they'd been celebrating my return with my bride to be in tow. That *El Diablo* would finally have his heirs to continue the Ibarra legacy and give them the stability I'd been unable to provide without Isa.

I touched a hand to her hair, brushing it back gently as I pushed her legs wider and settled my hips between them. She flinched back from the touch, her body able to feel the violence barely restrained in me.

The time would quickly come when I showed Isa what it could mean to be with me. If she didn't want to accept the man, then the nightmare would fuck her in the dirt and break her body into submission.

The choice was hers to make.

"I knew the moment I saw you that you would be my wife," I murmured. Her eyes widened at my words, and I wondered how they could come as a surprise. My intention to get her pregnant should have been enough to communicate to Isa that this was not a temporary situation for me.

"But I don't want to be your wife. I just want to go home." The words faded, the melancholy sound like that of a woman as she realized her home was gone. That it had been destroyed, and in a way it had.

It would never be her home again.

The shorts clinging to her sweat-slicked body kept me from touching what was mine. I grasped her around the back of her thighs, lifting her legs and ass off the ground to rest against my body. Sliding my hands into the elastic waistband, I pulled them down and over her ass while she stared up at me.

"You will never try to leave me again. I am sure you can see that it is pointless now," I said, watching as she nodded slowly. The movement was as hesitant as I would have expected, as if she was barely there.

Drifting away in the ocean, lost to the tide of my possession.

It would take the flames of Hell to bring her back to life, to resurrect her as *Mi Reina* so she could withstand the fires to stand by my side.

I dragged the shorts up and over the tops of her thighs as she watched me, blinking up at me in her shock. Tossing them to the side, I shoved her legs back down to part around me so that I could lean forward and pull the collar of her tank top down until her breasts spilled free.

I placed her bandaged hands on my chest, longing to feel her bare skin on me. To feel the torn flesh of her hands as she touched me and know that the marks on her skin were mine.

That they were part of us, for better or worse.

Even as I wanted her to look at me as if I was the man she'd fallen in love with in Ibiza, I couldn't deny the appeal of knowing she saw the darkness in me. That she stared in the face of the nightmare and held her ground where others might have continued to run. Isa could play innocent all she wanted, but she'd always seen hints of the darkness in my eyes.

She'd seen it, felt it against her skin, and she'd welcomed it with open arms. Like coming home to the place her soul was always meant to belong.

She didn't speak, just stared up at me with teary eyes as she shook her head from side to side. I knew there was nothing left she could say as she tried to work her way through the inescapable nature of her life with me, but accepting it was the first step in our battle toward happiness.

I reached between our bodies, dragging the waistband of my pajama shorts down until my cock sprung free in the gap. I notched my head against her clit, dragging it through her pussy and rubbing up and down through her until I was wet with the arousal she wouldn't want to acknowledge.

The brokenness faded from her eyes, the little demon rising in response to my attempt at sweet seduction. Isa had never been one to simply let me make love to her, instead preferring to push me until I couldn't resist the temptation to take her roughly. To push her past the limits she'd probably thought she had for herself.

But there were no limits to what I would do to Isa. No parts of her that I wouldn't claim as mine.

Even understanding that the defiance came from a place of not wanting sweet and romantic from a man she was determined to hate, that it was a defense mechanism as strong as any, I still felt nothing but frustration as I met her glare with one of my own.

"I did warn you what would happen if I caught you, Princesa," I warned as I lined my cock up and drove inside her. She screamed as I filled her, crying out into the night with the violence of my possession.

I covered her body with mine, shoving myself as deep as I could go in my attempt to fuse our bodies together. If I could spend my life inside her, I would.

I never wanted to be anywhere else.

She whimpered as I drew back, gliding through her tender and swollen tissue that hadn't been ready for me. "Scream my name when you come," I ordered, pounding into her furiously in my need for all the men in my village to hear it.

For them to know exactly who owned her.

She didn't say my name, defying me in one small way that only made me more determined to pull the word from her mouth as I fucked her. She grunted, taking what I had to give as I knew she always would. She was my perfect fit, the perfect match designed just for me.

I kissed her, forcing her to taste, to acknowledge that our connection went deeper than simple biology. That the emotion behind it was there, pulsating beneath the primal fucking in the dirt. I'd break her body down until her walls disappeared and she let me inside her head.

Then I'd own that too.

When I drew back, I grabbed her legs behind the knees and lifted until she bent in half for me. With her ankles around my shoulders, I pounded deep inside her with hard and fast strokes that stole a whimper from her each time I struck the end of her.

"Fuck!" she groaned, clenching her eyes closed as I fucked her harder than I probably should have in my desperation to hear my name as she came.

"Say my fucking name," I ordered again, shifting the angle of my hips as I drove inside her. "Whose pussy is this?" My dick hit her g-spot, bringing a shocked expression to her face as I dragged my head over it and worked her higher and higher into her orgasm.

"Fuck you," she moaned. Smirking down at her, I pressed forward until her legs touched her chest and she heaved out a ragged sigh. Leaning my weight over her, I took her bottom lip between my teeth as I shoved inside her in a downward motion. There was no reprieve with the ground at her back and my weight crashing into the top of her, forcing her to take everything I gave without escape.

"Soon, I'll lay you out like this and fuck your ass," I murmured against her mouth. She gasped into my space, reaching out to grab my forearms in her grip as her nails dug into my flesh and she tried to bleed me. "My name, Princesa."

Those nails dug harder as I drew back and moved inside her more gently, pulling her away from her orgasm until she gave me what I wanted. She whimpered, desperation taking over her features.

When she couldn't take it any longer, she whimpered my name in defeat. "Rafael, please."

Leaning forward, I kissed her and fucked her in harder furious drags of my head over that spot inside her that drove her as wild as I felt in my anger with her. She came, spasming around my cock while I kept pounding her through it. After a few more minutes of enjoying her as she panted beneath me, I followed her over the edge.

Filling her with my release once again, which she glared down at in the space between her legs as I pulled out. She didn't protest as I drew her into my arms and carried her back down the hill and toward the bed that waited for us.

No one dared to look at her half naked form as I made my way home.

Mi princesa was for my eyes alone.

She was too exhausted to care about anything other than going back to sleep, but I knew the argument regarding condoms would come soon enough.

She'd see it my way in time.

I forced my eyes open slowly, the coolness of the bed at my side alerting me to the lack of Rafael's presence even before they'd fully focused. I stretched a hand over despite my best intentions, touching his pillow and dragging it closer.

His scent filled my lungs as I inhaled, then shoved it away immediately after in my anger at my own ridiculousness. Instead of feeling grateful that he was gone, I was left with an unfortunate emptiness within me that I wishfully attributed to the newfound reality that I wouldn't be able to get off the island.

That escape would be impossible without help, because the last I'd checked I'd never even been on a boat before coming to Ibiza. Let alone driven one.

Sitting up and dragging a hand over my forehead, I squinted at the fabric bandage that touched my skin as my eyes adjusted to the bright sun shining in the windows. With a swallow, I pulled the fabric back slowly to reveal the torn mess of skin on my hand. Spots had already scabbed over where the scrapes went deeper, puncture wounds in the areas that the glass from the lantern had stabbed me.

There was no doubt certain spots would scar, but the majority of the wounds on my hands were superficial. Nothing but the road burn of falling on the street. Painful and stinging, but without lasting effect. I pulled the blanket off my body, unraveling the bandage around my knees as well and feeling satisfied that the covering wasn't necessary for those.

A glance down to my feet made me shudder. The repeated abuse they'd suffered since waking up in Rafael's bedroom meant they were a torn mess beneath the bandage, confirmed by the pain as Rafael had cleaned them when we came back in the middle of the night.

I wanted to hate him, but it felt impossible to do it when he took care of me nearly as well as he scared me.

I knew the most logical thing would be for me to spend the next couple of days healing, but I'd never been one to lounge in a bed. I'd been a terrible hospital patient after the accident, driving my nurses crazy with my insistence that I couldn't be stationary. Nothing had changed in the years that had passed since then.

I stood from the bed, making my way into the closet and grabbing a comfortable dress to pull on over my head. My back stung as the fabric slid over it, a reminder of the night before and the brutality of Rafael's thrusts inside me as he claimed me in the dirt.

It was filthy. It was instinctual, as if his very being called to him to mate and to make me his in a way that was animalistic.

As if the clean lines of his suit and the breathtakingly handsome face were an elaborate disguise for the beast that lived within him. He knew what words to say. He knew exactly how to lure me right into his trap.

And all along, I'd been nothing but his prey.

The man I'd known hadn't ever really existed. He'd made me fall in love with a gentleman tinged with darkness, when he was really the devil in a suit.

I grabbed a pair of lacy underwear out of the drawer in the closet, scowling at all the delicate fabrics and feminine items meant more for him than they could ever be for me. Tugging them up my legs, I nearly tumbled over in my rising frustration.

I wasn't a doll he could dress up in designer clothes and smooth silks, waiting to strip me down when he wanted to fuck me. I wasn't a toy to be locked away in his bedroom until he felt like gracing me with his presence.

After using the bathroom and rebandaging the wounds on my feet, I made my way to the door and tried to turn the knob. It refused to turn, locked from the outside.

Fury rose in my throat, knowing there was no reason to lock me in a bedroom when the entire island was a prison in itself. His cruelty knew no bounds. I banged the side of my fists against the door, screaming his name in the hopes that he was close enough to hear me.

Maybe I could annoy him until he let me go. That was always a possibility. If I couldn't force myself to smother him in his sleep, then perhaps I could just smother him until he grew tired of my demanding antics.

My eyes turned to the corner, glaring at the camera I'd seen sitting where the wall touched the ceiling the day before. I hauled the end table up off the floor where it had landed when I'd thrown it, positioning it beneath the camera before turning back to the bed.

Tearing the pillowcase off his pillow, I stood on the table

and stretched to swing the fabric over the camera. When it hung from it the best I could manage, I carefully lowered myself to the floor and moved to stare out the window and wait.

If nothing else, I'd find out how often Rafael watched me on the cameras. The sun had long since risen over the water, leaving me with a breathtaking view of the sparkling Mediterranean. It only made me miss my view of the neighbor's house a mere feet away back home.

Our cramped and crowded house seemed far more welcoming than all the luxury that surrounded me, knowing I was just another piece of property to Rafael. My family loved *me.* They would miss me as soon as they realized I wasn't coming back.

That was what a home really was, and I hated all the times I'd taken it for granted.

He didn't make me wait for long before the locks clicked on the bedroom door and he stepped into the room. A man followed at his heels, carrying the chess board I recognized from Ibiza into the space. He didn't so much as glance at me as he deposited it onto the end table and moved it to the front of the sofa.

Rafael dismissed him with a nod after he set the pieces on the board carefully, lining them all up and depositing the bag into his back pocket. Once the door was closed and the man was gone from sight, Rafael grabbed the cushioned chair from beside the bed and dragged it into the little sitting area. Claiming the side with the black pieces, he slowly unbuttoned his suit jacket and draped it over the back of the chair.

I didn't know where he'd gone during the morning while I slept, but he was back to the immaculate appearance of a businessman. Dropping into the seat carefully, he turned playful eyes my way after raising his brow at the covered camera. "Did you really think that was the only one I had in here?"

I swallowed back my fury, leaning against the window as I faced him and looked around the room. With none of the others easily visible, there would be no chance of me knowing if any corners were safe from prying eyes. No chance of me obscuring his view of me when he insisted on locking me away.

"Why would you need cameras in your bedroom at all?" I asked, narrowing my eyes on his intent gaze. The thought that maybe I wasn't the first woman he'd watched on those cameras unsettled me, turning what the darkest part of me hoped was a twisted obsession into something far more common. If Rafael was just another powerful man with a complex for raping innocent young women, then I was nothing more than a statistic.

A pawn in a game that countless women had already lost.

He leaned forward, resting his elbows on his knees as his pointer finger touched the pawn with the fissure on the top. The same piece he'd moved first in our very first game. "Does it still bother you to think of other women in my bed, *mi princesa?*"

"Of course not," I snarled, denying the jealousy coursing through me. That forbidden part of me wanted to rise up in response to the taunt, to claim him in the way he'd tried to make me his alone. But he wasn't mine to claim.

A woman couldn't tame a nightmare who wore skin to disguise the monster within.

"They're for you," Rafael said, lifting the pawn into his hand and nodding his head toward the sofa across from me and inviting me to take a seat in it without another word.

"So that I can watch you when I can't be with you. No other woman has been in this bed, Princesa," he said, setting the pawn back down in its designated starting position.

"Please," I scoffed, rolling my eyes to the ceiling as I stepped away from the window and took the seat on the sofa. I swallowed back the traumatic response that tried to well up within me being so close to the chess pieces he'd tortured me with. I perched on the edge of the cushion, dropping my hands to wrap around the edges and sinking my nails into the smooth fabric to center myself against the need to lash out. "You expect me to believe that?"

"I'm a man," he said with a shrug. "I am no virgin, but you are the first woman I've ever desired for longer than it took to get off. That is why you angered me when you insinuated this was nothing but sex. Had that been the case, our relationship would have been over before it began."

"This isn't a relationship!" I argued. "That term insinuates that I have a choice."

Rafael smirked, adjusting his legs as he watched me with darkening eyes. Every time I spoke, every opportunity I took to argue, the monster showed in the lines of his face a little more. From the tense line of his jaw to the purse of his lips and narrowing of his eyes, he wore the monster under his skin more visibly.

He had nothing left to hide.

"You're right," he conceded, shocking me into silence. My mouth dropped open as I stared at him. "A relationship isn't the best term to describe what is between us."

I swallowed back my fear as his lips curved into a challenging grin. I opened my mouth to speak, floundering for what to say in the moments where I was entirely caught off guard by his agreement. I hadn't anticipated it.

"You're to be my wife, after all," he said, the line of his

teeth showing between his lips as his smile broadened. "I believe that makes engagement a much more appropriate term than relationship. I've never particularly thought of myself as your boyfriend. I find the title doesn't appeal to me much. Too common for my place in your life."

I stared at him in horror, trying to will my breathing to return to normal as I swallowed back my scream. "What is wrong with you?"

"Husband feels more up to par with who I am to you. Yours, irreversibly," he said, ignoring my question. "As to what is wrong with me: I saw something I wanted. I maneuvered the pieces to take it for myself. You were outmatched long before you even knew we were playing, *mi princesa*."

"Divorce exists," I spat. "Nothing is irreversible."

"It is for you," he replied, sweeping out a hand to the board. "I didn't come here to debate the semantics of our engagement. Play a game with me," he said.

"I'd rather stab you with the pieces, my fiancé," I said, giving him a saccharine smile.

His eyes dropped to my lips, watching them form the words as something clicked into place on his face. He ran his tongue over his teeth, studying me thoughtfully. "Husband will be better," he said.

I glared at him, turning my face to the chessboard in front of me and considering my options. "What do you say we raise the stakes?" I asked finally, even knowing the chances of winning were next to nothing. In our previous games, Rafe moved pieces around the board like a professional. Cunning and manipulative, he barely had to glance at the game to know how to trap me.

"Let me guess: if you win, I have to let you go free?" he asked, watching as I nodded my confirmation. It couldn't come as a surprise, given my freedom was all that I wanted from him. "And what do I get if I win, *mi princesa?*" he murmured, tipping his lips up with his amusement as he leaned forward and into my space across the small table. With his eyes so close to mine and studying me intently, I swallowed as I tried to come up with a response.

With something I could stand to give him.

"I'll stop trying to run," I offered with a swallow.

He chuckled darkly, leaning back and crossing his arms over his chest as his teeth sank into his plump bottom lip and he grinned at me. "You can try to run all you want," he said with a shrug. "What difference does it make to me when there's nowhere for you to go?"

I clenched my eyes closed, trying to rack my brain for something that I could offer to the man who would only take what I didn't give anyway. There was nothing I had that wasn't already at his mercy. "What do you want?" I asked through gritted teeth.

I opened my eyes as he reached out a hand suddenly, catching my chin and tipping my head up to look at him. His thumb dragged over my bottom lip, pulling it to the side harshly before sliding into my mouth. I bit down on the offending appendage, sinking my teeth into his flesh as he chuckled. "I want your mouth, *mi princesa.* I want you on your knees in front of me, worshiping my cock with your pretty pink tongue without fear that you'll bite me."

He retracted his thumb, dragging my lip away from my teeth as he drew his entire hand away. "It's your move, Princesa," he said, sitting back in his chair. His hands touched the arms of it, his posture relaxed as my body vibrated with need. The memory of the bite of the shower floor against my knees the first time I took him in my mouth set my skin on fire. My cheeks heated as I leaned forward, touching a pawn and staring at the board intently.

I started with the King's Pawn Opening, the irony not lost on me.

That was what I was to Rafael despite his words about a King protecting his Queen, but it was also one of the few openings he'd taught me in the little time I'd known him. He grinned as if he could sense my realization, the knowledge that I would never win against him.

It was foolish to even try. Chess wasn't a game that was mastered through beginner's luck, but by studying the board and strategy relentlessly.

I watched him counter with his Sicilian Defense. "Who taught you to play?" I asked, making the effort to take his fixation off the game as I studied it intently and moved my own piece.

"My father," he said. "Initially anyway. He didn't appreciate it when I started winning, so I played with my uncle and cousins in the summers when I would visit them. Sebastian was a worthy opponent," he said as we continued playing.

"Who did you play when you were home?" I asked, my nerves rising higher. I couldn't distract him from the game, because he never paid any attention to it. He simply went through the motions as if he'd already won, and I knew it to be true.

I heaved out a sigh, glaring at the pieces as if they were to blame for my stupid wager. I might not have been free without it, but I wouldn't be settled between his legs and trying to fight off the attraction I knew I shouldn't feel as I gave him the one part of my body he wouldn't dare to take by force.

He stared at my mouth as if he could already feel it wrapped around him, leaning forward and looking down at the board more fully for the first time. "No one regularly. Most men tire of losing fairly quickly."

He moved his piece, turning his eyes up to mine with a grin. "Check." I turned my eyes down to the board, finally realizing just how long he'd drawn out our previous games past what he could have done. His lack of focus on the game wasn't because he didn't want to play, but to give me the opportunity to think and learn.

Fuck.

I touched my hand to my bishop, watching as he pursed his lips. Taking my hand off the piece hastily, I reached for my Queen and moved her. He took it ruthlessly, announcing that if I'd had any doubt, the game was as good as done.

I moved, capturing a pawn in what seemed like the only move I could make. "Checkmate," he said, not bothering to use his turn. With the space I'd vacated, I'd given him a clear line to my King as he toyed with me.

He stood partially, pushing his chair back from the little table between us and giving space in front of his body. With his legs spread, he leaned back and looked like the devil on a throne of sin. "A deal is a deal, *mi princesa,*" he murmured.

I stood on shaking legs, suppressing the desire to deny him what he'd been promised. Walking to the space in front of him, I swallowed back my anxiety as I stared down at him. With his knees to either side of my legs, I touched a hand to each arm of the chair and lowered myself to my knees in front of him. "Good girl," he murmured, reaching out to stroke my cheekbone with his thumb.

I glared at him despite the nerves making my hands shake as I touched a hand to the belt buckle at his waist. His eyes dropped to the contact as I pulled the leather through. Unbuttoning his pants and tugging down the zipper on his pants came after, his eyes on mine as I stared up at him with a nervous glance.

I chewed the corner of my mouth and hesitated, unsure if I could really proceed. Already the thought of pulling his cock free from his pants made heat bloom between my legs. It was a perversion, a sick twist of my body turning against me in a way that shouldn't have happened. There was nothing normal about desiring the man who'd kidnapped me.

It all came back to the part of me that should have never been set free. That part that should have stayed hidden beneath the surface until the day I died.

I considered not following through, backing away from him and letting him take it out on my pussy in the way I was sure he would. But setting the tone for our bets to not be followed through wouldn't work to my advantage, and he'd make me enjoy whatever he did to me. Whether he used my mouth or my pussy should have been inconsequential.

I slid my hand inside his pants and reached into the boxer briefs that covered him and helped hide his bulge from innocent bystanders as he went about his day. He groaned as my palm wrapped around him, pulling him free from the layer of fabric until he hung free, heavy in my hand. I stroked him from his balls to the tip of his head while I held his eyes.

He reached out one of his hands, tangling it in the hair at the back of my head and pressing me down until his head brushed against my lips. I opened my mouth, letting him guide me down until the taste of him exploded in my senses. He slid over my tongue, releasing his grip at my head to grab the arms of the chair and leave me to do it on my own.

Filled with the knowledge that he'd meant his words about wanting me to worship him, I knew it would be different than the time in the shower. He'd used my face then, pushing me to take him harder and faster as his hips thrust in and out of me.

Now he leaned back in his chair, watching me with rapt attention as I stretched my mouth wider to accommodate his girth and slid up and down on his length of my own will. He took my hand in his, wrapping my fingers around the base the best I could and guiding me into working what I couldn't fit into my mouth.

There was something intoxicating about his eyes on me, about the heat in his stare as he watched me hollow my cheeks and suck. I shifted my hips as it brought a physical reaction in my belly that begged for relief.

I closed my eyes, focusing on the mechanics of what I was doing and trying to tune out the rest of everything. "Look at me," Rafael commanded in his deep voice, forcing my eyes to open with the words. I glanced up at him as his hips shifted up, driving a little deeper into my throat. With his eyes on mine, there was no denying the heat blooming between my legs or the way I wanted him inside me. "If you want me, then take me," he said.

I shook my head, focusing my attention back on his cock and getting him off as quickly as possible. Admitting I wanted him wasn't something I was willing to do. Letting him come inside me was something even less tolerable, and we both knew that was what would happen if I let him fuck me.

"Fine," he grunted, his frustration evident in his scowl. "Touch yourself." I drew back off him, releasing him with a wet sound as he popped free of my mouth.

"No."

"Put your fucking pretty little fingers between your legs and play with my pussy until you come all over them, *mi princesa*," he said. He pushed to stand, making me back away on pained knees as he wrapped a hand in my hair and pulled me back to his cock. His other hand guided himself to my mouth, slipping inside and shoving deep as I gagged around him. "You should have just hopped on my cock and gone for a fucking ride."

I mumbled around him, touching my hands to his thighs and digging my nails in. The fabric of his pants interfered with me hurting him the way I wanted as he hit the back of my throat with hard drives that made my eyes water.

"Don't make me fuck your ass today, Isa. Touch yourself," he said. I glared up at him, dragging one of my hands down between my legs and lifting my dress as he used my face. Dipping into the front of my underwear, I touched two fingers to my clit and circled it in the way he always seemed to do. My hips squirmed at the contact, a strangled gasp escaping around him as he groaned his pleasure. "You think you can deny that you want me? I can *hear* how fucking wet you are just from my cock in your throat. You can try to lie to yourself, but your body tells me no lies."

I moaned around him, watching as his lips twisted into a pleasurable snarl with his anger.

He pulled out, working his hand up and down his length furiously. "Open your fucking mouth." With a swallow, I did. Even suspecting what was coming as he angled himself toward my face. He pressed the head inside, jerking himself off until the taste of his release coated my tongue. "Show me."

He pulled back, leaning forward until his face was in front of me and he stared at his cum on my tongue. I swallowed as he pulled me to my feet roughly, planting me in the chair and dragging my panties down my thighs. His hand covered mine, helping me work myself higher and higher toward an orgasm as he leaned in and devoured my mouth in a rough kiss. Uncaring of the fact that he'd just come there, he swept his tongue inside and used his quick fingers at my clit to send me spiraling into an orgasm.

I moaned against him, both desiring more and hating him for giving me the climax I hadn't wanted. The one that betrayed everything I should have been.

Good girls didn't have sex with murderers, and they most certainly didn't *like it.*

I woke up to the sound of the shower running the next morning, and Rafael's side of the bed empty. Sitting up, I clutched the sheets to my chest and looked around the room. He'd left shortly after getting me off the day before, only returning to the room to bring me food before leaving me alone once more. If his intent was to bore me to death, I feared he would win that battle sooner than later if he forced me to stay in a bedroom with nothing to do for another day.

He stepped out of the bathroom, a cloud of steam following him as he made for the closet. Dressing in one of his suits, he stared at me as I watched him move around the space. "You understand there is no way off the island, yes?" he asked.

I nodded solemnly. I still didn't know what I'd do to get off the island, but I knew the solution wouldn't come without Rafe's involvement, and if he'd chase me back home, then escaping at all was futile. It would only endanger my family and friends needlessly if he meant his words about dragging me back.

"If you would like, you can spend the day with Regina while I work. My office is in the main part of the house, and you would be welcome to join me there as well. Somehow I suspect you would rather help Regina in the kitchen."

I looked up at him hopefully, biting my bottom lip thoughtfully. "I can leave the bedroom?"

"If you cause problems, I'll bring you back here. But so long as you're kind to Regina then I have no problem with you having freedom around the house, but for now I'd like you to stay with her. Just until you have a better sense of the island and your place on it. Is that acceptable for you?" he asked, buttoning up his shirt.

"Yes," I agreed. "I'll take anything over being locked up in here. But who is Regina?" The jealousy in my voice couldn't be missed, and I mentally scolded myself for it.

He smirked at me knowingly. "My step-mother, I suppose," he said. "My housekeeper now that my father has passed."

I nodded with flushed cheeks, scurrying for the bathroom to shower quickly while he finished dressing. It seemed ridiculous to embrace the freedom as if it was a gift when I'd still be trapped on his island.

I hated myself for the gratitude I felt, when true freedom should have been my right.

His palm came down in a firm slap against my ass as I passed him, making me turn a shocked glare at him over my shoulder briefly before I continued on my way.

Given everything that had happened, scolding him for touching me seemed irrelevant. If there was one thing I knew about Rafael Ibarra, it was that he did as he pleased.

And to hell with what anyone else thought.

"*I* want to talk to Chloe," I demanded as I stepped out of the bathroom and into the bright bedroom, where Rafael sat on the same chair he'd occupied during our game of chess the day before. He lifted his hand from the sleek cell phone where he'd been reading something intently, quirking a brow up at me as if to remind me that I was in no place to make demands. "She's supposed to go home today. Will she make it home?" I asked, dropping my eyes as my lip quivered slightly. I wanted nothing more than for my friend to have made it home safely and be out of Rafael's reach.

Even if it meant she would tell my parents who I'd gotten involved with and about my sudden disappearance when I didn't come home with her.

He stood slowly, pushing his cell into his slack pockets as he studied me. "Your friend made it to the embassy the night she called you. They put her on her plane two hours ago, and she is safely on her way back to Chicago, despite her best efforts to convince the authorities that you'd been taken by a mad man and needed help. The police informed her they had spoken with you, and you merely made the choice to extend your vacation indefinitely."

I swallowed back the rapidly building saliva in my mouth as I considered the reach Rafael must have to be able to manipulate the police into such a lie. "But that's not true!" I argued, feeling like a petulant child as I tried to consider how to communicate my frustration without stomping my foot. He'd seen me as an innocent girl who was too naive to understand what she was getting herself involved with and used that to his advantage.

He'd been right, but I wouldn't further add to that image

by throwing a tantrum. Besides, stomping my foot wouldn't be nearly as fun unless his face was beneath it.

"In Ibiza, the truth is whatever I say it is, *mi princesa*," Rafael murmured, his voice deep but smooth like a soft caress as he stepped closer to me. He reached up a hand, stroking the side of my face delicately. Despite the storm brewing in his eyes with his anger hovering just beneath the surface, the lines of his face were oddly tender in an unusual moment of sincerity. "It would have been the truth, had you only trusted your love for me and not believed the rumors a teenage girl whispered in your ear to turn you against me."

"I don't think they can be called rumors if they're true," I hissed. I bit my lip in frustration as I tried to deny the feelings I'd developed for him in our short time together before everything had come crashing down, but the words wouldn't come. I didn't love Rafael; I couldn't.

But I had loved Rafe and losing him felt like tearing out yet another piece of me that I would never get back.

"If you had only chosen to stay, I could have shown you the benefits to being with a man like me. You could have known the beauty my lies afforded you through ignorance, but now I have no reason not to expose you to the reality of the man I am."

"I was never going to choose to stay. No matter how I felt about you or what you made me believe. I would have *never* chosen you," I told him, watching as his eyes darkened. "The fact that you thought otherwise shows you don't know me at all."

"I know you better than you think, Princesa," he said, clenching his jaw and then relaxing it as he shook off his anger at my words. "But here we are. Regardless of whatever you would have chosen, it is my bed you share every night. It is my cock that slips between your legs and sinks into this wet fucking pussy." He dropped his hand to touch me through my sundress, his hand cupping what he could of me with my legs pressed tightly together in shame. Heat exploded through me the moment he made contact with me, proving his point that no matter what I said to him, my body told him no lies. His hand raised up to my stomach, resting his palm against the flat surface as he stared down at it. "And soon enough it will be *my* child that grows in your belly. Do you really think what you want matters to me?"

"I think you're awfully angry for someone who claims not to care," I argued, grabbing his wrist and shoving his hand off my stomach. "I think it kills you to know that I don't want you enough to walk away from everyone who loves me."

His eyes lit as something passed behind them, a thought I knew instantly he wouldn't allow me to be privy to until he was ready. His lips curved into a smirk despite my harsh words, the punishment he'd no doubt crafted in his mind taking the sting away from him.

I could try to hurt him with my voice, but Rafael and I both knew that he was the one with all the power. He could crush me with a glance, break my heart with a word.

Destroy my soul with his touch.

"I suppose we will find out how much it matters in the end," he murmured, taking my hand and guiding me toward the door of the bedroom without another word. While his mood had improved with whatever terrible plan he'd concocted to torment me, I grumbled at his heels as I followed. Knowing that Chloe was at least safe, Hugo was in the front of my mind. My concern for him grew, knowing that he lived close enough to be readily within Rafael's grasp should I disobey him in a severe enough way to make him follow through on his threat to my friends.

I'd pressed enough for one conversation, but I'd need to ask after Hugo and his brothers soon enough, though part of me wondered if Hugo might be better off if I never mentioned him and hoped Rafael simply forgot he existed.

That didn't seem likely for the man who saw everything and used it to his advantage.

As we moved through the halls, the house seemed different in the light of day. The shadows of the corners weren't ominous, but brightly lit with the Mediterranean sun. He turned to stare at me as we emerged from the labyrinth of halls, waiting until I stepped into the open space where he'd reminded me of the consequences for failing to escape him.

I'd never stood a chance against Rafael. I'd never had a hope of protecting my heart from him, of keeping him out of my soul. He'd claimed it as his. Even as I stared up into his dangerous eyes, I knew that no matter what he'd done, I would never get it back.

We all lived with formative events in our lives, moments that defined us as people. The day I'd placed my hand in Rafael's and let him take me to bed had been the day that would define me as a woman for the rest of my life. For better or worse, he'd stained my soul with his darkness, tangling it with my own until I couldn't deny what stared back at me from the shadows.

I'd never been meant for the light.

He wrapped his arm around my waist as I jolted in his touch, guiding me toward the kitchen and the woman who faced away from us. Stirring something on the stove, she spun slowly as we approached and Rafael pulled me forward with gentle hands. "Regina, this is my Isa," he said as her warm brown eyes dropped to mine. So like my mother's, the immediate comfort in them made tears burn the back of my throat irrationally, even as my irrational heart swelled at hearing Rafael call me his.

I missed my family in a way I'd never thought to experience, something that only came with the knowledge that I might never see them again. That they may never know what had happened to me. Forcing a smile to my face and resisting the tears that threatened at my eyes, I nodded to her in greeting. "It's nice to meet you."

"Oh, *mi hija*," she said softly, patting her hands on the dish towel she'd grabbed off the island in front of her and stepping around to meet us on the other side. Rafael's eyes were heavy on my face, his stare weighted by the confused furrow to his brow. She reached out a hand to slip a gentle finger beneath my chin and tilt it up to look at her. "She's so beautiful," she said warmly, turning a proud smile to Rafael. He never looked away from me, staring at my face as I turned my gaze away in a hurry to escape the questions in his eyes. "His mother would have loved you."

"You don't even know me," I said, whispering as I sniffled. The last thing I needed was for Rafael's mother to approve of me, but I still couldn't help the irrational grief I felt for a woman I'd never known.

For the closeness I felt to a ghost.

"It's in the eyes, *reinita*," she said, cupping my face in her hands. "You are everything she would have wanted in a daughter, and you wear that in them like a window to your soul." The words reminded me of my grandmother, of her assertions that you could tell everything you needed to know about a person with one search in their eyes.

The mouth could lie, but the eyes only ever spoke the truth of our souls.

If it was true, I wondered what she would see if she looked at Rafael. I'd seen the darkness in him that first night, but I'd thought it something I could withstand and then walk away. I hadn't seen the truth, but I wondered how much of that was because of my own desire *not* to see it.

"Go and work, *El Diablo,*" Regina said teasingly as she waved him off. "I will take care of your Isa for now."

"Are you alright?" he asked me, ignoring her attempt to shoo him away. I turned my gaze to his finally, nodding my head even if the movement felt fragile. I wanted nothing more than to break down into tears, and I knew that point would come.

Every day, every second felt like another revelation. Another strike against the walls of my sanity, and there was only so much more I could take before it crumbled.

"I'll be fine," I said shortly, not trusting whatever words I might speak. He leaned down to kiss me, not seeming to mind in the slightest that his step-mother watched the interaction with a happy smile on her face.

"Behave," he murmured against my mouth, reaching up a hand to tangle in the damp hair at the back of my head. The warning was clear as he held my eyes while he kissed me gently, defying the sweetness of the kiss itself by tugging just enough to make me inhale sharply.

As quickly as he'd touched me, he disappeared down a separate hallway from the labyrinth we'd emerged from. This one went off the kitchen, ending in only two doors a short way down.

Regina cleared her throat, moving to the stove to turn back to whatever she'd been cooking. She hummed as she stirred, filling the space with the comforting and smooth sound of her song. I took a seat at the island, fiddling with my hands and glancing around the space. "How long have you known Rafael?"

"Since he was born," she said, smiling at me over her shoulder. "He was such a happy baby, though you would never guess that now. Very close with his mother, which his father hated of course. Men like Miguel thought the boys belonged with men, not attached to their mother's hip." My hand went to my own stomach, to the memory of Rafael's proclamation that his child would soon occupy the space within me.

I couldn't let that happen. Not while I had any chance of finding a path to freedom and a life without Rafael Ibarra breathing down my neck.

"He wants me pregnant," I whispered, leaning across the island counter with a glance toward the hallway where Rafael had retreated. "I don't want that. Please." I didn't know how to voice the request, and the words felt too dangerous to speak even if I had been able to find a way.

She turned off the stove, stepping around the island and standing next to me. "Such things are beyond my control, *mi hija*. Just as they are now beyond yours."

"But it's my body. If I don't want a child, I should have access to birth control," I whispered back, furrowing my brow at her in frustration.

"It *was* your body, but that is not how things work in Rafael's world. It is his now, and he will do whatever he pleases with it. Far easier to accept it than to fight the inevitable," she murmured, stroking a hand over the top of my hair and then stepping back. "Come. You look like you could use some fresh air. We'll just go out by the pool. The sun heals all wounds." She winked as she glanced toward the hallway Rafael had disappeared.

I nodded despite the sinking feeling that Rafael

wouldn't like it, letting her guide me to the French doors that led to the infinity pool. The pavers of the deck felt hot through the bandages on my feet as we stepped outside, staring out at the Mediterranean as I tipped my face up to the sun. It felt like it had been a lifetime since I'd been outside in the day.

Like the time we'd spent in the sun in Ibiza was nothing but a distant memory.

"Thank you," I murmured, turning my gaze back to her. She smiled kindly, her lips parting as if to speak as I shifted my gaze to the village behind her. To the people who had abandoned me to suffer whatever fate Rafael deemed appropriate. I hoped to leave the island in one piece, but if I couldn't find a way, I didn't know that I'd ever forgive the people for what they'd done.

For leaving me to die here.

As I watched them move about in the distance, my heart stopped. The familiar and imposing figure stepped out of one of the houses, glancing up to meet my gaze as he froze solid. The recognition in the motion confirmed everything I suspected and couldn't know was true, considering the distance.

I sprung into action, sprinting across the pavers and onto the grass at the other side of the pool area. "Isa!" Regina gasped, stretching out a hand as if to catch me. But I shook her off, determined to cross the distance between us.

Joaquin stepped closer to me, heading me off before I could get to the village, with a nervous glance behind him. His hands wrapped around my upper arms as I flung myself into his arms. I grinned up at him when I found him unharmed, only happy that Rafael hadn't hurt him.

"*Mi reina*," he whispered, his face pinching as he tried to guide me back toward the house. Regina closed the distance between us, her hand covering her mouth as tears stung her eyes. "Let's get you home."

"What are you talking about?" I asked, spinning to stare at him once more. The house he'd stepped out of loomed in the background, Hugo's smiling face appearing as he and Gabriel emerged from it.

The happiness I'd felt at seeing them unharmed fled, replaced by a sudden emptiness as I tried to understand what stared me in the face.

Victims of abduction didn't smile as they stepped into the sun, unless they were free. They didn't look horrified when their eyes locked on mine.

Hugo mouthed my name as I backed away from Joaquin, the stinging bite of betrayal striking me through my confusion. "Let's go home," Regina said at my back, reaching down to take my hand in hers. Her bottom lip trembled when she met my eyes, and it hit me that out of all of us, I was the only one who was lost. I was the only one who didn't know the truth.

So much for the promise of no more secrets.

Hugo closed the distance between us slowly, swallowing and licking his lips as he and his brothers watched me for a reaction. "What's going on?" I whispered, tears burning my eyes.

I tried to connect the dots. I tried to put the pieces together, but where there should have been connections, there was only blinding betrayal and pain.

"What are you doing here?" I asked when he didn't answer. His silent stare met my words as he swallowed, then clenched his eyes closed so he wouldn't have to look at me. *"What are you doing here?!"* I screamed, backing away a step as my brain tried desperately to find an excuse that didn't mean it had all been a lie. That I'd been set up from the very beginning.

"Gabriel, go get Rafael. Now," Regina ordered. The middle Cortes brother nodded and gave me one last sad look, sprinting up toward the house above us.

"This is my home," Hugo said, swallowing around the words. He gave me nothing else, didn't take a step toward me or move to comfort me as Regina tried to pull me into her arms. I shrugged her off, filled with the determination to stand on my own two feet as my world crashed down around me. I'd known I would lose Hugo when I came to Ibiza.

I just didn't know it would be like this.

"Did you—" I paused, wincing when my lip felt wet with tears. "Did you tell Rafael about me? Did you set me up for *this?*" I asked. He shook his head, his face pinching as if it pained him to stay silent. "I don't understand," I cried, shaking my head.

"I didn't choose this for you. Please know that," he said, his voice catching on the words.

"You didn't choose this?!" I screamed, stepping into his space. My hand collided with his cheek, the stinging of my wounds bursting to life as the slap echoed through the clearing. The pain grounded me against the tumult of emotions swirling inside me.

Rage like I'd never known felt like it would consume me. Like it would pull me to the depths of hatred and never let me go.

My body trembled as I raised my hand again. He stood there, just waiting for the second blow as if he knew he deserved it.

It only made it worse.

"Settle, *mi reina*," Joaquin said, wrapping his arms

around me and pulling me away from his brother. "That's enough," he murmured softly. The soothing sound of his voice felt like a betrayal against everything I'd thought I knew about the brothers. Like the fact that it had all been a lie would split me in two and I'd never be the same.

"Take your hands off her." Rafael's deep voice barked the order. There was no hesitation as Joaquin obeyed, stepping away from me with his hands raised innocently. Regina stared at Rafael in horror, shaking her head in a silent plea. "I gave you one rule," he said to her. "She was not to leave the house for exactly this reason. Are you happy?!" He spoke in that calm, deadly measured voice of his that was more intimidating than most people yelling, swinging a hand out to me where I stared at Hugo with a tear-stained face.

"Rafael," she pleaded.

"Go," he ordered, turning his back on her as he stepped up to me. He put himself between Hugo and me, demanding my attention in a way that might have felt jealous if it hadn't been illogical.

"I don't understand," I said, staring up at him as he moved closer into my space. His huge hand cupped the side of my neck, his thumb moving gently over the surface as if he could feel me shattering beneath his touch.

"I sent the Cortes brothers to you in Chicago," he said. I froze, blinking up at him blankly and biting my bottom lip as I thought back to how long Hugo had been a staple in my life.

"That's not possible. It's been over a year," I whispered, trying to back away from his touch.

"Sixteen months," Rafael said, watching my face as I tried to do the math. "It's been sixteen months since the first time I saw you, standing on the sidewalk across from *Fists of Fury*."

All the air expelled from my lungs as my body sagged. The day came crashing back over me, the way I'd stared at the mysterious man across the street and thought about the darkness that surrounded him.

I'd wanted him even then, but known that he would never be anything other than disaster for a girl like me.

"That was you," I whispered, backing away from him and stumbling over my steps. I fell to the ground on my ass, staring up at the devil in front of me in horror. Joaquin looked like he might try to intervene, his body jerking as if he meant to protect me. But even he stilled with a glare from Rafael as he reached down and plucked me off the ground. "Why?" I couldn't possibly begin to comprehend that choice. To wrap my head around the months of planning and manipulating that must have happened for us to end up right where we were.

He ignored the question, continuing on with his story as he wanted. "A few days later, your sister and her friend drugged you," he said. My body went still, remembering the vague recollections I'd had of the phantom in the night. The fact that Joaquin had never made me feel the way he supposedly did when I'd been drugged. "Two weeks later, I killed him for what he tried to do to you. To what was *already mine,*" he rumbled.

His grip tightened around my upper arm as I cried, shaking my head from side to side as I tried to deny the truth that stared me in the face. I tried to find another explanation, but instead of reassurance there was just nothing.

"I watched you. I studied you. And when the time came for you to finally come to Ibiza, I used what I knew to make you fall in love with me," he said.

I opened my mouth to speak, but found myself suddenly stripped of my voice. Something inside me cracked, breaking open while they watched and it felt like I bled all over the ground.

Everything I'd thought I'd known had been a lie.

Nothing but a game to a man who'd violated me before I'd even known he existed.

*S*he nodded her head, the only sign she'd even heard me as she snapped right before my eyes.

I'd wanted her broken.

But not like this.

She turned on her heel as I released my grip on her arm, moving toward the house while I followed. The others trailed at my heels, the concern etched into the lines of their faces echoing the splintering I felt in my soul. Objectively, I knew this moment had always been inevitable. I'd known it the moment I sent Hugo to insert himself into her life, and it had only been confirmed with every day that I spent watching her.

Watching her grow closer to Hugo. Watching her trust the three of them, but particularly Hugo, in a way she never should have trusted anyone but her husband.

Anyone but me, even if trusting me was foolish in reality.

I'd thought there would be a fleeting moment of happiness when I ripped away the last of her bonds with a male rival, but instead there was only a deep, cavernous self-loathing.

When she reached the pool area, she crawled up onto the daybed where I'd fucked her the night before. Sitting in the middle, she hugged her knees to her chest and stared out at the water.

Her body went still, as if she'd shrunk back inside that place she went when nobody watched her in her bedroom at night.

The place where she ceased to exist.

I stepped toward her, determined to draw her out of the shell she'd crawled inside of. While I'd known she'd hurt when the truth of my deception was revealed, I never could have expected her to fade away before my eyes.

"Leave her be, *mi hijo*," Regina said as she stepped out of the kitchen. Her face was set with determination, despite the fact that she'd fled my wrath only moments before. "She needs some time."

"You don't know her," I said, shaking my head as I watched her. I'd never seen her in her bedroom when she went silent because of my refusal to put cameras in her room when she was underage, but when I thought of what a person must do to be so quiet? This was the exact image that came to mind. Her sitting on her bed, trapped in her head and overthinking everything.

It should have been simple to understand. I saw her. I wanted her. I *took* her. I wanted to be the one to bring her back to life. To remind her what it was to be mine and to welcome my possession.

"I know what it is to be a woman grieving the loss of a friend," Regina said. "She'll come around, *mi hijo*. But the greatest kindness you can give her now is the freedom to process in her own way."

I nodded my head as I watched Isa. Joaquin stepped up at my side. "I'll watch over her," he said.

"She doesn't leave your sight. I have a feeling she'll come out swinging when she gets out of her head." I sighed, turning to the house and forcing myself to try to get some work done.

I'd have a long wait while Isa worked through her grief.

🙾

*J*oaquin stood guard over her like a sentry, determined to keep her safe from anything that might harm her while she cried silently. Night came before she ever moved, her eyes glued to the horizon as the sun set and she didn't stop to appreciate the vivid colors. I sipped my scotch as I stepped outside, staring at her back and the unnatural stillness in her body.

"She's still grieving," Regina said sadly. "She wouldn't eat."

"She's grieved enough," I said, handing her the empty tumbler as I turned a glare to her.

"Be gentle with her, Rafael. With her like this, you'll never know the damage you cause until it's too late."

"Is that how it was when my father murdered your brother on your wedding day?" I asked, turning a cold stare her way. "Were you grieving the first time he raped you?" Even I recognized that I was overly harsh, but I blamed her for the way Isa had retreated.

She shouldn't have learned the truth yet.

"You are not your father," she said, but she turned her eyes away and swallowed. "He was a brutal man, and I knew what was coming the day he killed your mother. He'd never been secretive about his intentions for me to replace her. I only wish that my brother hadn't tried to intervene and been hurt in the process. What you did with Hugo was cruel, but the intention was to protect her and not to hurt her. Eventually, she will come to see that." She patted my back reassuringly and disappeared around the corner of the house. Making her way to her own home to hide out for the rest of the night.

Watching Isa process what I'd done before we met made me feel closer to my father than ever despite her words. I felt like more of a monster in those moments than I had with any of the people I'd killed in cold blood.

Regret wasn't something I knew how to feel, but if anyone came close to bringing those emotions to the surface in me, it was Isa.

She was my only weakness and the only person I cared for. The one thing that my enemies could use to hurt me. She was my vulnerability and my distraction.

My greatest sin.

I stepped up to the side of the daybed, staring at her profile as she gazed at the water. Her eyes were half-closed, as if the exhaustion of holding one position for so long threatened to put her to sleep then and there. "Come to bed, *mi princesa*," I murmured.

Her gaze never left the water, but the miniscule twitch of her body confirmed she'd heard the words. That even when she'd withdrawn, I could reach her. "Isa," I said, waiting to see if she would look at me. When she didn't, I stepped around the daybed and directly into her vision. "Come." I held out a hand for her, and she shifted her gaze down to it.

There was a moment of recognition in her eyes as she remembered all the other times I'd asked for her consent in the same way. As she realized they'd all been a ploy, because she'd never had a choice.

Her life had become mine the moment I laid eyes on her.

Her lips were dry as she turned her stare up to mine, a glare in it as they met mine in fierce challenge. I watched the moment *mi princesa* died on the pyre, her innocence lost as the last pieces of my deception snapped into place.

Mi reina was born from the ashes, her face twisted in fury as she uncurled her legs from her body and slid along the mattress. The night before, Isa would have fled off the other side of the bed. She'd have craved the distance between us.

Instead, she welcomed my darkness, meeting it with her own as storms swirled inside her green gaze.

"I hate you," she whispered, sliding off the edge of the daybed to stand before me. With the defiance in her face, I almost didn't doubt the words.

But that pulsing attraction between us couldn't be denied, no matter what words her mouth formed. I knew the truth that tormented her twisted little soul.

"Such a pretty lie," I murmured, stepping closer. Her breasts grazed against my chest as she drew in a deep, steadying breath. "You love me, and you fucking hate yourself for it," I said, lifting a hand to touch her face. I wanted to bottle her anger, to remember the fierce look in her eyes as she proved that everything I saw in her hovered just beneath the surface.

She'd always been one break away from unleashing her darkness on the world.

She slapped my hand away before I could touch her, the crack of her hand against mine echoing through the silence around us. "Don't fucking touch me," she growled. There was no fear in her face, no moment of recognition where she realized I'd killed people for less. I lifted my hand to stare at the pink skin where she'd struck me in surprise, before turning a smirk back her way.

"You shouldn't have done that, *mi reina,*" I purred, tilting my head to the side as a sick smile transformed my face.

"Sorry to disappoint the great *El Diablo,*" she said mockingly. "But I don't live to please you." She planted her hands on my chest, shoving me away from her hard enough that I stumbled in a moment of shock. She spun away from me, moving to walk back toward the house and leave me staring after her in the night.

I stepped forward, snatching her arm up in a tight grip. She twisted it and slapped me away again, glaring at me as if she could tempt me into her trap.

But she already owned me, and Isa was slowly realizing the depths of my obsession.

"You don't get to touch me anymore," she snapped, her glare faltering for a moment as she wondered how far I would push the envelope. The truth was, even I didn't know the answer to that.

I suspected there were no boundaries I wouldn't cross when it came to her.

"Another pretty lie. We both know this is going to end with you coming on my cock, *mi reina,*" I said, tugging her into my chest. She pushed me away again, unwilling to give up the fight so easily.

It was a good thing her resistance and the fire that burned inside her turned me on. Anything was better than the empty shell who'd stared at the water, but watching her come into her own and become my equal was unparalleled. The Queen I'd always sensed hiding beneath the surface and smothered by everyone else's expectations of her could finally be free.

Because their opinions no longer mattered.

"Fuck you," she hissed, jerking in my grip.

Chuckling, I lifted her into my arms as she struggled. She buried her fingers in my hair, gripping the short strands with all her strength and pulling so harshly that my scalp burned beneath her assault. Nails dug into my head, but I persevered to get her to our bedroom. I kicked the door open when I made my way through the labyrinth of hallways designed to give us time to escape in the event of an emergency, using my foot to close it behind me.

"That is the idea," I chuckled, dropping her onto the bed. She landed on her back, bouncing as she stared up at me where I stood at the foot. "And you'll love it, just like you love me," I said, my confidence in her feelings growing every time I said the words. No matter what she said to me, it was never a denial of our connection.

"There's something wrong with you," she hissed, watching as I stripped off my suit jacket and tossed it to drape over the back of the chair next to the bed. "Why did you bother with that charade in Ibiza if we were always going to end up here? What was the fucking point?"

I unbuttoned my shirt, sensing the vulnerability in her words as I watched her. The vague traces of the broken-hearted girl peeked through the cracks, trying to return despite her resolve and her evolution. As much as I loved her innocence, Isa would need to be stronger than that if she was going to stand by my side through everything I'd put her through in the future.

"I gave you the chance to fall in love with me. To *choose* me," I said, giving her a rare moment of complete honesty. "You didn't."

"Of course I didn't," she laughed, her face twisting as if the thought was absurd. It probably was. "I met you a week ago. I can't just abandon my family for a man who will toss me aside the moment he finds a new toy."

I glared at her, stripping the shirt off my chest and tossing it on top of my jacket. Her eyes tracked down from my face, gliding over my chest and to my abs as I gripped my belt and kicked off my shoes. "That isn't going to happen. I waited sixteen months to have you. I won't be so easily distracted from my obsession with you."

My pants and boxer briefs followed as I kicked them off, standing naked in front of Isa. "How the fuck was I supposed to know you were some kind of stalker?" she asked, rolling her eyes as she huffed in disbelief.

"Not some kind of stalker. *Your* stalker," I corrected her, reaching out for her. I grabbed her by the ankle, dragging her over to the edge of the bed. She kicked at my hand, but nothing would change the fact that she'd laid there and watched me strip.

Nothing would change the fact that she wanted me, in spite of her better judgement.

There'd come a time when she wasn't afraid of my darkness, where she welcomed it as part of her because she was just as twisted as I was. There'd come a time when she accepted that was who she was.

For now, I held her squirming legs still long enough to shove her dress up her hips and tear her panties down her legs. They bunched at her knees as she fought me, but it didn't matter for what I had planned. If anything, the restriction at her knees only helped as I pinned her legs to my chest and drove inside her.

She screamed from the sudden invasion, her pussy clenching around me to protest the brutality of it. I reached around her legs when she rose up onto her hands, pulling down her dress until her breasts sprang free from the fabric so I could watch them bounce as I fucked her.

With hard drives, I bottomed out inside her as her ass hovered at the edge of the bed. She grunted with the force of my thrusts, taking what I demanded of her without a verbal complaint.

Even while she glared at me, her pussy clenched me like a vice and tried to keep me locked inside her. As if her body needed it as desperately as I did.

When I wasn't inside her, I was thinking about it. When I was, I already dreaded the moment it ended. Her lush mouth twisted with pleasure as I struck the end of her, her hips rising to meet my thrusts as she sought more pleasure.

Wanting to feel her pressed against me, I tore her panties down her legs since she was feeling more cooperative and spread her wide so that I could lean my body over hers. I crashed my mouth against hers, tasting her as my tongue swept inside and claimed what was mine. I cupped her breast in my hand, squeezing it gently and working her nipple with my fingers while she moaned into my lips. "Tell me again how much you hate me, *mi reina*," I teased, pounding deep enough to shift her on the bed. I slid a hand into her hair, pulling her back down so I could drive into her with furious strokes as she glared at me.

"I hate you," she hissed, wrapping her legs around my waist to defy her confrontational words. Her arms followed, wrapping me in her embrace as she pulled me tighter to her body. With only the fabric of her dress bunched at her stomach between us, the lines of my body touched hers.

Every inch of skin vibrated as if electricity pulsed between us, the same shock of knowing I'd felt the moment her eyes connected with my own.

We were made for each other, no matter what I had to do to get her to see that.

She twisted her body, pulling me forward into the bed with her and rolling me to my back while I grinned at her. Instead of moving to separate us as I might have thought, Isa rolled her hips and took me deep. I tore the dress off her head, wanting to see every line of her body as she moved on top of me. The traces of the innocent girl who was insecure in her body were gone, replaced by the temptress who knew how deep my obsession ran.

I'd seen every inch of her, and I was still as obsessed with her as the first day I'd touched her, if not more.

Her body trembled and she ground her clit against my pubic bone as she rode me, chasing after her own orgasm with a brutality that threatened to make me explode before she had the chance. But I watched her dance on me, watched her face morph with pleasure as her pussy clenched down on my cock.

I'd thought to flip her to her back when she came, but she rode me through the orgasm despite her panting breaths. I groaned as my release approached, gripping her hips as she rocked hers back and forth on me. With her eyes intent on mine, the intimacy of the moment seemed unparalleled. My teeth sank into my bottom lip, and Isa shifted her hips suddenly to pull me out of her. I coated my stomach in my cum as she rubbed her pussy along my shaft to work me through the rest of my climax.

"Next time, wear a fucking condom, asshole," she hissed, swinging her leg over my hip and standing from the bed.

She disappeared into the bathroom, leaving me to laugh alone in her absence.

I woke up the next morning, the early sunshine streaming through the floor to ceiling windows making my eyes peel open. In the suite, Rafael had rarely slept later than me. He'd often been awake and working in the living room by the time I stumbled out of bed to eat a quick breakfast before he shared his plans for the day.

I'd naively thought he was some kind of sales manager, and I still didn't understand if that lie related to how he was a murderer or if it had been a complete fabrication. I got out of bed and moved to the windows, staring at the private little dip pool on the private terrace with a roll of my eyes. Given the extravagance of the main pool, having a separate one was just wasteful. It disappeared over the side of the cliff this side of the house rested against, the water of the pool blending in with the water of the Mediterranean. I touched the button on the side of the glass, jolting in surprise when the window whirred to life with a quiet murmur and retracted into the ceiling.

I glanced over my shoulder at Rafael, amazed that he would have slept through the noise. He always woke up so easily that I fully expected him to spring from the bed before I could step outside. I wrapped my arms around myself, eyeing the tall partition walls that kept the private terrace free from wandering eyes as people moved around the house.

I hadn't seen too many of them the day before, not with how quickly Regina had led me outside and I'd seen the brothers, but as I stepped outside I heard the soft murmur of voices on the other side.

There were none that I recognized, but the unmistakable sound of men and women conversing couldn't be denied. I imagined if the entire island was loyal to whatever El Diablo did, they were probably a fairly regular part of his life. Stepping onto the deck, I stared at the sun as it rose over the water. My body protested every movement I made after sitting for so long the day before, drawing a groan from me as I inhaled the fresh air.

I knew the moment Rafael woke up behind me, the sudden commotion of his body as he sprang into action when he found me missing from his bed. The movement stopped when he spotted me, and then the faint sound of footsteps came as he slowly made his way across the bedroom. His nude form pressed into the back of mine and the nightgown I'd thrown on before coming to bed the night before. Sweeping the hair off my shoulder, he touched a light kiss to the skin there.

My flesh raised in response even though I wanted nothing more than to hate the way his lips felt on my flesh. I'd seen him with blood on his hands. I knew one of the people he'd murdered. His crimes weren't innocent, and his sins were unforgivable. He'd forced me to grieve the loss of a friendship that had never really been mine to begin with.

"I thought you'd run," he murmured.

"Where would I go?" I asked flatly, wincing when his arms squeezed me tighter. He'd made certain I knew that there was no escaping him. That he would cross over oceans and all boundaries in his pursuit of this twisted obsession he had with me. He didn't respond, because there was no answer to that question. There was nowhere I could run. "Why do they call you *El Diablo?*" I asked. He nuzzled his face further into my neck, breathing in deeply as if he could draw me into his lungs.

"More questions? Is *mi reina* ready for the answers?" The sound of his voice rumbled against my skin, the vibrations pulsing through my body. I knew what it was to have all that power between my thighs, to have his mouth worship my flesh as if it was his favorite meal, and I could never seem to separate myself from the physical response he elicited in me. Was that how it was for everyone when they lost their virginity? Was it something that was unique to us or was I just too naïve to know the difference?

"I don't see how it matters if I'm ready for the answers at this point. You took that choice away from me when you brought me here," I murmured, stepping out of his grip to turn to face him. His multicolored gaze fell on mine, searching my face for something I didn't know that he'd find.

I felt like a stranger, like the cold had crawled out of the depths to embrace me in a shroud of emptiness and only my moments of rage could bring me back to life. Nothing about my life back home felt safe. He'd tainted that with his stain before I'd ever known he existed.

He could and would have my body, but I had to find a way to shield my heart from the pain he caused. Rafael was a raging inferno, consuming everything in his path without regret.

He turned my mind into chaos, threatening to make me need him in a way that I never should have. I needed answers to the burning questions circulating in my head if I was ever going to shove him out of my soul. If I'd ever find a way to cleanse myself of his darkness.

"*El Diablo* means the devil," he said.

"I knew that much, thanks," I said sarcastically. "That doesn't tell me why they call you it. What do you do, go around the world murdering innocent people for fun?"

"I do a great many things, *mi reina*," he said, grasping my chin in his grip so that he could hold my eyes with his. "I own legitimate businesses like *Lotus* and *Moon* in Ibiza, but I also own the underbelly of the island and some of the territory on the mainland."

"The underbelly?" I asked, squinting my eyes as I tried to understand what he was saying. I'd lived a sheltered life, so caught up in the safety of my routine that I couldn't help but feel like I was outside my realm of comprehension.

"The criminal side of the city. The term you would probably be most familiar with is the mafia, but my ranks are not limited by the same kind of familial bonds as those are. My men work their way up the ranks by proving themselves loyal, not by being born to my father's men."

"The mafia? Don't they sell drugs and weapons? Don't they sell *people*?" I asked, flinching back from him. Those fingers held my chin steadily, refusing to release me as I struggled against his touch. Wayne had been an asshole, and I could almost convince myself that he deserved what he got. But there were some lines I couldn't tolerate, and selling people was so far beyond that limit I didn't know what to do with myself. "No wonder you thought it was perfectly acceptable to abduct me off the streets!"

"I assure you, *mi reina*, you are the first person that I have ever kidnapped in this way. Human trafficking isn't something I tolerate, especially after seeing you standing on the side of the road. Completely unaware that a war raged around you in Chicago when one side of the war fought for the right to sell young girls just like you into sexual slavery. My alliance with the Bellandis is what brought me to your city when I saw you, and my desire to stop trafficking only grew when I thought of what might have happened to you had I not offered you my protection." His words felt like they unlocked a piece of my heart, with the worst of the crimes he could have committed off the table.

"But drugs?"

He nodded. "I am not a good man, *Princesa*. My men sell drugs. I negotiate arms deals with governments all over the world, and I care little for anything beyond how much they will pay me. Women work for me *willingly* in the sex trade. My crimes are extensive, but I do what I can to mitigate the fall out on innocent people."

I shook my head as angry tears threatened my eyes. "Except for me," I whispered.

"Except for you," he confirmed, leaning forward to tease my lips with his.

The kiss was gentle as he willed me to feel something he couldn't say. I didn't know what there could be to say beyond the fact that he was a murderer. That he was a criminal beyond redemption.

It went without saying that he'd never let me go.

I just didn't know why.

"*F*uck!" I screamed, clawing for purchase along the shower wall. Rafael's hands gripped the underside of my ass, lifting it up to give him a better angle as he powered through my tender tissue. The ridge of his cock stroked over my back wall as the rain shower head dropped water onto my back and where he took me.

"You'll fucking take it," he grunted, shoving into me so harshly that my hands slipped along the wall and the side of my face planted into the tile. One of his hands left my ass, his massive arm stretching over my body to press the palm of his hand to the side of my head as he held me completely immobile.

Each thrust forced me up onto my toes, his balls slapping into the backs of my thighs in a sound that bounced off the shower walls.

"Touch my pussy," he groaned, using his other hand to grab my wrist and shove my fingers between my legs. I stroked my clit, building the pleasure higher and higher as he took me.

"Oh God," I whimpered.

His hand came down on my ass in a sharp slap, stinging the skin with his reprimand. "There's no God here, *mi reina*. Only *El Diablo*." My fingers stroked faster, pressing harder into my clit as something brushed against my *other* entrance. I jolted in his grip, trying to move away from the added sensation as he applied pressure slowly.

The water eased his way as he slid a finger in my ass, the burn of it drawing a ragged groan from my lips. "Rafe," I whimpered.

"Fucking come, Isa," he ordered, pulling his finger back and then sliding it back inside me. He thrust inside me sharply, pushing me over the edge into a blinding orgasm as my body felt too full. Too taken by him and consumed.

He groaned behind me, shoving deep as he flooded my body with cum before I came down from my orgasm. I groaned my frustration into the shower wall, trying to push off and dislodge him. But he held me still with his hand at my head, keeping me trapped as he slid through my pussy slowly.

He slid his finger from my ass as he released my head finally, leaning back to watch his length as he pushed in and out of me twice more before finally pulling free. "I think I won round one today," he murmured with a chuckle, wrapping his arm around my chest and pulling me up until my back pressed against his front. "We'll see who wins round two later."

"You're a bastard," I groaned, shoving off from his body and washing myself furiously. "I'm eighteen. You could at least give me time."

"Time for what exactly, *mi reina*?" he asked, reaching between my legs with his bare hand to help me clean myself off. His fingers slid inside me as he watched my face, teasing me as if he wanted me in a constant state of desiring him. "For you to think you've found a way to leave me?"

"To figure out what the hell is going on!"

"I've already told you exactly what is going to happen. You're just too stubborn to hear it," he said, stepping out of the shower and grabbing a towel from the rack. I hit the switch for the shower, turning off the water as he dried himself off quickly and wrapped the towel around his waist. He grabbed another, holding it out for me to step into.

"I'm not stubborn. You're unrealistic," I argued.

"We'll see," he murmured with a laugh as he moved into

the closet and grabbed one of his suits. Watching him dress was to watch him don the persona of a gentleman.

But if there was one thing he'd taught me, it was that the devil was a gentleman. He'd pretended to be whatever he needed to lay his trap, and by the time I'd realized I was his prey, it was too late.

I was already caught.

He tossed a dress onto the bed, the dark apricot fabric with a subtle white pattern standing out against the white bedding. I sighed and resisted the temptation to reject it.

Picking out my clothes was a new level of controlling, even for him.

But the shape of it looked comfortable, and since I had no intention of walking anywhere on my throbbing feet that day, all I wanted was something easy. I pulled on the white bra and panty set he tossed to me, shrugging the dress over my head and smiling when he glared at the low neckline where it dipped to show the top of the valley between my breasts.

"Maybe you should change," he murmured, twisting his lips as he retreated back into the closet. I turned for the door, striding out while he chased at my heels with a disgruntled noise of frustration.

"You picked it," I teased. While I might have felt uncomfortable wearing it, I'd never resist the chance to torment him. I had no power in our relationship, if you could even call it that, and I'd take whatever small victories I could when they came.

My confidence faltered when we emerged into the main space and Rafe guided me to the kitchen. Joaquin sat at the island, sipping a cup of coffee as he ate an omelet and Regina flipped something on the stove.

I gave Rafe a look of condemnation as he sat me in the

chair next to Joaquin. My cheeks flushed as Regina turned a bright smile my way, feeling like it couldn't be possible they hadn't heard me scream my orgasm into the shower wall as Rafael fucked me into it. Neither of them said anything to that effect, but her gaze felt too knowing as she flipped an omelet on to a plate and slid it in front of me. My stomach grumbled with hunger, knowing I hadn't had much to eat at all since leaving Ibiza.

I hadn't exactly been in the right mood to eat, but the plate in front of me was too appetizing to resist. She slid a bowl full of fresh fruit in next to the plate, pouring orange juice into the glass. "Joaquin is going to keep an eye on you from now on," Rafe said, touching his lips to the top of my head and then making his way around the side of the island. I leveled his back with a glare as he made his way past me, picking up my fork and stabbing into a piece of banana before popping it into my mouth and chewing.

Rafael moved to the coffee maker on the counter, clicking the buttons on the machine as he spun to look at me. His face twisted into a smirk as he met my glare, gripping the counter and leaning his ass into it. "Don't look at me like that, *mi reina*," he murmured, his hands gripping the surface. "You might find out just how much I like your glares."

I blushed, darting a glance to Regina and then to Joaquin at my side. The traitorous ass never looked up from his food, minding his own business despite the innuendo to Rafe's words. Regina only smiled, trying to hide it as she cleared her throat and forced her mouth back into a neutral expression.

"Rafael!" I scolded, my voice a strangled whisper.

He pulled his coffee cup from the machine, blowing on the scalding liquid gently and leveling me with a smirk. "I'll never hide our sex life in my own home," he said. "Are you offended, Regina?" he asked.

The older woman shook her head, smiling through the motion. Rafe strode over to me, tilting my face up and kissing me gently before continuing across the kitchen to the little hallway that led to his office. "You didn't ask me," Joaquin said to his back.

"Because I don't care what you think," Rafe called back, making Joaquin chuckle at my side.

"Eat your breakfast, *mi hija*," Regina said, drawing my attention away from Rafael's retreating figure. "You've gone hungry too often lately, and this is good for fertility," she added.

I dropped my fork to the plate with a clatter, turning disbelieving eyes up to Regina. She smiled in response, as if there was nothing unusual about discussing fertility with a woman she hardly knew who had already expressed the desire to not be pregnant. I picked the napkin up off the counter, wiping my mouth as I thought over a response. "I've lost my appetite."

"Rafael will not be pleased if you don't eat," she said, a smirk tugging at her lips. "I think I would take my chances with the food, as I suspect his displeasure will be more likely to cause pregnancy than simply eating a healthy breakfast."

Joaquin snorted at my side, covering up the sound by taking a sip of his coffee. It didn't escape my notice that nobody bothered to offer me any. Whether that was because of my distaste for it or the seemingly unanimous desire for me to fall pregnant quickly, I couldn't know. "You have no issues with the fact that I'm eighteen and don't want his child?" I asked her, picking up my fork as my stomach grumbled. I wish I could have said the spinach and mushroom omelet was gross, but to my famished stomach it was one of the most delicious things I'd ever tasted.

Second only to the *ensaimada* Rafe had hand fed me in *Dalt Vila*.

She turned her lips down into a frown. "I can understand why it might seem odd for you, coming from how you were raised, but Rafael is thirty-three years old. He needs to consider the future of his legacy. To be honest, he should have started producing heirs years ago, but by the time he realized he was interested in it, he'd found you. His plans have already waited longer than I would have thought him capable." She said the words as if they should reassure me. Instead they only confused me more.

"Why should that have mattered? I can't imagine he would have cared if he brought me here when he already had a spawn to call his own. He doesn't seem to give a shit if anything he does affects me," I said, glaring at her before turning my glare to Joaquin.

"I can understand how it might feel that way now, but Rafael loves you. He will do what it takes to have you, but he doesn't enjoy hurting you unnecessarily, aside from what had to be done to bring you here and to make you see that it isn't temporary," she said. Her words echoed in my head as my vision blurred.

I shoved the thoughts away with denial. "He doesn't love me. He would have told me if he did."

"Just as you've told him that you're in love with him?" she asked with an arrogant smirk. "Rafael doesn't understand emotions. His father beat them out of him when he was a boy and killed all traces of them along with his mother." I froze as Joaquin went still at my side. Regina closed her eyes as she realized she'd probably said something she shouldn't have.

"His father killed his mother? He told me she died in a fire," I said, shaking my head. Of all his lies, I thought that one might have been the worst.

"She did," Joaquin said at my side. I turned my stare his way, wishing I could undo the way that his face hurt me. It shouldn't feel so familiar, not when every word he'd ever spoken to me had been a game. A job. He might not have hurt me as much as Hugo, but I'd grown close to Joaquin in my own way. "He burned her alive," he added, holding my stare with deep brown eyes that sucked all warmth from the room.

Regina nodded her confirmation as tears stung her eyes, and I turned back. "But why?"

"He became unhinged as he grew older. There was never an official diagnosis since he didn't trust doctors, but he thought she was a witch. Things got worse when Rafael was born and had her eyes. He said it was the mark of her witch-craft." Regina shook her head, her lips moving as my world spun. I knew better than most how judgmental some people could be about even the most miniscule of differences, but to kill someone over their eye color was...

Deranged.

That was the man who had birthed Rafael. In the event he did get me pregnant, what would my child grow to become? Another monster?

"Is that what Rafael will do with me when he tires of me?" I whispered, staring up at her in shock. No matter what Rafe said to try to assure me I was a permanent staple in his life, I couldn't imagine there hadn't been a time where his father fed his mother the same pretty lies.

"He won't grow tired of you, but even if he did, he's not his father," Regina reassured me. "He may be cruel, but the only thing that would cause him to become that unhinged would be losing you."

"Everyone gets tired of fucking the same person every day when there's no love involved," I said bitterly.

"Rafael will tell you he's obsessed with you. He doesn't know it is love yet, but he'll get there," Regina repeated, echoing her words from before as she stared at me intently and I forked a massive bite into my mouth to avoid having to respond.

"Men like Rafael have two outlets," Joaquin said at my side. "Killing and fucking. He lost one of those when he saw you and you were too young for him to touch. Trust me when I say that his men spent the last year parading all manner of tempting women in front of him to try to get him to fuck, because his cruelty knew no bounds when he didn't have you with him. He killed. He punished his people more brutally than he would have if he'd had a warm body in his bed," he said. "But never once did he show the slightest interest in any of them. Men who are only obsessed do not give monogamy to a woman who doesn't know he exists. He gave you monogamy because he loved you, even then."

I laughed, the smile fading from my face as his eyes held mine intently. "Are you saying Rafael hasn't been with anyone in sixteen months?"

"I'm saying he hasn't so much as *looked* at another woman since he saw you," Joaquin said.

"Why are you telling me all this?" I asked, glancing between the two of them as they leaned in closer. As if whatever came next, they didn't want Rafe to overhear.

"Because you're so desperate to be free that you haven't stopped to consider something. You look at Rafael like he's your captor. Like he took you from your life and made you his prisoner," Regina said. "But you imprisoned him long before he ever touched you."

"The game is over when the King is lost," Joaquin said, glancing at the chessboard sitting in the breakfast nook as the sun shone in the windows. I hadn't even noticed it when I walked in, but the same pieces sat on the board.

The same ones that had haunted me in the streets of Ibiza.

"But the Queen is the most powerful piece on the board," I said, turning my head to face Joaquin in my confusion.

"You have all the power, *mi reina*. He's already tried to tell you as much." I bit my lip, considering his words. "All that's left is for you to use it."

When the sun had started to set over the horizon, Alejandro knocked at the side door of my office, avoiding the main space as I'd requested.

Until I felt she was ready, I thought it best to keep her as isolated as possible. Certain events would prohibit it from being entirely true, but I'd do what I could to let her acclimate. Putting Alejandro's mauled hand and his limp directly in her face didn't seem like it would be the best path forward if I wanted her to relax, especially with what was coming once the sun went down.

"Everything is ready for tonight," he said as he dropped into a chair on the other side of my desk. "Are you sure you want to go through with it?"

There was no hesitation in my response. "It's tradition."

"She won't like it," he said, shaking his head in warning.

"It's part of life here. She'll have to come to terms with it eventually," I said, continuing on with the next task I had for him. "I want you to find Pavel's sons."

He nodded, pursing his lips to the side. "Which ones?"

"All of them, but start with the oldest." He widened his eyes, biting his bottom lip.

"Are you sure that's the wisest move? He's already restless after your interaction in Ibiza."

"He could have cost me Isa," I warned. "With his relentless need to insert himself into my vacation with her, he put everything I'd planned at risk. He needs to suffer for it. His sons were going to die anyway. Knowing he'll watch me kill each and every one of them before I finally come for him will be his punishment."

"You'll leave Isa here to go hunt Pavel's sons?" he asked, questioning my motives. It would kill me to leave Isa behind, but there would always be business I needed to tend to off the island. She wouldn't always be able to accompany me, as much as I very much liked the idea of having her waiting for me when I finished and went back to our hotel room at the end of it.

But the reality was, she was much safer on *El Infierno*.

Most of her time would be spent here, particularly once our child was born. That would give her a distraction, because *mi reina* had never been good at inactivity. Boredom would be her worst enemy.

"Yes. She'll remain here for now. Hopefully there will come a time soon enough where I can trust her," I said, dismissing him as I stood from behind my desk. As night fell through the windows, I made my way toward the door to the rest of the house.

Isa was curled up in the breakfast nook, a book in her lap as she studied the words intently. The cover brought a smile to my face, the chess pieces staring back at me as she glanced up from the book. She studied the board, moving a piece with her expression deep in thought.

In the yard behind the pool area, a fire raged in the pit

halfway between my home and the start of the village where my most trusted people lived. Regina met my gaze as I made my way to the French doors that led to the yard with Alejandro at my heels. Isa's face twisted as she realized I intended to walk past her without greeting, but the events of the night required a certain detachment.

I regretted nothing I would do that night, but that didn't mean I wasn't weighed down by the reality of what was still to come. Penance was necessary, a tradition that kept people from failing me. That kept them from betraying the loyalty I expected of my men.

Hugo had failed me months ago, but his connection to Isa had prevented me from giving him the penance he'd earned. Nothing stood in the way of him paying the price for that failure now that Isa was aware of his involvement with me. I stripped off my suit jacket, tossing it onto one of the stools at the island as I glanced toward Isa one last time. She pushed her chair out from the table, looking as if she might follow me into the night.

But women had no place at the pyre, not unless the penance was theirs to pay.

That day too would come.

My shirt followed, draping over the stool as she held my eyes in confusion and glanced toward Regina who wisely held her tongue. "What are you doing?" Isa asked when I didn't move to strip my pants down my legs.

"Stay here," I ordered her as Alejandro swung the doors open and stepped outside. I followed, pulling them closed behind me with a meaningful look. Turning my back on her finally, I hardened myself to the mask my people saw.

Only Isa threatened to make that mask slip, only she could make me realize that it was a mask at all.

The pyre loomed closer as Hugo approached from the

other side. Gabriel accompanied him, standing by his side to help him stumble home. Hugo's first penance—there was no telling how he would react to the skin melting off his body.

The brand already burned in the fire as he stripped off his own shirt and knelt at my feet. I held his eyes as some of my other most trusted men gathered around to bear witness to his penance, to offer their support in the fact that he willingly accepted the punishment for failure. Giving ourselves to the fire was the only true way we could cleanse our bonds of the negative responses to such things.

Never again would I blame Hugo for what happened with Isa all those months ago. His penance would wipe his sins from his skin.

He'd be free to continue to work for me, without the disappointment of his failure influencing his future.

"Do you accept your mark?" I asked, staring down at him. He swallowed down his nervousness, his dark eyes glittering in the flames beside me that heated my skin. My own brands burned with the memory of skin melting, and I remembered what it had been to anticipate the first mark.

The terror I'd felt looking up into my father's eyes when I'd dared to cry as my mother burned. The same fire that burned her had been the flame to give my first penance.

"Yes, *El Diablo*," Hugo said, his voice carrying through the night air. Heads around me nodded their agreement, the soft acknowledgement of the ways that had been ingrained in our history for as long as I could remember. The tradition might have been barbaric to some, but it was ours.

And it was an honor to continue a tradition my people held to so strongly.

I picked up the glove and slid it onto my hand, reaching to the fire and grasping the handle of the branding iron in my grip. Isa's scream pierced the night as the doors of the house flew open. I watched in confliction as Joaquin grasped her around the waist, working to restrain her and keep her away from the pyre.

She struggled in his grip, yelling my name as if she could stop Hugo's penance. She didn't yet understand that it was as much for him as it was for me, or that he came to receive the mark willingly.

She would soon enough, when it was her who knelt at my feet to accept the penance for her betrayal.

"*Let go of me!*" I screamed, shoving at Joaquin's grip. "That's your fucking brother!"

"Isa, it is better that you don't watch," Regina said, stepping out from the kitchen to speak softly. "This is part of life here. Rafael does what he must. But you do not need to see it," she said.

I shoved at Joaquin's arms one last time, dropping to the ground when he released me suddenly. Looking back toward the fire, Rafael stood watching us and holding up a hand for Joaquin. The order was clear.

I hurried to my feet, glancing around the fire as I approached. My eyes widened as I realized that the majority of the men standing there wore the same scars on their chest as Rafael. The same tally marks marred their skin. I stopped in the space between Rafael and Hugo, putting myself between them.

"Isa no," Hugo sputtered behind me. He didn't move to touch me, not when Rafael watched us both with a stubborn set to his jaw.

"Move, *mi reina*," Rafael said as my eyes dropped to the

red hot brand in his hands. To the mark that would soon occupy space on Hugo's skin if I didn't intervene.

"I won't let you do this," I said, shaking my head from side to side as men around the fire looked at each other in surprise. "Why would you even want to?" I asked.

His jaw clenched as his free hand grabbed me by the arm, jerking me to the side and away from Hugo. "Do not ever choose another man over me, *mi reina*. If you seek to protect him from my wrath, choosing him over me is the wrong move. You will sign his death warrant instead." He paused, willing me to see the truth blazing in his eyes that seemed to spark with madness as the fire cast shadows on his face. "Hugo came to the fire willingly. He accepted his penance because he knows he failed me. Will you do the same when it's your turn?" he asked, making me flinch back from him.

"When it's my turn?" I asked as tears stung my eyes. "You would do that to me?"

Silence hung in the air as his men waited for his response, my heart in my throat as I watched him swallow. "Yes. You earned a mark for your betrayal."

"What betrayal?" I asked, staring in the face of a monster. The conversation I'd had with Regina and Joaquin that morning seemed a world away from the reality of who he was.

He was not a man who could love. He was not a man at all.

He was nothing but a nightmare waiting to drag me to the pits of Hell.

"*You left me!*" he roared, the sound of his anger echoing off the house in the background. His men flinched back, their faces shocked by the extreme display as Rafael lifted the brand. I stepped back from him, shaking my head frantically as he shifted his grip from my arm to my chin, digging his thumb and fingers into my cheeks. He squeezed tightly, holding my gaze as he moved forward quickly and pressed the brand into Hugo's flesh.

It sizzled beneath the heat of the brand, crackling as it melted and the smell of burning flesh filled the fresh night air. Gagging against Rafael's grip on my face, I fought to step back when he tossed the iron to the ground at his feet once he finished with Hugo. Those burning eyes never left mine, his glare intense as he turned toward me and forced me to turn my face down to Hugo's pained expression. "He allowed you to be drugged. He let you be nearly raped. *This* is his penance for that failure."

"That wasn't his fault," I sputtered. "How could you do this to people..." I gasped as his grip tightened more, reaching up my hand to touch the marks on his chest and caressing the skin there despite the harshness of his grip on my face. "When someone did it to you?"

"It's our way," he said, covering my hand with his as he walked me backward toward the house.

"It's not my way," I argued. "This will *never* be my way."

Releasing me suddenly, he ducked low and pressed his shoulder to my stomach. Lifting me over his shoulder so my head dangled and blood rushed to my brain as he carried me back to the house. I didn't struggle, knowing it would be entirely futile. I had to hope the nightmare I'd seen at the fire had been a glimpse of *El Diablo*, of a man who wouldn't *really* brand me for leaving him. Regina stared on in horror as he strode past her and made for our bedroom, hurrying toward the doors as I watched her leave. The house was silent in her absence after she made herself scarce in the face of Rafael's anger.

He smacked my ass sharply as he walked. "*Never* question me in front of my men again," he growled, a tight warning in the words.

"Then you'd better hope you never fuck up in front of your men. I won't just sit quietly and look pretty while you *torture* people," I argued, wincing when another sharp swat burned my skin. The glove he wore dropped to the floor as he turned the corner to the bedroom, turning the knob and stepping inside the private space that must have been his oasis from prying eyes.

It was nothing even close to the sort for me.

He flipped me over his shoulder, dropping me to my feet as I fought to find my balance and my blood fled my head finally. "It isn't torture when they're willing, *Princesa*," he said. "I will give you leeway where I can in finding your place in my life, but I will not tolerate what happened tonight. Those men are my concern. They are mine to keep obedient so that I can *keep you safe*. If the consequences for betrayal are too lenient, that is when men come to my home and think they can get away with spying on me. That's when your life is in danger."

"You expect me to believe you give a shit if something happens to me? You said you would *brand me!*"

His face twisted, a moment of regret slipping into the fierce expression. "And I will when your time comes. Even the devil is a product of other people's expectations, *Princesa*. I have to do to you what I would do to others."

"When?" I asked as tears stung my eyes. "When will you—"

He studied my face, watching my reaction with a gentle expression. "Tomorrow night."

My jaw dropped as my breath caught, my eyes immediately drawn to the brands on his chest. To the marks that scarred his skin and the knowledge that he could do that to me settled over me. "No," I mumbled, shaking my head furiously as he wrapped his arms around me and clutched me to his chest. *"You can't!"* I screamed, shoving against his body as his face touched the top of my head.

He surrounded me. Overwhelming me with his presence as if he should be a comfort.

But he couldn't protect me, not when he was the one who would hurt me.

"You can't," I repeated, the words coming on a whisper.

He held me still, wrapping my hair around his fist and tilting my face up to meet his intense eyes. He searched my gaze, sighing into the void between us. "There are pains worse than the physical. Give me a different scar. Show me the ones on your soul," he murmured.

"What are you talking about?" I sputtered, reaching up to wipe away one of the tears that stained my cheeks.

He raised his hand to the space over my heart, the beating of it muffled against his palm. "Why does Odina hate you so much, *Princesa*?" he asked, watching as I drew in a ragged breath. Disbelief consumed me that he would ask such a thing of me in that moment.

I sniffled back my fear, pressing my lips together as I glared up at him. To use my terror against me, to pry to get inside my head in such a way was diabolical.

Given everything Hugo knew about my life, there wasn't much I had left that was safe from Rafael's invasion of my life. There was nothing left that was just mine.

But this one thing, the shame I felt for my actions as a child?

That was mine.

And I'd be fucking damned if I gave that up for anything. Even if I should have told him, because he'd never want to be with someone so fucking *stupid*.

I glared up at his hopeful face, at the confidence he felt that I would do what it took to avoid the branding, and I took joy in denying him something that he wanted. Something he couldn't know without me giving it to him. He might be able to take everything else.

I'd be damned if I gave him the last piece of me.

"No."

*H*er mouth formed the word. Her eyes glared up at me. But my brain struggled to wrap around the strength in her voice.

She defied me so beautifully, even knowing it would end in nothing but pain for her. I'd known men to promise me the lives of their children to avoid a brand if they hadn't been raised on the island and in the culture that dominated our community. For a moment I wondered if she thought I wouldn't do it.

If she suspected that my obsession with her would be enough to save her from the pyre. But the steel to her green eyes and the posture of her spine as she squared her shoulders left little doubt. She knew I would do it.

She believed me when I said I'd hurt her. She just didn't care.

Her secrets were more important to her than protecting her flesh.

It confirmed something I'd always known about Isa. She felt safe inside her mind. Whatever had happened in that river, she knew her body was just flesh. That the core of who she was lurked deeper within, and that the place where nothing else could touch her was her ultimate defense.

I knew with sudden clarity that it was where she went when nobody was watching. Why she was so silent in her room at night. The safety of her mind was a haven she couldn't resist when there were no distractions around her.

"No?" I asked, walking her backward. She didn't resist the fact that I steered her toward the bed. There wasn't the slightest attempt to diffuse the situation or deny me access to her body.

Her body was just a shell. *That,* I could have. Just not her mind. Not her soul or her heart.

I'd find a way to pry them open, but until that happened there was one part of her that I hadn't yet possessed.

"No," she repeated, holding her own despite the fury I felt on my face. My skin felt hot, as if I was the pyre myself and I could burn her with my touch. I'd cleanse her with the flames if I could, but I didn't know how to do it when I never wanted to hurt her.

Not like this.

I wanted her to bear my mark, not the mark of a failure. I wanted to not have to hurt her, but she couldn't give me that. She couldn't meet me halfway, so intent in her own damn stubbornness to cling to her secrets. As if her sins were horrible, when they could never compare to mine.

"You'd rather accept a brand than tell me why your sister hates you?" I asked, my voice a grumble in my frustration. I lifted her onto the edge of the bed, setting her on her knees so that she was closer to my height. Leaning forward, I touched my lips to hers and held her eyes. She held perfectly still for my kiss, not returning it or fighting back. Then she suddenly opened her mouth, grabbing my bottom lip between her teeth and sinking them into my flesh until the metallic taste of blood exploded over my senses.

I grabbed her by the hair, wrenching her head back so sharply that she had no choice but to release me. I trailed my blood stained lips down over the front of her throat, leaving a red stain on her delicate fawn skin as I nipped at her flesh sharply enough to mark her. Her gasps fueled me on, her attempt at denying the fact that she wanted it set to fall on deaf ears before she ever murmured a word of protest.

But *mi reina* was coming to terms with her sexual appetite, with her desire for the nightmare who haunted her from the dark. She reached up to grasp my hair, tugging firmly to pull me closer rather than push me away.

I dragged my tongue up over the cord of her neck, baring my teeth one last time when her nails drifted down to my shoulders to claw at me. I took her mouth with mine, catching her bottom lip between my teeth and biting down the same way she'd done to me. Her eyes held mine as the flavor of her blood burst over my lips, staining my teeth as I dragged back slowly. Her delicate pink tongue darted out to soothe the wound, wincing when I settled the palm of my hand over the scar on her thigh.

With my request for information so at the front of her mind, the physical reaction she had to being touched there was even more prevalent. I'd punish her for her refusal to give me what I wanted, for her rejection in not giving me the last pieces in understanding the shards of her history.

But the way she glared at me with her blood-stained lips brought out the other part of me. The Devil who wanted to worship his Queen, because even my hatred of the denial couldn't quiet the simple truth of what she'd done.

Nobody dared to deny me anything.

Nobody but *mi reina.*

I slid the fabric of her dress up her thighs, staring at the smooth expanse of skin as it revealed her body to my gaze. Once the fabric snagged around her hips, she lifted her arms for me with a tiny smirk. So confident that she could take whatever I would give her, she had a surprise in store when her punishment finally came.

Even before the brand, there was a part of her I hadn't claimed. A part of her that wasn't yet mine.

It would be before the night was over.

Raising the dress off and over her head, I lifted her off the bed as soon as she was in her bra and panties. Twisting and striding for the bathroom, I carried her into the room and quickly stripped her of the rest of her clothes before lifting her to set her on the counter. Her shoulders pressed into the cool glass of the mirror as I lowered myself to my knees on the tiled floor.

The same way she'd kneel at my feet the next day to receive her penance. I leaned in, licking her from her entrance to her clit and sealing my mouth over her pussy. She moaned, reaching down to pull at my hair as I worked her with slow strokes of my tongue. Tasting her, laving her with my mouth, I watched her through hooded eyes as her breasts heaved.

She held my gaze, watching me worship her on my knees. She couldn't understand the significance of the moment, but I'd made myself a promise as I watched my father burn alive.

I knelt for no one.

Except her.

Shoving my hands behind her knees, I pushed them high and spread her wide as I pulled my mouth away and stared down at her. Rising to my feet while she clung to me,

I ignored her groan of frustration as I shoved my shorts out of the way and slid inside her. I worked her with slow pumps meant to tease her. Meant to drive her closer and closer to an orgasm that I'd only let her have when I spread her ass wide.

I licked the seam of her mouth playfully, smearing her essence all over her mouth and the wound I'd left with my teeth. Opening for me, she let me tangle my tongue with hers in a duel of willpower. Her hips rose on the counter to the best of her ability, pressing her tight pussy higher on my cock as she sought out her own orgasm.

I pulled out, abandoning her mouth to draw a nipple between my teeth and nip at her sensitive flesh sharply. She moaned as my fingers slid between her legs, stroking in and out of her and tormenting her g-spot. Getting them wet enough for what I'd need next. I slid them free, staring down at her swollen and needy pussy as my finger drifted lower.

Her eyes widened when I touched a wet finger to her puckered hole, pressing against it firmly and persistently until her flesh parted to let me in. She whimpered as it slid inside, meeting the resistance of her body as she tensed. Reaching over, I opened one of the drawers and pulled out the bottle of lube that waited for exactly this purpose.

I hadn't thought to do it when I was angry with her, when my frustration made my body tense with the need to fuck some sense into her. But Isa loved everything I did to her. She met me stroke for stroke even as pain crashed over her when I took her too roughly.

Once she got over the shock of the adjustment, she'd love taking my cock deep inside her tight heart-shaped ass.

I squirted the gel all over my second finger before gliding it in next to the first.

"Rafe," she whimpered. "I can't."

"You can and you will, *mi reina*. You think you can deny me and decide your own consequences? You'll take me in your ass tonight, and then tomorrow you'll kneel at my feet and let me brand you. It would have been so much simpler to give me the answer I wanted," I said, curling my fingers inside her ass and scissoring them apart. Stretching her as she tried to squirm away from my assault. I stilled her with my free hand at her throat, wrapping my grip around her jaw.

"It hurts," she whined, trying to lower her thighs to restrict my access. I pulled my fingers free, yanking her down from the counter and turning her around. I lifted one of her legs up, resting it on the counter to spread her open for me as I slammed inside her pussy and moved my fingers back to her ass while I fucked her slowly. She grunted as I stretched her while feeling my cock move on the other side of the thin barrier inside her. I moved in and out with opposite strokes to the way my fingers worked her, gliding over tender tissue until the moment when her pained gasps changed to reluctant moans.

"Rafael wait!" she begged as I pulled my cock free from her tight sheathe and covered it in lube. I pumped it in my grip, pressing the head against her hole as she tried to climb up on the counter to escape. I grabbed a fistful of her hair with my other hand as I applied pressure to her while she clenched.

"Relax, *mi reina*," I ordered. "It will hurt less." She whimpered as my head popped inside her, her hands clawing at the surface of the counter. She gripped my cock like a vice as I fought my way inside her. Her back strained as she drew in deep breaths, unable to move as I pulsed in and out of her in shallow thrusts. Watching her body stretch to accommodate my invasion, I used my grip on her hair to lift her up until she had to stretch to support herself against the mirror. Watching her reflection, I shoved through her swollen tissue until my groin touched her ass and she screamed. "Touch yourself," I ordered, staring into her eyes in the reflection.

Her hand slid down off the mirror slowly, gliding to the space between her legs to touch her clit with firm fingers. She circled it fast as she whimpered, her breath catching when I pulled my hips back until only the head of my cock was inside her. Gliding back in with a smooth thrust, I watched her eyes drift half closed, watched the moment she tried to deny how much she liked the forbidden pleasure that built inside her.

"You like it when I fuck your ass, *mi reina*?" I asked, repeating the motion. She struggled as I took her relentlessly, squirming in my grip, but those determined fingers of hers never stopped working her clit for me.

"Yes," she whispered, the admission vibrating through my body and straight up my cock. I pounded into her harder, forcing her to take it even if I was being too rough. With her tight heat strangling me, I had no chance of lasting long.

"I want you to watch yourself come with me in your ass," I ordered, sinking my teeth into her shoulder savagely enough to break the skin. She came, her ass clenching down on me as she screamed out her release and sent me over the edge with her.

I roared as I shoved deep and filled her with it. It wasn't until I came down that I tasted her blood in my mouth, running my tongue over the bite marks I'd left on her as I helped her lower her cramped up leg down from the counter. Pulling free, I moved to the deep soak tub in the corner of the bathroom and turned the water to hot.

She stared at me blankly, wincing as she moved to step

over to the tub. I took sympathy on her, knowing I'd been too rough in my need to consume her and remind her of who she belonged to. Lifting her in my arms, I lowered us both into the tub. She flinched as the hot water touched her abused flesh, jerking in my grip as I forced her to settle.

We sat in silence as I mulled over my options, trying to find a way to work myself inside her head until she gave me the truth.

Until she gave me everything.

*I*sa spent most of the next day locked in the bedroom, trying to ready herself for what she knew was coming. Normally, I might have hated the separation from her. I would have detested the distance she tried to put between us. But knowing what I needed to do, I didn't want to look her in the eye and feed her lies.

It would be agonizing for her. The first time always was.

I wanted to be able to hold her through the pain, to comfort her as she suffered her penance. But the public spectacle of it prevented that. I couldn't be seen as weak in front of my men, and I'd need to be the *El Diablo* they all expected me to be, to prove that my relationship with Isa wouldn't make me more lenient for their transgressions.

My phone vibrated in my pocket as I watched the sun set over the horizon, the fires of the pyre already blazing as my people prepared for Isa's penance. "Yeah?" I barked, lifting the phone to my ear.

"I found your cop," Ryker snapped on the other end of the line. "You aren't going to be happy about it."

I spun away from the window, moving to my desk so that

I could write down his name. "What did he have to say?" I asked.

"Not a damn thing, because he's fucking dead. He mysteriously committed suicide a week after the accident. Nobody ever followed up on his report, since it was just a drowning accident and nobody died...." His voice faded as I thought over the implications. Shaking my head, I focused on the rest of what he had to say even though I wanted to strangle Isa.

A murder disguised as a suicide would mean someone else had been involved. Someone that very much wanted to keep the truth a secret.

"His wife says he was never depressed until the week before his suicide. She thinks he got himself wrapped up in something he shouldn't have been involved with, and that his guilt consumed him to the point that he had to end it."

"Did you look into the suicide?" I asked, lifting a paperweight off my desk. The last thing I needed in the moments before Isa's brand was to be this furious with her for her secrets all over again.

"Yeah, single gunshot to the temple. But not a speck of residue on his hands. There's no way he did it, Rafe," Ryker said. "He was shot in the right temple, but this guy was left-handed."

"Fucking Christ," I muttered. "They didn't even try to make it look legit."

"Not one bit. I found the cops who signed off on the suicide. They both retired a couple years ago and left Chicago, but I'll hunt them down and get our contacts on it. She's still not talking about it?"

"Not a word," I grunted. "Not even under duress."

Ryker paused, his sigh vibrating the phone with static.

"Go gentle. This is fucked, Rafe. I thought she fell in that river, but this?"

"Someone threw her in," I said, voicing the words he didn't dare to say. "Somebody tried to fucking kill her, and she won't even tell me it happened. Let alone who." I growled, "Get. Me. That. Name."

I jabbed my finger into the red button on my cell, tossing it down on the desk. I roared my frustration as I threw the paperweight at the wall, my immediate temper only somewhat abated when the glass shattered and the sound echoed through the house. Regina hurried into the room, flinging the door open in her worry and staring at the mess.

Her face twisted with sympathy as she wrongly assumed that she knew the cause. "You don't have to do this. Nobody will blame you for letting her off this once when she didn't know the rules until last night."

I stared at her, wishing it could be true. If I hadn't given her the chance for an alternative the night before, it might have been. But Isa had made her choice.

And mine along with it.

"It has to be done," I grunted, wiping my hand over my mouth and trying to embrace the familiar cold of being uncaring. Of not giving a shit about who I hurt.

Isa's pained eyes haunted me as if she already knelt in front of me. The betrayal I knew too well because I'd seen it in my mother's eyes the day my father killed her. "Men who love their wives do not do such things," Regina said, pleading with me to see the reason in her words.

I didn't dare to deny my feelings for Isa again, not after I'd already started to come to terms with the way she'd consumed my every waking thought since I'd seen her.

Obsession wasn't a strong enough word for what I felt for *mi reina*. Love didn't seem like enough either.

She was just mine.

"You have to accept your feelings for her if you ever expect her to do the same," Regina said, reaching up to touch my cheek gently.

"Is she ready?" I asked, stepping away from her hand. She closed her eyes, heaving out a sigh as she nodded.

When she opened her eyes, I found disappointment staring back at me for the first time. I swallowed down the confliction I felt in seeing it, stepping around her and moving out of the office.

The time had come for Isa to understand exactly who would be her husband.

She couldn't have me without *El Diablo*. She couldn't be mine without embracing the devil.

I just hoped she would be strong enough to withstand the flames.

I stared out the window, watching as the fire burned, with my heart in my throat and tears in my eyes. Regina had promised she'd try to talk some sense into him, racing in when she'd heard the shattering of glass in his office.

I didn't bother to go to him, knowing reasoning with him would be futile.

Any man who could look me in the eye and talk about scarring me for life knew nothing of remorse. He knew nothing of love. Whatever it was he felt for me, I wanted no part in it. I turned my gaze down to the photo in my hands. Rafael's mother's face stared up at me, far too young to have died, especially in such a brutal way. Her eyes were similar to Rafe's, one blue and the other light grey compared to his green.

He looked like his mother. She possessed the same ethereal kind of beauty that hid his darkness when he wanted.

Rafael stepped up behind me. He brushed the hair off my neck, touching his lips to the bite mark on my shoulder briefly. "She was beautiful," I murmured, feeling him still as his stare settled on the picture of his mother.

"Where did you get this?" he asked, taking it from my hands gently and setting it on the bed.

"Regina gave it to me," I replied, watching as he turned his back on the photo like he couldn't bear to look at her.

"Are you ready?" he asked, shifting his focus back to me.

"Would it matter if I begged you not to do this?" I asked, turning my head to look at him over my shoulder. His bright gaze met mine, something missing in the way he stared at me.

All hints of warmth were gone, replaced by a numbing cold that chilled me to the bone.

"Do you have something you want to tell me?" he asked, stepping forward to put his hand on the doors that led to the pool and fire.

I clenched my eyes closed as my bottom lip trembled briefly. When I opened my eyes to find him waiting, he already knew my answer. Nodding, he pulled the door open and grabbed my hand in his as I tried to back away.

"Come, Isa," he commanded, dragging me through the door. I stumbled over my feet as he set a brisk pace, his footsteps too large for me to keep up with. The flames danced in the night as my heart pounded in my chest.

"Rafe," I said, trying to appeal to the man who'd held me as I cried. The man who'd shown me tenderness as he took my virginity and showed me Ibiza. But all traces of him were gone, and he ignored my pleas.

Joaquin stepped into our path, blocking the fire as the two men waged a silent war. I watched helplessly as Hugo hovered in the distance, his chest bare for the ceremony, the angry red of his brand echoing the flames. I swallowed down my nausea, knowing that my skin would look like that in just a few moments.

Joaquin heaved a conflicted sigh as his lips twisted and his eyes came to mine, but he stepped aside to allow Rafael to guide me past him.

The heat of the fire kissed my skin as he guided us right in front of it. I watched as the smoke billowed into the night sky, mingling with the stars as it carried messages to the ancestors. Rafael turned me to face him, pausing to give me one last chance to give him what he wanted.

But his determination to know the truth only made me more resolved to keep my secret. If this was the man he was, if *this* was the kind of monster he would be, then I'd do everything I could to keep some part of me for myself.

He was no less a monster than a man who would throw a child into a river.

Tearing the strap on my dress to bare my shoulder, he pushed me to my knees as tears fell down my cheeks, my breathing ragged with my fear. His nostrils flared as he stared down at me, his teeth clenching as he prepared to mark me permanently. "Please don't," I begged one last time, finding nothing but brute determination in his gaze as he lifted the brand from the flames.

I closed my eyes slowly, hearing my grandmother's voice in my ears. The soothing sound of her telling me our lore beside the fire in our yard, carrying the passage of our heritage up to the ancestors so they could know that their stories lived on in us.

Fire cleansed. Fire healed all wounds.

I opened my eyes, and I stared the devil in the face while I waited for the pain. Despite my fear, all I could focus on was the determination to look him in the eye as he hurt me. To make him see what he did to me. His eyes flashed with regret as he watched me cry, finally showing a moment of *something.*

His mouth twisted into a scowl as he yelled his fury into the night sky. He moved his arm so quickly I flinched back, expecting the blinding pain of my skin burning.

But it never came.

The logs in the fire shifted and sent embers into the air as he threw the brand into the flames. Rafael spun, disappearing into the night as he stalked off and left me hyperventilating by the fire. Regina raced out of the house on the other side of me as I watched Rafe fade into the dark, wrapping me in her arms as she touched my chest frantically.

"He didn't do it," I whispered, staring up at her in bewilderment.

"No, *mi hija.* He didn't do it," she whispered, tucking me into her chest as sobs wracked my body. She knelt at my side, drawing me away from the fire's edge and folding me more firmly into her embrace as the others dispersed amongst shocked whispers. The brothers closed the distance between us, hovering around me and refusing to leave even though I didn't want to speak to them.

"Why didn't he do it?" I asked Regina, my voice sounding too loud as the fire crackling was the only other noise around us. Joaquin's hand came down on the top of my head, relief in his eyes as he studied the unscarred skin on my chest in something akin to wonder.

"Because he loves you," she said with a smile that faded as she looked up. "And now everyone knows it."

I stood at the top of the island, looking down on the people who relied on me. On the people who counted on me to keep order in a world full of chaos. I'd never failed them before tonight.

Alejandro followed, stepping up behind me in near silence. He didn't speak, but I could feel the intensity in his gaze. The judgment that I'd never hesitated with marking a woman for her betrayal before.

"Isa never betrayed *El Diablo*," he said. "She never endangered the operation. Marking her was never something that should have been done in the same way," he added, making me spin to look at him with incredulous eyes. "Penance is for people who fail *El Diablo*. It's for people who put our safety at risk through their actions. We were never in danger because Isa tried to leave you, Rafael."

I nodded, staring past him to watch as Regina knelt beside Isa below us. Illuminated in the lights of the flames, shadows danced over *mi reina's* fawn skin.

"She left *you*," Alejandro added. "Whatever you need to

do to make amends with her for that choice, it should be between the two of you. It shouldn't be a spectacle."

"That would have been nice to hear a few hours ago." I barked out a disbelieving laugh. "Now everyone knows my weakness."

"Would you have listened? This is something you needed to discover for yourself. It isn't a weakness to spare someone from harm when you love them, Rafael. It takes strength to recognize love for what it is, because it's far easier to deny it and reject those feelings. Especially when all you've ever known is pain and regret." Alejandro had grown as the son of one of my father's advisors. He'd been on the receiving end of their cruelty as often as I had. He understood what it was to be raised by a monster. "I like to think if I ever find *my* Isa, I'll have the courage to tell her how I feel."

"She knows," I said, voicing the fact that it would take a fool not to see how obsessed I was with her.

"She knows of your infatuation with her, but that doesn't mean she knows that you love her. I don't think you've even admitted it to yourself. You might start there." As he retreated back down the hill to the village, I turned to watch Regina guide Isa into the main house.

She wobbled on her legs, the fall from such an adrenaline spike taking its toll on her body without the outlet the brand would have supplied. Even despite the tremors in her body that were so apparent I could see them even from my distance, she held her head high. Joaquin glanced back my way, and though I knew he couldn't see me because of the light from the fire, he nodded once.

Isa turned to look for me once she reached the house, her striking gaze searching for the phantom she couldn't seem to find. The strength in the lines of her face brought a smile to mine. She might have knelt at my feet with tears in her eyes, but the unmistakable crown of a Queen rested on top of her head. She accepted her fate. She didn't act like a simpering fool.

She hadn't closed her eyes, afraid to look the devil in the eye as he delivered her punishment. She'd met my gaze with strength and quiet determination. She defied me.

Without ever saying a word.

It was in those short, breathtaking moments that I came to terms with my truth. The one that pulsed inside me, demanding I give it a voice despite all my denials.

Love wasn't a strong enough word for how I felt for Isa, but it was the only one that existed. She was my weakness. My everything. She was the heroin I would willingly inject into my veins, even knowing it would be the end of me one day. She owned me, body and whatever remained of a soul inside me. That feeling only grew with every day she spent on the island, growing into the woman I'd known she could be.

I couldn't have her without the darkness lurking in her soul. She couldn't have only the pieces of me that she could handle, not without embracing *El Diablo* as well. The only path forward was for our demons to dance together, to entwine until we were one nightmare moving through the darkness.

We'd come together under the moonlight. We'd love under the stars if we survived the night.

I sat on the edge of the bed, staring out the window and waiting for Rafael to show his face. Joaquin and Regina had helped me to the room on wobbly legs, depositing me there to wait alone. There was nothing to be said in the moments where we all tried to wrap our heads around what had happened. They seemed both relieved and shocked at Rafael's decision not to brand me.

I was still hung up on how close he'd come to following through. On the fact that he'd been so close to scarring my flesh permanently, simply because I didn't choose a man I hardly knew over the family who had raised me.

It had been hours since he'd stormed off from the pyre and left me in the dirt. Hours since he'd left me to cry in Regina's arms as I came down from the overwhelming adrenaline rush of what I'd prepared myself for. After an entire day anticipating the brand, my body still trembled with the energy of it not happening.

In the absence of the brand, without Rafael present for me to either rail against for scaring the shit out of me or hug for not following through, I didn't know what to do with myself.

So I sat, trying to retreat into my head so I could process what had happened, but the normal emptiness that welcomed me was gone. Vanished as if it had gone up in flames instead of my skin.

My gaze darted around the room as I thought over Regina's words. The fact that she seemed to think it would be a negative for people to know Rafe cared about me didn't bode well for my safety. I clenched my teeth, trying to wrap my head around the implications of having a mob boss love me.

I still didn't believe it, but there was *something* there. Something had prevented Rafael from branding me when he'd shown no remorse for what he'd done to Hugo.

The bedroom door suddenly opened as he stepped in, barely glancing my way as he went straight for the bathroom.

I stood from the bed, staring after him in enraged disbelief. After everything he'd put me through, he thought he could just *ignore* me? He emerged a moment later, staring at me across the space. He closed the distance between us slowly, reaching up a hand to cup my cheek gently. I swatted it away, glaring at him as he dared to look at me with all the affection I'd needed hours ago.

"You were going to brand me!" I yelled in his face. I pounded my fist against his bare chest once. Repeating the motion over and over, I wanted nothing more than to mark him for what he'd put me through. To make him feel even just a hint of the terror I'd felt knowing that he would hurt me.

He accepted the assault, not moving a muscle as he let me vent my frustrations into his skin. Only when tears fell down my cheeks did he reach up with both hands and cup my face in his grip. I wrapped my hands around his hips, staring up at him.

"I didn't," he murmured gently, pressing his lips to my forehead. The soothing sound of his voice shouldn't have felt like a comfort, not when he'd been the one who wanted to scar me, but the lack of all harshness from it reminded me of the hints of the man I'd loved in Ibiza.

The man beneath the monster.

He moved one hand to my neck, putting pressure there and holding me steady as his other hand dropped to his pants pocket. Pulling out a black switch blade, he pressed the button to free the knife itself as I reeled away from his grip. But he refused to release me, turning it in his hand until the point faced him.

"Show me your darkness," he murmured, pressing the hilt of the knife into my hands. He dragged it up and over his bare torso, the blade leaving a thin, raised pink trail as it slid over his skin. He stopped when the tip of the knife rested just over his heart, his hands pressed firmly into mine as he pulled it closer. The tip pierced his chest, the give of his skin popping beneath it vibrating up the blade and through the hilt in my hand.

"What are you doing?" I asked, my horror mounting as he held my grip steady.

"You want your freedom? The only way is if I'm dead, *mi reina*," he said, digging the blade in more firmly. I winced as blood coated the edges of the knife where it protruded from his skin. His eyes were gentle on mine, intense and probing as he lifted one of his hands off mine and cupped my cheek in his hand. "It belongs to you. Whether it beats or not."

"Stop," I gasped, pulling my hand back. He held me firmly to the knife, refusing to let me release it until he was good and ready. My freedom was literally in my hands, but tears stung my eyes as I tried to picture sinking the blade into his flesh. As I thought of what it would be to see the life fade from his stunning eyes. A tear slipped free, gliding down my cheek as he watched me intently.

"Eres el amor de mi vida, mi reina," he murmured as my hand trembled on the knife. His stare was trusting and resigned all at once, like it didn't matter to him if I killed him. "I won't live without you."

His hand moved the blade, carving into his skin as I stared at his chest with a strangled sob. He didn't flinch back from the pain, accepting it with nothing but affection in his eyes as he stared down at me. I clenched my eyes closed as the first letter came into view when he pulled our hands away, moving slightly to the side so that he could continue on. "Stop," I whimpered, watching him slice through the curve of the second letter. The last letter took more time as I fought his grip, trying to make him stop.

Only when he'd finished carving my name into the center of his chest did he lift the blade away one last time, centering it back to the space just below the word and pressing it into his flesh once more.

"I'm not a good man. I'll hurt you. I'll demand things of you that I have no right to ask, but I'm yours. If you don't put this blade through my heart now, know that you're accepting all of me, *mi reina.* My way of life, my home, my cruelty. You will never get this chance again. So think very hard before you make your choice." He leaned down to kiss me gently, the knife pressing deeper into his flesh as he moved without a care. "If I live, you'll be my wife. You'll never be alone in the space inside your head again."

My lips trembled as he kissed away my tears. I stared at the knife in my hand as he watched my face, uncaring for the fact that his life could end with just a moment. "Aren't you afraid?" I whispered, glancing up at him.

"Why would I want to live if I don't have all of you?" He smiled sadly, dropping his second hand from the knife and lifting my empty one to wrap around it. I clenched my eyes closed, my palms squeezing around the hilt as I tried to force myself to end it all.

To take back the freedom he'd stolen from me.

"Meet me in the moonlight," he murmured softly, echoing the words that had started it all. The words I'd thought had brought me to him. Memories of our time in Ibiza fluttered through my mind. From our first meeting to walking on the beach after dinner.

And I knew I couldn't do it. I couldn't kill the only man I had ever loved, no matter what he'd done to me or would continue to do.

The knife clattered to the floor as I dropped it, landing inches from my foot as I stepped back hurriedly. His lungs heaved with relief as he watched me across the space between us.

"You made a mistake, *mi reina*," he said. "You fell in love with your nightmare."

I didn't deny the words as he closed the distance between us and crushed his lips against mine.

How could I, when I'd chosen him over my freedom?

*R*afael spent the next day away from me, leaving me to ponder my choice and stress over the outcome relentlessly as Regina tried to get me to focus on anything but the void inside my head.

Freedom had been within my grasp. My family had nearly gotten the peace they deserved and me home with them where I belonged.

I stepped out onto the private terrace, my bare feet soaking in the warmth from the tiles even though the sun had set long ago. Rafael's business had required him to work through dinner, and I hadn't quite been able to convince myself that I would be welcome in his office. He might have thought my place in his life was clearly defined by the unrealistic expectations he had of what we would be, but I was less than convinced.

I couldn't kill him, but that didn't mean I should have stayed. That didn't mean that I could let myself enjoy my life with him.

The sky faded into deep purples as the sun disappeared behind me, leaving me to consider the impossible choices I'd need to make. What the fuck would I tell my family?

Would he let me tell them at all?

The fact that he hadn't been able to follow through with branding me meant there was something there, and I might not speak much Spanish, but I knew what *amor* meant. In some way, Rafael had admitted he loved me.

I hadn't given him the words back, and I didn't know that I would ever be able to.

His arms wrapped around my waist as he stepped up behind me suddenly, moving through the bedroom with the kind of stealth that would never cease to amaze me. Like he was one with the darkness and it was his to claim.

His mouth touched the mark on my shoulder where he'd drawn blood, the wound pulsing to new life under the gentle pressure. His tongue ran over the healing flesh, somehow erotic when it should have been nothing short of gross.

When he pulled away, he unbuttoned his dress shirt and held my eyes as he revealed the inches of his flawless skin. The moment my eyes landed on the red marks where he'd carved my name into his chest, I couldn't help the surge of possessiveness that came over me. The satisfaction in knowing that it was *my* name on his skin.

He was a beautiful enigma, a devil that no one could control. And yet he'd willingly carved my name into his flesh for all to see, unconcerned with the fact that other women might see it.

Because he was mine. Just as I was his.

His hands went to his pants, unfastening them with an arrogant smirk as I watched. "Take off your dress," he ordered.

I swallowed back my nerves, instinctively knowing that

Rafael planned to take me into the pool. Even if I knew how to swim, I would never be free of the panic I felt at just the thought.

At the reminder of what the water could do.

"Will you be faithful?" I asked, slipping my dress off over my head as Rafael shoved his pants down his legs and stepped out of them and his socks and shoes. He stood naked, without care for the fact that we were outside. Entirely confident in the privacy of his little haven within his home.

He smiled as he stepped up to me, reaching behind my back to unclasp my bra and help me pull it down my arms. He was meticulous about the way he touched me, carefully controlled and making sure to only trail his fingers over my arms lightly enough that goosebumps rose on the flesh in his wake.

His body stayed a hair away from mine, the warmth from his body kissing my flesh as he raised my hand to touch my name. "I always have been," he murmured, his dark smile hinting at the truth to what Joaquin and Regina had told me.

Rafael hadn't been with anyone else since the first time he saw me. It was fucked up. It was baffling. It was far sweeter than I would have thought him capable of being. "I'll put your name on me permanently if it will help convince you," he said, dropping to his knees in front of me. He drew my panties down my thighs as he stared up at me, tossing them to the side and then standing so he could take my hand and guide me into the water.

I hesitated slightly before walking down the steps, enjoying the cool water against my skin even if it made me feel a moment of panic at the first touch. But somehow, some way, the moment he wrapped his arms around me and pulled me into his chest, it all faded back into my memories.

"I love you, *mi reina*," he murmured softly, touching his lips to the top of my head as he moved us through the water beneath the stars. "All I could think of today was the fact that I never said it in English, and you might not have understood. There will be no other women for me. All that I am is yours, for better or worse."

I looked up into his eyes, gliding my hands over his chest and the wound I half hoped would scar. "How do you know you won't get tired of me?"

"Never, Isa. I'm yours," he said sternly, lifting a hand to cup my cheek. "Until forever ends."

*T*he tattoo gun buzzed as Elías worked. With my left arm extended and braced on the edge of the chair he'd dragged into the office, I didn't bother to glance down at what he inked onto my skin.

He'd hand-designed it with me at his shop the night before, setting everything into motion before I returned to Isa and put the knife in her hand. It might have seemed like it could have been an unnecessary waste of time, but I knew *mi reina* too well.

She loved me, and now even she couldn't deny it despite the fact that she hadn't given me the words. They would come in time. I'd left her in my bed in the very early hours of morning, making my way behind the closed doors of my office so Elías could get started on the tattoo that would take him hours to complete.

There needed to be time remaining for him to do Isa's on the same day. Before she could see my tattoo and ask questions.

I picked up the stencil for hers from where it rested on the desk, staring down at the intricate design that was a perfect match for mine. The black King chess piece, surrounded by flowers and flames that bled into shadows and darkness would wrap around her entire left forearm, fitting against mine like a puzzle piece. The words *El Diablo* would be etched into her skin in permanent ink, marking her as mine in a way a generic brand wouldn't have done.

Penance and a promise, all in one.

"You're sure you want to do this?" Elías asked, raising an eyebrow to me as he put the finishing touches on the white Queen wrapped in barbed wire and surrounded by black waves that bled into the same shadows as Isa's tattoo. He moved to the position of the words *Mi Reina* beneath the Queen, pausing as he waited for my response. Undoubtedly, it seemed unusual for a man like me to mark his body with the ownership of a woman.

But Isa wasn't any other woman.

"I promise," I said with a sarcastic smile. He set the tattoo gun to my skin, inking her claim on me into me permanently.

Soon she'd wear my name in return, in more ways than one.

She just didn't know it yet.

*R*egina plied me with food to try to pull me out of the mood that had consumed me since I'd woken up alone that morning. Rafael and I hadn't spoken since we'd fallen into bed the night before, and I was left with the feeling that I'd made a grave mistake.

What could I do about a life I didn't want, but hadn't chosen to escape? What I shared with Rafael was too dark and twisted to explain, but I couldn't kill him either. My poor family was probably worried sick about me, and here I was eating lunch in a glamorous kitchen while they thought I was lying dead in a ditch somewhere. Even with a day to consider my choice, I was no closer to coming to any real decision. It didn't help that I spent more time away from him than I did with him. Was that what my life with him would look like?

He'd offered me my freedom. I'd stayed, despite everything I had waiting for me back home. We'd had sex in the pool, pushing me past all my limits that I would have thought I had for myself. And despite all of that and his words that he would be faithful, at some point in the middle of the night, he'd slipped out of the bed we shared to go do God knows what in his office. Music played over the speakers, drowning out any sounds I might have heard when I'd been brave enough to go looking for him.

It only drove my suspicion higher, wondering what he could be so determined to hide from me.

"It's not a woman," Regina assured me, reading the expression on my face as I looked down the hall toward his office.

"What?" I forced myself to shovel another skewer of *melon con jamon* into my mouth. The salty serrano ham complemented the honeydew perfectly as Regina turned back to the stove to stir a soup while I ate. Joaquin lurked in the breakfast nook, a smirk forming on his face at Regina's words. "What's so funny?"

"Rafe with another woman," he laughed, shoveling a bite of food into his mouth. "Even if he was tempted, he's smart enough to know you'd cut him before you shared him."

"That's not true! I'm not violent," I argued.

"*Mi reina,* did you know that Rafael allows the men to use his personal gym in the basement?" Joaquin asked with a broad smile. "He regularly displays your claw and bite marks for all to see. It is a point of pride for him that his woman marks him so."

I blushed as my eyes darted back to my plate. If those marks had been scandalous enough, my name carved into his chest was ten times worse. "Shit," I muttered, refusing to meet Regina's eyes as she looked between us.

"Love marks are not so bad," she said sympathetically. "Spanish women are passionate, and your mother is Latina is she not?"

"Do you often cut your name into your lover's heart?" Joaquin asked her, grinning broadly as I tried to sink down into the stool. My stomach turned suddenly, the melon and ham no longer seeming appealing as I thought about what he'd made me do.

"He made me do it!" I said in shame, shaking my head to protest the insinuation that it had been my idea. "I could have killed him, but I didn't. Surely that says that I am the exact opposite of violent."

"Ah, but if you were so against violence, wouldn't you have wanted to kill the criminal who murders without thought? You had the chance to rid the world of a monster, but instead you let him live. Because you do not blame him for his violent impulses. I would guess the very same ones run through you," Joaquin said.

I forced another bite into my mouth, knowing there was truth to his words. I wanted to be free of Rafael because it was what I *should* want, but not because I felt any level of disgust when he touched me. Not because I wanted to turn him in to the police or see him go down in a rain of gunfire.

He could murder someone right then and return to me with the blood of his enemies staining his hands. I'd still welcome him to my bed, and that was *wrong*. I'd become a product of what he made me, a demon to match his devil. But I couldn't cross that line and be violent myself.

Accepting it as part of him was one thing, becoming it myself was another.

Right?

The devil himself appeared at the entrance to the kitchen, leaning into the wall with a smile as if he hadn't abandoned me for an entire day and left our bed in the night.

The insecurity in me drove me to ask the question that burned in my mind as I glared at him. "Where have you been?"

He crossed his arms over his chest, smirking as if he could feel the jealousy in the words. He was just the type to want me that way, to want to drive me mad with it until I had no choice but to verbally confess the words I'd withheld from him. I couldn't bring myself to say them, not when there was so much undecided and up in the air between us. I had no idea how our relationship could work, but it didn't seem possible for it to have a happy ending, given how we'd begun.

My eyes narrowed in on the skin of his forearm and the black ink that swirled and covered his flesh in an intricate design. The Queen chess piece stood out, the negative space of her not filled in and gleaming in contrast to the dark ink. The barbed wire wrapped around her made my eyes go wide as my hand drifted down to touch my thigh with a loud swallow.

He'd permanently inked my greatest shame onto his skin.

"I have something to show you," Rafael said, holding out a hand for me as he stepped into the kitchen. I glanced at Regina, nervous about going anywhere alone with him.

"You mean aside from *that*," I said, the breath leaving me in a sudden gasp as I stood from the stool and placed my hand in his. The tattoo bled lightly in the darkest areas as I looked down at it.

"Yes," he said with a slight chuckle, guiding me down the hallway. As we rounded the corner into his office, I looked around the room for the first time. If I'd expected trophies from his victims to line the walls, I was sorely disappointed.

The space was distinctly masculine, with a black built-in unit of shelves on one wall and the accent wall painted a matching ebony to contrast the stark white paint of the other three. Natural light flooded the room, from one end where Rafael's desk sat to the other where a brown leather sofa sat in front of the built-in unit. Two black upholstered chairs and a round table completed the sitting area, though I couldn't imagine many people spent their free time in his workspace.

Directly in front of his desk, a Spanish man stood facing the leather tattoo chair they'd presumably brought in for Rafe's ink. He worked to take the back off the chair, unscrewing the bolts where it connected to the base. I swallowed down my apprehension, watching as he finished with that and grabbed a bandage off the desk. Fixing it to Rafe's forearm now that I'd seen the artwork, he didn't so much as glance at me despite my presence. I was instantly reminded of the day in the Penthouse when Rafael had forbidden the man from looking at me when he delivered our breakfast.

"What did you want to show me?" I asked, stepping farther into the room. Rafe grabbed something off his desk, turning it to show me a sketch of his tattoo. I looked down at it, shock dropping my jaw when I recognized the differences from what already covered his arm. "No," I said, shaking my head.

"Yes," Rafael said simply. He pushed the tattoo chair up against the desk as the other man set a wooden plank on top of the desk along with two cords of rope.

"I don't want a tattoo," I protested, even if I had to admit the sketch itself was stunning. I couldn't justify putting something permanent on my skin, not when it related to one of the most terrifying nights of my life. The King stared up at me, horrific even if only because of my memory of finding that last chess piece and knowing the game had ended before I even had a chance to think.

"Consider it the replacement for your brand," Rafael said, guiding me to the tattoo chair. He picked me up as I squirmed, dropping me onto the seat on my knees. "Penance has to be paid in some form. I've paid mine," he said, gesturing down to the tattoo on his arm.

"What's your penance for?" I asked.

"For deceiving you," he responded, as if it was obvious. It might have been to me or any normal person, but Rafael didn't do regret. He didn't think there was anything wrong with his actions when the ends justified the means to his twisted sense of logic. Grabbing my right arm in his grip, he held me still as the other man took a razor to my skin and carefully shaved off the hair on my entire forearm. Then he rubbed some kind of solution over the area while Rafael held my gaze.

"You can't be serious," I protested as he handed the other man the stencil from my left hand. He worked to apply it and smooth it out carefully as I watched, frozen in place and knowing that even if I fought it would be pointless.

There was nothing but that familiar, steely determination in Rafael's gaze when I turned my eyes up to his.

"I'm very serious," Rafael said. Once the stencil was in place, he put a hand between my shoulder blades and pressed me down until my torso lay flat against the surface of the desk. He carefully lifted my right arm in his grip, setting it down on the wooden plank and curling my hand around the edge.

While his friend tied the rope around the top of my hand and around my bicep, securing me to the plank fully, Rafael pulled my hair into a ponytail at the nape of my neck and secured it with a hair tie.

"She'll need to hold perfectly still," the other man said in warning. I looked at him in confusion, the position of the tattoo seeming incredibly unorthodox. Why not just put me in the chair?

"She will. You just worry about keeping your fucking eyes on her arm, Elías," Rafael scolded. "If I catch you looking anywhere else, I'll cut them out and feed them to your children for dinner tonight."

Elías chuckled, nodding his head as he picked up the tattoo gun and opened a fresh pack of needles before getting himself set up. "You can't tattoo your damn name on me!" I yelled, glaring at Rafael as I turned my head away from Elías.

"Technically *he's* tattooing my damn name on you." Rafael shrugged. He leaned down to kiss me as the gun buzzed to life and drew a whimper from my lips.

"Rafe, please," I begged. It wasn't even that I was afraid of the tattoo itself, but the repercussions of it. One day, I'd see my family again even if I had to do it with Rafael at my side.

What would they think?

"Your name is on me twice, *mi reina*," he said, settling his hand onto my shoulder blades to help keep me still as Elías touched the needle to my skin for the first time. The vibration traveled up my arm, the light stinging taking over my senses as I turned my head back to glare at him.

"You asshole," I hissed. He didn't glance up from my arm, obeying Rafael's orders even as I continued to curse at him under my breath. "Do you often tie women down for other men?"

"Enough, Isa," Rafael warned, gliding his hand down my spine until he touched the hem of my dress. The one he'd set out on a chair for me before he left in the middle of the night. I hadn't thought much of putting it on in my hurry to find where he'd gone earlier, but as he slid the hem up my thighs, I winced and wished I'd worn shorts.

I flailed my free arm as I spun to glare at him. The

bastard ignored me with that cold smirk on his face, disappearing behind me until I couldn't see him.

"What are you doing?" I gasped, flinching away as he flipped my dress up onto my back and scraped his teeth over the globe of my ass.

"Distracting you from the pain," he murmured gently. "Elías won't look. He values his vision too much." He grasped the waistline of my panties, dragging them down over my thighs until they bunched around my knees. He slid two fingers between my legs, stroking me slowly and building desire within me. The pain of the tattoo only drove me higher, conflicting the pleasure he built in my core.

"Stop it," I hissed, clenching my eyes closed as I resisted the urge to moan. I couldn't get off with another man in the room. Even if he didn't look at me, he'd *hear* me.

"Put on your headphones," he ordered Elías, who moved at my side as the gun left my arm. "Her moans are mine alone." The quiet murmur of metal came from Elías' direction as he followed Rafe's order wordlessly. Rafe slid his fingers inside me, pumping them slowly and drawing a ragged groan from my lips. "Not so bad, is it?" he asked, teasing me with both his words and his touch.

"You're the reason God created the middle finger," I growled, earning a deep rumble of laughter in response.

"God has no place on my island, *mi reina,*" he said, drawing his fingers away. In the absence of them, I resisted the urge to squirm. Wanting his touch back on me, even though I knew I shouldn't. Even though I knew what he did was wrong. "Getting a tattoo like this is a lengthy process," he said as the heat of his breath hit my needy flesh. "How would you like to spend that time?" He swept his tongue through my slit, sliding it through me until he pressed it firmly against my clit. "With my fingers in my pretty little pussy? My tongue?" He paused, groaning into my flesh as he licked me again. "Or is it my cock you want, *mi reina?*"

"I want to not get a fucking tattoo," I groaned, and I would have liked to claim the sound was out of frustration. But it was the sound only Rafael could drag from me. The one of pure bliss as his wicked tongue explored me, building temptation in my veins.

"My tongue it is," he said, leaning back in to eat my pussy from behind. With meticulously well-planned strokes of his tongue on me, he kept me at one level of arousal as he worked me over.

It would be the longest tattoo in history if he kept that up.

*E*lias' brow furrowed in concentration as he leaned over Isa's arm. Finishing the final detailing on the back, he looked as exhausted as he must have felt. Five hours with headphones on would be enough to give anyone a migraine, let alone the vibration of his tattoo gun in his hand and the concentration it took to perfectly execute Isa's ink. If he fucked it up, he just might lose his hand.

Isa had long since stopped squirming, clenching her eyes shut to fight off the waves of arousal as I kept her in a steady state of needing to get off. I'd never thought to toy with orgasm denial before, never given a woman enough time in my bed for it to even be a remote possibility until *mi reina,* but the desperation in the lines of her face appealed to me in a way that felt similar to watching a man beg for his life.

It called to the nightmare inside me that craved control in all things, the part of me that wanted to see Isa begging on her knees for my cum.

She leaned over the desk, slumped forward with her face pressed into the surface as I stroked my fingers through her drenched pussy and watched Elias draw the tattoo gun away from her arm. He turned it off, staring down at the newly tattooed skin in concentration and giving it a last look over after wiping the blood and excess ink away from the final piece. Satisfied with what he saw, he set the tattoo gun to the side and untied her arm at the shoulder. Isa didn't move despite the change in freedom, and I had to assume she *couldn't* move. Forcing her to kneel for such a long time was cruel, an even larger part of the penance she had to pay to make up for the lack of a brand.

The tattoo was her mark, but it was more about my claim on her than the pain. People willingly chose to get tattoos every day, and while the sting of the process might have seemed uncomfortable to Isa, it was nothing compared to the searing heat of a brand.

Being forced to kneel for five hours, that was another story.

Her knees were an angry red where they peeked out of the chair whenever she shifted, and the internal pain she felt must have been enough that she'd be walking funny the next day. I couldn't decide if it would bring me pleasure or regret to know she walked down the aisle with the pain of my claim all over her body.

We'd find out soon enough.

I pulled my hand free from Isa's pussy, flipping her dress down to cover her ass and tapping Elias on the shoulder. He didn't look at her as he pulled his headphones off and rolled his shoulders as he untied her wrist and lifted it to show me the design more clearly. I nodded my approval, trying to suppress what the sight of my mark on her skin did to me long enough to get Elias out of the room.

He immediately set to wrapping a bandage around her arm. I watched the motion, noting how Isa didn't respond to his touch in the slightest even as he lifted her arm off the board and cradled her with all the gentleness I would expect of a man handling his Queen. She was totally lost to her surroundings, hidden in the haze of lust that consumed her.

Once Elias gently placed her arm back on the desk, I looked to him with the storm I felt raging in my eyes. Toying with her for hours didn't only torment *mi reina*. My cock was like steel within my slacks, painful as it throbbed with my own need and my balls drew up.

"Get the fuck out," I ordered Elias. He nodded, turning and dashing out of the room. He'd need to collect his tools later, but I couldn't give the first shit about them right then. I suspected after a solid ten hours of work following a mostly sleepless night, he didn't either.

The moment the door clicked shut behind me, I shoved Isa's dress back up over her back and pulled my cock free from my slacks. I slammed inside her in one smooth drive, my groan echoing off the walls as my body relaxed into the feeling of her tight sheath surrounding me. "Fuck," I grunted, pulling back and snapping my hips forward.

She whimpered as her eyes opened finally, staying draped over the desk like I'd left her. With the pain in her body, she was a completely passive participant. I took her hard. I took her fast. Driving her toward the release she so desperately needed with each drive of my cock inside her.

"Rafe!" she screamed, her pussy clenching down on me as the first of her orgasms crashed over her. Her hands scrabbled along the desk surface as I fucked her through it, determined to give her a second for all that I'd put her through.

"You look so fucking good with my name on you," I

grunted, even though I couldn't see the ink past the bandage. I knew it was there.

I'd watched with rapt attention as Elias marked every line of *El Diablo* into her skin. It was better than her brand ever could have been, more specific to who she was to me. "I let you off the hook once," I said, grabbing her by the ponytail and slowly lifting her off the desk.

She whimpered as her body moved, the shift bringing all her aching joints ablaze with a fresh wave of pain. "It hurts," she whimpered as I wrapped my free hand around her and stroked her clit while I thrust my hips up into her sharply. Pounding into her and claiming my pussy as she begged me to stop the pain.

"Do not ever disobey me again, Isa. I will not be so kind a second time," I warned. I didn't look forward to the day she tested those limits, but I knew it would come.

Mi reina wasn't the type to take my kind of ownership lying down, and eventually I'd have no choice but to show her I meant business. But my conscience would be lighter knowing she knew the rules now. That she understood her choices would have consequences.

"I will fucking *brand* my name on you next time," I growled, working my pussy as I fucked it.

She whimpered with her second orgasm, her weight sagging in my grip. With her second release out of the way, I took pity on her and roared out my own inside her. It seemed unending, built up from five hours of deprivation alongside her torment.

By the time I pulled out of her and tucked myself back into my pants, she was boneless in the chair. Despite no longer being tied down, she groaned. Since she was unable to move, I reached forward to grasp her around the waist and lift her off her pained knees. Turning her to sit on the chair, I knelt at her feet.

Stretching her legs for her, slowly easing them back and forth as her knees cracked and popped and she stared down at me with hate fueled eyes. I dragged my lips over her right knee, willing the red and sore flesh to stop tingling with pain, before moving to her left.

Lifting her into my arms carefully, I carried her to the bedroom and the hot bath I would run for her.

Mi reina would need it to survive the next night.

♟♟♟♟♟

*D*espite the fact that my home was known as *El Infierno*, and the fact that it was literal Hell on Earth for my enemies, my great-grandfather had been a very religious man.

As had my grandfather and my father after him. I was perhaps the only Ibarra heir who would have allowed the chapel to fall into disuse, if not for the religious among my people who sought comfort in the promise of an afterlife. Of a God who would allow them to repent for their sins and gain a magical ticket to heaven.

Isa's faith was an eclectic mixture of her mother's Roman Catholic upbringing and the Native American Church that her grandmother practiced. It didn't seem entirely appropriate for her, given the connection she felt to the land. My island may not be her ancestral home, but it was Earth.

It was the Earth she would be buried in at my side when we eventually passed. It was the land our children would be raised on.

It seemed only fitting for Isa that I marry her on the

land, but to appease the Catholics among my people, I arranged for the ceremony to happen in the backyard of the church. It butted against the back side of the island, a fairly modest building in and of itself, but offered enchanting views of the Mediterranean.

I stared out at the water as the women scurried around behind me, arranging flowers onto the arch the men had carved for Isa. For the Queen they planned to welcome as their own that day, when Isa was finally ready. She'd slept in after her ordeal the day before. I was a cruel bastard for not giving her a day to recover, but I needed her tied to me in every way.

My people already knew she was special to me. She already knew I loved her, and she'd made her choice to stay when she could have killed me and taken her freedom. Instead, she slept in my bed until Regina woke her and helped her through preparing without giving away any specifics until the moment I would arrive with her white dress in hand.

As the women finished with the flowers, the men hauled the arch into place and lifted it, securing it to the ground with spikes to hold it firmly for the day. The women smiled at me encouragingly, draping light beige fabric over the arch artfully.

I turned on my heel, heading for the SUV and climbing in next to Alejandro. He grinned, a dark smile that rivaled one of my own. He knew the fight I would have coming. Isa may have agreed to stay with me, and I'd told her she would be my wife.

I just don't think she understood that I meant immediately.

"Let's go get your wife," Alejandro said as Santiago started up the SUV and turned onto the dirt road that would lead us around to the front of the island where the main house sat. The journey wasn't long, but I stared out the window as my home passed us by. The beauty of the woods and pine trees on the back side were such a contrast to the sandy beaches down below. I truly believed my island offered the best of nature that the world had to offer.

"Can you stop twitching?" Alejandro asked as the car turned up the road that would lead to the house. I glanced back at him, relaxing my fingers from the fists they'd clenched into. "You already know she's going to say no, so what has you so antsy?"

"You mean *aside* from the fact that the woman I'm about to marry will need to be threatened into saying yes? Not a thing," I grunted, turning my gaze up to the house as we pulled into the driveway. I sat in the passenger seat for a few more moments, until Alejandro sighed behind me.

"You've never cared before. What difference does it make now?" he asked.

"It doesn't," I said finally, shoving open the SUV door and climbing out. I grabbed the dress bag out of the back seat before making my way inside. Regina was missing from her usual post in the kitchen, the only confirmation I'd get that she'd done as I asked and pushed Isa to get ready.

The bedroom door was open as I rounded the corner, stepping into the room. Isa sat at the vanity I'd had the brothers haul in for her when she was being tattooed the day before, her stunning face staring into the mirror as she swept a coat of mascara onto her eyelashes. She turned her uncertain gaze to me in the mirror, the green of her eyes standing out against the soft and dewy look her makeup gave her.

She stood slowly with a slight grimace as Regina stepped in to offer her a hand and help her, wobbling on her bare feet as her knees protested the movement. "What is all this?" she asked, glancing at the dress bag in my hands.

Regina looked at me as she guided Isa to me, placing her hand in mine so that I could support her as I dropped the dress bag onto the bed. I nodded back, and she smiled with tears in her eyes before she ducked out of the room and closed the door behind her. "Rafael?" Isa asked, swallowing her nerves as her eyes fell to the garment bag. "You're scaring me."

"There's no need to be afraid, *Princesa*," I murmured, leaning forward to touch my lips to her forehead. She leaned into the touch, exhaustion written into the lines of her face as her eyes drifted closed. With everything I'd thrown at her since bringing her to *El Infierno,* I knew this would be the last hit for a little while.

She needed to rest. She needed to come to terms with her place in my life, and there was just one more piece to move into position before she could do that.

"Then what's going on?" she asked. "Are we leaving the island?"

I released her slowly, giving her the chance to find the balance to stand on her own. She swayed slightly without my support, but persevered through it to stare down at the dress bag and watch as I unzipped it carefully. The simple white dress had been made by Alejandro's mother. With thin straps that would hang off her shoulders and a fitted bust that fell to delicate layers of hand stitched lace that would trail lightly behind her.

It was understated, but fit for my Queen in a way that I knew would suit her. She stared down at it, shaking her head in protest quickly as she tried to back up a step. "It's too soon," she argued, not even bothering to deny that she would marry me one day. She'd agreed to it by not killing me when she had the chance.

"I've waited long enough," I told her, stepping forward to grab the tie on her robe. She swatted at my hand, trying to push me away as I unknotted it and bared her body to my gaze. With only a strapless bra and matching panties to cover her, it would take every ounce of control in my body to keep from taking her then and there.

Such was the sight of *mi reina* in all her glory.

But the next time I came inside her, she would be my fucking *wife*.

"Rafael, this isn't fair. I'm not ready for this!" She winced as I slid the robe off her shoulders, letting it pool at her feet. She was in no state to fight me, perhaps one of the benefits to being cruel and marrying her when she was sore. "You've known me for over a year, and you're older. But I'm only eighteen, and this is all so new to me. Please, just give me some *time*," she pleaded, watching in apprehension as I pulled the dress out of the bag and unzipped the back.

"Time will not make a difference for you," I murmured, trying to keep my voice patient with her as I bunched the fabric in my hands. I slid it over her head, tugging it down and being careful not to disrupt her carefully arranged hair that she'd styled in waves. I maneuvered her arms into the straps while she stared at me. Her brain worked behind her gaze, trying desperately to come up with an excuse that I would accept.

She sniffled, her bottom lip trembling as she fought back tears. A sliver of guilt crept in, not wanting her to cry on our wedding day. With her dress still unzipped, I cupped her face in my hands and leaned down to run my nose along the side of hers. Taking care not to muss her makeup, I kissed her gently. Coaxing her to remember the reason that I needed to marry her so urgently.

I loved her. I would always love her.

I wouldn't waste another day without her as my wife.

"Will it always be like this?" she asked, shrugging her shoulders as her face twisted with pain. "You deciding things for me? Forcing me into things I'm not ready for?"

I stepped around her, zipping her dress and sweeping her hair to one side. I touched my lips to her shoulder as my hand drifted down to the bandage on her arm. Pulling it free slowly, I stared down at the ink that claimed her as mine. Knowing that soon my rings would rest on her fingers as well appeased the beast in me, letting me be gentler with her in our private moments than I would be if she challenged me at the ceremony itself.

I had no doubt she would, and I'd taken precautions to ensure her complete cooperation. Even if it bothered me that I would need them.

"It won't always be like this," I said. "Things will settle. You'll adjust to your life at my side, and eventually you'll come to embrace who you are when you're with me. It would be easier if you didn't fight me every step of the way, but then you wouldn't be you," I said, smiling into her skin as she sighed.

She nodded absently as I zipped up her dress, but the move was anything but an agreement. We both knew that the real fight had yet to come.

*T*here was a church on the forsaken island from hell. A place that should have been abandoned by God or the ancestors, a mockery of all that my mother would consider holy.

And yet, it was one of the more modest churches I'd ever seen, as if the people truly used it as a place to connect with God, despite the wealth of the village on the island and the riches Rafael commanded. He clearly didn't care for the church or its teachings, embracing the name of the devil as his pseudonym so fully that he'd marked it on my skin permanently. I stared down at the fresh ink staining my skin, the black so opposite to the delicate white lace of the dress Rafael had dressed me in.

As he opened the door to the SUV and guided me out carefully despite my flats, I couldn't help but notice that the inside of the building was empty. I wouldn't have pegged Rafael as the type to hold a fancy ordeal, but I'd have thought his people would want to support him if they were so loyal.

It was only when he guided me around the corner with

his hand at my waist that I realized we weren't actually going to step inside. "Will you burst into flames?" I asked, the snark of my discomfort soothing me. My voice was all I had left in the situation Rafael had dealt me. My ability to refuse him, even if it would be inevitable, was my only power.

I could deprive him of my will. Keeping it for myself so that I could continue to hold on to that last piece he hadn't claimed for himself. It sounded stupid even to me, but I'd fight with him until my dying breath before I went quietly with everything he planned.

I would never be voiceless.

"No, *mi reina,* but I thought you might like to have an outdoor wedding," he murmured as the backyard came into view. The simple chairs on either side of the flower lined aisle were filled with people I didn't recognize, the only exceptions being the brothers, Regina, and Alejandro who I'd seen in passing moments. He'd never bothered to introduce himself, averting his gaze whenever I was near as if I was nothing of consequence to him.

I supposed I wasn't.

The flower-and-fabric decorated arch at the end of the aisle was something from a destination wedding, breathtaking despite its simplicity. A priest already stood at the end of the aisle with a smile on his face as he waited. Rafael moved to walk forward, halting when my feet didn't move to follow at his side.

His eyes were knowing as he looked to me, and I knew he'd expected this moment.

I hadn't. I hadn't thought I'd bother to resist aside from voicing my displeasure, but seeing the set up that was so close to what I might have chosen for myself, if I'd had a say, struck too close to home. I'd never dared to dream of being married. Of starting a family of my own when I was the root cause of the dysfunction within the one I had.

But I realized in those moments that I wanted that. I wanted the white picket fence and the husband who adored me. I wanted the man who would treat me like a queen and the children who would drive me insane despite the over-whelming love I felt for them.

When I tried to fill in the gaps of the image, it was a face-less man. Rafael Ibarra wouldn't fit in that picture, because he would never be a normal man. He would never give me a white picket fence, but an island so entrenched in security that I couldn't leave without his permission. He wouldn't treat me like a queen in the way I thought I should want, but he'd drive me mad with the extent of his obsession and the steps he would take to ensure he kept me as his.

"It's time, Isa," Rafael warned, dropping his voice low enough to a growl that vibrated in my ear. He leaned into my side, saying the words I didn't know I needed to hear. "I will force you."

I knew with a sudden clarity that it was what I needed. He knew it too, his gaze disappointed but not angry as I turned my face up to study him. I couldn't go willingly down the aisle, not with Rafael when he wasn't what I would have chosen for myself given the chance. I loved him, but I shouldn't have. I should have wanted someone safe, someone who would support my relationship with my family and foster my independence.

Instead, I loved Rafael. A devil with no conscience who took lives. A devil who had lied to me, stalked me, and drugged me to bring me to his island paradise. It was wrong on every level, and unlike him, my guilt wouldn't allow me to go willingly with him into the setting sun on the horizon.

He nodded his head, and Alejandro sighed before standing. He snatched Hugo from his chair by his shirt, pushing him toward where we stood at the end of the aisle. Hugo went along willingly, his shoulders sagged as his brothers watched and did nothing to intervene. Rafael dropped his hand from my waist, reaching into the back of his pants beneath his suit jacket and pulling a gun from his pocket. I blinked at the sight of it, my eyes going wide as I thought over the possibilities of what he might mean to do.

Hurting Hugo because I wouldn't marry him was *insane* on another level, but it was far from beyond the realm of possibility when it came to *El Diablo*. "What are you doing?" I asked, my voice a harsh whisper as Alejandro pushed Hugo to his knees. In the same position as he'd been a few nights prior and I'd gotten between them. Rafael's gun pressed against his forehead as his eyes came to me.

"Will you make me kill him, *mi reina?*" he asked as my lungs heaved. I turned my gaze down to look at Hugo, at the nervousness on his face. It was no act, or if it was, he hadn't been let in on the secret. Joaquin stood from his seat in the background, his eyes pleading as they connected with mine. "Or should I find Chloe and make her suffer for what she told you after all?" Rafael asked, drawing my attention back to him. The devil danced in his eyes, his fury rising with every second that I hesitated.

Part of me could almost justify letting Hugo die. The darkest part of me tried to say that he would deserve it for what he'd done to me. But Chloe was an innocent. The friend who'd risked everything to tell me the truth I'd been too naive to see for myself. There was no justifying letting her suffer for my problems, but I still couldn't make myself say the words to end it all.

Rafael pulled his gun back, slamming it into Hugo's face

brutally as I watched the skin split open before my eyes. "Make your choice, Isa," he growled, fury growing more as I clenched my eyes closed and separated myself from him in that final way. I wouldn't give him the victory of my eyes when I caved to his demands, knowing there was no other choice.

Even if I hadn't resisted at all, there'd never been a choice.

"Okay," I whispered, my eyes flying open as Alejandro grabbed Hugo and hauled him out of the way. Rafael took my hand in his, storming up the aisle quickly as I scrambled to keep up on my aching legs.

The moment Rafael and I stood before him, the Priest spoke. "We are gathered here today to celebrate one of life's greatest moments, the joining of two hearts. In this ceremony today we will witness the union of Rafael Ibarra Vasquez and Isabel Alawa Adamik in marriage." Rafael's mother's maiden name was another piece of information I'd never known about him, hanging on the end of his name like a sign of everything I still didn't know.

My heart dropped into my throat, my heart catching in my chest as I stared at the priest in front of me. The crowd of people behind us was eerily silent, the heavy weight of their gaze on my spine making tears sting my eyes. An island full of people, and no one would intervene.

An island full of people, and they'd happily watch Rafael force me to be his wife.

"Rafe," I murmured, turning to look at him. I couldn't do it. I couldn't condemn myself to *this* for the rest of my life. He slid his massive hand beneath my hair, grabbing me around the back of the neck and turning my head sharply until I faced the priest.

"Get the fuck on with it," he ordered. The heavy weight

of his hand never left me, holding me still as I stifled the strangled sob that tried to claw its way up my throat.

"Why are you doing this?" I whispered, clenching my eyes closed. "I stayed. When will it ever be enough?"

"When you're my wife," he growled, his fingers gripping my flesh so harshly I almost fell to my knees at his side. "When you're pregnant with my son. When I am imprinted on your very fucking *soul*," he snapped. "Only then will it ever be enough, *mi reina*."

"Do you, Rafael, take Isabel to be your wedded wife, to cherish in love and in friendship, in strength and in weakness, in success and in disappointment, to love her faithfully, today, tomorrow, and for as long as the two of you shall live?" The Priest's words crawled over my skin, the meaning something entirely different for most people than it would be for me.

There would be no divorce for me. No matter what he did, Rafael would never let me go.

"I do," he said, the words cracking against the evening air. I glanced up at him from the corner of my eye, finding his bright gaze turned to me. I bit my bottom lip as I waited, never looking at the man who would help Rafael condemn me to my fate as he spoke.

"Do you, Isabel, take Rafael to be your wedded husband, to cherish in love and in friendship, in strength and in weakness, in success and in disappointment, to love him faithfully, today, tomorrow, and for as long as the two of you shall live?" the Priest asked.

"I can't," I mumbled, flinching back against Rafael's grip.

"Say the fucking words, Isa," Rafael ordered, raising the gun he still held in his grip. He lifted it in my direction, touching the barrel to the side of my head as I looked at him out of the side of my eye.

The gasp caught in my lungs, echoed by the sound of the people standing behind us. "Rafael," the Priest protested. Blood roared in my head, the shock of his gun touching my face making everything beyond the two of us seem fuzzy.

"This is the only way you leave here without my ring on your finger, *mi reina*," he said harshly.

"Rafael," I whispered, tears falling as I stared at him in betrayal. I'd thought him incapable of surprising me, I'd thought I'd known exactly what he was capable of, but the violent storm in his eyes dared me to test him. There was no doubt he would follow through if I pushed him.

"I will not live without you as my wife. So say the fucking words, or we'll both stain the ground with our blood," he ordered.

I clenched my eyes shut, the hollow of my life settling over me. Rafael was a raging inferno, destroying everything he touched. I'd been foolish to think I might survive the flames. "I do," I whispered, sealing my fate.

Rafael dropped his hand from my neck and turned me to face him as he shoved his gun back into his pants. Alejandro stepped up at his side, depositing two rings into Rafael's outstretched hand as he grabbed my left in his grip and lifted it. He lined up the rose gold bands, sliding the engagement ring with a large, round moonstone at the center into the middle of the double banded wedding ring. The top of the band was studded with diamonds, resembling the crown on the Queen, and the words *hasta que la muerte* were engraved into the bottom band as he slid them onto my ring finger.

The moonstone stared back at me, gleaming in the setting sun as the sky tinted orange.

Alejandro held out a ring, the brushed black gleaming with the golden words *nos separe* etched into the surface as

Rafael lifted a hand. I sniffed back tears, plucking it out of his palm carefully and sliding it up his finger and accepting him as my husband.

"By the power vested in me, I now pronounce you husband and wife. You may kiss the bride!"

Rafael's face loomed closer, the fire in his eyes dying down to a burning ember as he cupped my face in the palm of his hand. His lips touched mine in our first kiss as husband and wife, a crushing and claiming touch that echoed everything he'd already made clear.

I would never be free.

The cold metal of his ring touched my skin as he devoured me, a physical reminder that I wasn't just me anymore.

I was the wife of *El Diablo.*

*T*he ride back to the house was silent as I stared out the window. I'd signed the marriage contract Rafael shoved in front of me, realizing it would be the last time I signed as Isabel Adamik.

Something told me Rafael would never let me keep my maiden name, even knowing that it gave me a connection to my heritage when he'd taken all the others away from me. When we arrived back at the house, he lifted me into his arms before I could approach, carrying me over the threshold and into the home I would never escape.

I should have stabbed him when I had the chance.

My anger vibrated in my body, boiling my blood in a way I'd never felt before. I'd thought I'd felt anger. I'd thought I'd known what it was to hate someone so completely.

I knew nothing.

He set me on my feet in the kitchen, walking over to the stunning white cake that hadn't been there when we'd left. I watched as he picked up the knife, looking at me as if he knew that I would stab him if he handed it to me. He would have been right.

Suddenly the idea of being a widow so young felt like a blessing.

He placed my hand on the hilt of the knife, covering it with his own immediately and guiding it toward the cake. With everything else in our relationship, I didn't know why he required my participation. It wasn't like I had a choice either way. We carved out the first slice, the lack of people in the room growing more and more noticeable as we set the slice on a plate.

He set the knife to the side, placing it as far from my grasp as he could manage before he picked up a fork. Cutting through it, he raised the red cake with white frosting to my mouth. It brushed against my lips, and I parted to let him feed me even though I would have preferred to take a bite out of his finger instead.

I had to suspect that was the reason he didn't feed me by hand like tradition dictated.

He smirked at me as if he could see the path my thoughts gravitated to, turning the fork to offer me the handle. I took it from him, cutting a piece off the slice of cake and raising it to his mouth. He opened, letting me slide the red velvet onto his tongue. I pulled back the fork, hating the smile that transformed his face as he chewed.

I hated everything about him.

My grip shifted on the fork, holding it firmly as if my life depended on it. For all I knew, it did.

He was still chewing thoughtfully when I lifted the plate and slammed the remaining cake into his face. The ceramic shattered in my grip, and I raised the fork in my hand and drove it toward his body.

Stabbing him in the shoulder, I winced as his flesh parted, offering resistance as the tines pushed through his suit and his skin. Like stabbing into raw meat, I fought back the urge to gag, and dropped my hold. He cursed, wiping cake from his eyes furiously and grabbing for me as I backed away and narrowly avoided his grasp.

I didn't need a knife to stab the fucker, and he'd do well to remember that.

"There's your fucking penance," I growled, staring down at the spot where I'd stabbed him. His eyes followed, moving to the fork sticking out of his shoulder as his shirt stained red. In the same area as his brands, I had to hope it would be memorable enough.

It was all I had.

"My penance?" he asked, raising a brow at me and stalking toward me slowly. I grabbed at my dress frantically, pulling the small train up and out of my way so that I could back away as I glared at him. It would be pointless to run, and I knew it, but the impulse consumed me. I didn't want to suffer through the punishment promised in his smoldering eyes.

"You put a fucking gun to my head!" I yelled, horrified to find tears burning my throat. I shouldn't have been surprised, but I was.

"I did," he agreed. "And I would do it all over again to have you as my *wife.*"

I glared at him, watching as he gripped the handle of the fork and pulled it out of his shoulder slowly. He tossed it to the side, and I glanced over to watch it clatter on top of the island. With the red stain to the tines, I wondered if Regina would realize it was blood, or if she'd assume it was from the red velvet of the cake.

"You told me you loved me," I whispered, forcing my feet to hold still despite the urge to flee. "You do not murder people you love, *El Diablo,*" I hissed.

"Is that your issue? You think because I would kill you

that I cannot possibly love you?" he asked, stepping up into my space. His fingers ran through my hair gently, delicately brushing the waves back from my face. He sighed, gripping a fistful in his hand and snapping my neck back so that he could crush his mouth against mine. In a furious tangle of teeth and tongue, he swept inside and claimed me. Pulling back to glare at me, he turned my body with his grip at my hair. Leaving me no choice but to walk backwards toward our bedroom under his direction, I stumbled over my dress and only his support kept me upright.

"You don't," I gasped.

"My love for you is so consuming that I would die before I let you leave me," he murmured, leaning forward to nip at the end of my nose. "The words to describe what I feel for you do not exist. Do *not* question my love for you, *mi reina*. I am not the one in denial of my feelings," he said, guiding me through the open bedroom door finally.

"I can't be in denial of feelings that don't exist," I lied, glaring up at him.

"Such a pretty mouth to tell such ugly lies," he laughed, releasing my hair to spin me. His fingers pulled down the zipper on my wedding dress, his mouth biting into the flesh of my shoulder where his mark still tainted my skin.

"How could I feel *anything* but hatred for you after today?" I asked. I turned to face him, compelling him to feel my hatred in those moments before I knew he would take whatever he wanted from me.

He always did, and for some reason I was powerless to stop him. He made it so I didn't even *want* to.

He grinned, stripping off his suit jacket. His shirt followed and then his pants and shoes until he stood naked in front of me. "Then come ride my face and tell me how much you hate me, *mi reina,*" he laughed. My thighs clenched involuntarily, the thought of that wicked tongue of his nearly permeating the haze of my rage.

But I held firm to it, stripping off the wedding dress I wanted no part in wearing. I stood in front of him for a moment, only allowing him the sight of my lingerie clad body for a brief moment before I shouldered passed him and made my way to the closet to grab real clothes. He lashed out a hand, grabbing me around the waist and tossing me onto the bed as I screamed my frustration. "Let me *go!*"

He tore the underwear down my legs, laying on his back as I tried to scramble off the bed. He reached out with muscular arms, grasping me around the waist and lifting me while I flailed. He somehow got my legs spread so that I straddled his chest, grinning up at me victoriously before he wrapped his arms around the back of my thighs and shifted me up his body.

The grip of his hand on top of my thigh indented my skin, holding me firm even though I tried to get away from his touch. Once he'd shifted me far enough up that my pussy rested above his mouth, he used his grip to pull my hips down into him. He devoured me without preamble, no teasing torment of his tongue exploring me to work me up to the intensity of his onslaught.

Just his tongue sliding inside me as he fucked me with it. I reached down, grasping a fistful of hair and pulling as if I could make him stop. But he only groaned against me, pulling me down harder until all that peeked out from between my thighs were his intense eyes that he kept on mine. I looked away as pleasure consumed me, trying to shove down the building orgasm that defied all logic.

My body belied my anger, and I felt so fucking stupid as my hips tried to shift. He loosened his grip slightly, letting my body take control as I moved slightly on his face. Giving him more ability to touch other parts of me with that sinful mouth, I slid my hips back and forth on his tongue.

Riding his face despite my best intentions, I shoved down the guilt I felt. Rafael was all I'd ever known.

He'd taught me about sex. He'd made me into a nightmare like him.

Just when my orgasm was about to take over, he lifted me off his face and tossed me down onto the bed face up. Sealing his body over mine, he slid inside me in a smooth glide with an arrogant smirk on his face as I moaned. "I don't trust you not to bite my cock off," he laughed, fucking me in slow, deep thrusts as he stared down at me. "Would you miss it, *wife?*" he asked.

"Fuck you," I growled, baring my teeth. He leaned forward, giving me more of his weight and taking my bottom lip between his teeth.

"We both know you would. You need me just as much as I need you. So just fucking admit it already and stop goddamn fighting me," he growled. My eyes fell to the four puncture wounds where I'd stabbed him, a moment of fleeting regret threatening at the edges of my consciousness.

To feel guilt for hurting him was ridiculous after everything he'd done to me.

He kissed me, finally ceasing his verbal torment to take me the way he wanted. His drives inside me shifted us further up the bed with the force of them, until the top of my head hit the headboard. Still he kissed me, consuming me until I shattered beneath him. Hating myself, hating him.

He followed me soon after, coming inside me and sagging his weight on top of me. "We could be happy," he murmured. "And we will be, once you admit that you love me."

He shifted his weight off me, letting me retreat into the bathroom to clean myself up and compose myself. Staring into the mirror, I had to wonder if he was right.

I couldn't love him. But I did.

And at what point was fighting those feelings futile? At what point did I just give in and accept my new life?

I didn't know if I'd ever have the answer to that question.

My stomach rolled as I sat up in bed, the sun shining in through the windows feeling particularly blinding as I fought back the exhaustion that battered my body. My legs ached, the joints popping as I swung my legs over the edge of the bed and gripped the mattress desperately while I tried to work up the strength to stand.

I wanted to sleep for a week, to sprawl out and let my body recover while I rested so I wouldn't have to force it to move or feel every place that hurt.

"You should stay in bed and rest," Rafe reprimanded as he stepped out of the bathroom in a cloud of steam.

I shook my head, pushing myself to my feet and swallowing back my queasiness. "You said I could call my family," I reminded him, moving toward the bathroom. "Please don't tell me that was a lie."

"You can call them later today," Rafe said as I stepped into the bathroom and splashed cold water on my face and brushed my teeth. Rafe was dressed by the time I stepped out, wrapped in my orchid satin robe. He sat in the chair next to the bed, his cell phone held in his hands. He twirled it absently and waited for me to sit on the bed in front of him. "You should spend the morning considering what you plan to tell them. It's the middle of the night for them."

"What am I allowed to tell them?" I asked. "Can they know where I am? Can I tell them your name?"

"You can tell them whatever you want, *mi reina*," he murmured, tucking my hair behind my ear as he studied the tired lines on my face. "You can tell them I kidnapped you, if that's what you want to do. It won't make a difference to me, but if you want us to be able to have a relationship with them in the future, I would suggest refraining from giving them the full truth."

"You mean I should lie to them?" I asked.

"Yes," he said. "What good will knowing all the details of our marriage do for them? They can't change it any more than you can, and no matter how we got here, you had the chance to walk away."

I scoffed. "I just had to kill you to do it."

He caught my chin in his grip, a soft smile transforming his face. The hostility of the day before was gone, vanished from his face, and he appeared almost serene as he gazed down at the tattoo on my arm and the rings on the finger of my opposite hand. "I meant every word when I said that I will not live without you, my wife. It may be toxic. It's probably unhinged, but it is never going to change. The greatest kindness you can do for your family is protecting them from the reality of our life together."

I nodded, knowing there was truth to his words. My grandmother would be crushed to know that I wouldn't come home to live in Chicago and continue our legacy with the Menominee community as it was. Knowing that it was because of a crime and she was unable to help me would only break her more.

I couldn't risk her sadness, not when the consequences of it might mean I never got to see my family again. As much as it pained me to admit it, I would only see them when Rafael determined it acceptable. "When can I see them?"

"You mean when will I take you home to visit them? I'm not sure I can put a time stamp on that. It depends on too many factors," he said as he stood from the chair. I followed, getting dressed for the day while he watched.

As soon as I pulled the dress over my head, he stepped into my space and claimed my lips with his. The memory of the feeling of the barrel of a gun against my temple flashed through my mind, a vivid recollection of all the toxicity that was our relationship.

I should have thrown something at him. I should have fought off his embrace. Instead I sank into the feeling of his mouth moving against mine. The plump flesh of his bottom lip tensed lightly as it tipped up into a smile when he felt my unwavering devotion in the intimacy between us. He was nothing if not over-confident in the connection we shared.

It didn't matter to Rafael that I still hadn't given him the words to tell him I loved him. He didn't need to hear them, because he felt them every time my body yielded to his touch.

Even still, I'd protect the words deep inside myself. I'd shove them down to the place where I hid the secrets I kept. With the demons that lurked in my past.

"I have to get to work," he said ruefully as he pulled his mouth away from mine. With our foreheads touching and his eyes closed peacefully, I stared up at the devil himself. I studied the peace on his face, wondering if he suddenly seemed so at ease because he'd claimed me as fully as he always wanted to.

With his name on my skin and his rings on my finger, the last way to make me his would be to impregnate me. *To breed me*. And given his insistence on not using condoms, even that was an inevitability.

"So, go," I said, a teasing lilt surprising even me as he flung his eyes open and stared down at me in amusement.

"I don't want to be away from you," he murmured, the words caressing my skin with the freshness of minty breath.

I smiled up at him, the demented part of me enjoying the reminder of the softer, sweeter Rafe who had showed me Ibiza before reality crashed down around us. "I think you've got it bad, Mr. Ibarra," I teased.

He grinned down at me, running his nose up the side of mine sweetly before catching my bottom lip between his teeth and nipping me lightly. "I think you do too, Mrs. Ibarra," he said back, making my heart pause in my chest at the sound of the name. Knowing it and hearing it were two very different things, and I didn't think I'd ever get used to the sound of Rafael's surname in reference to me.

I shouldn't be his wife. I should be single, waiting for a boring accountant to come and sweep me off my feet into a life of normalcy where I didn't have to wonder if my husband would put a gun to my head the next time I said no to him.

Rafael was a sociopath, uncaring about how his actions affected the people around him, least of all me. He was unstable, driven by rage and violence and his own selfishness. But what did it say about me that I looked into the eyes of a nightmare and loved him?

I was unstable too.

"Maybe," I murmured, refusing to admit to the emotions

swirling in me as he stepped back hesitantly and held out a hand for me. I tried to drive my anger higher, to get back to the place where I wanted nothing more than revenge for the way he'd terrified me. Instead, all I could think of was the warm comfort of his hand surrounding mine. Of the way he enveloped me so firmly.

I understood why he didn't want to live without me. I might not have killed him if he didn't want to marry me so quickly, but I knew what it was to be terrified of returning to my life pre-Rafael. I never wanted to be without him, even if I spent most of my time wanting to strangle him for the things he'd done.

He guided me through the labyrinth of a hallway, taking me to the kitchen where Regina waited with *ensaimada* already prepared. I took a seat at the island with Joaquin in the seat next to me but spaced far enough away that we were at opposite ends of the large counter. Rafe went for his coffee as Regina put a glass of juice in front of me with a broad smile.

"Mrs. Ibarra," Joaquin greeted from my side, making me choke on my orange juice as I felt Rafael's intense eyes on me. He smirked, lifting his coffee to his mouth and leaning forward to snatch an *ensaimada* off the counter and take a bite. Leaning in with powdered sugar on his lips, he kissed me briefly before retreating down the side hall to his office and closing the door.

Part of me wanted to exist with him. To go into the office and just be in his presence, but I knew if I was going to stay on the island, I needed to find my own way to pass the time. The moment his presence left, I turned my eyes back to the kitchen and zeroed in on the bloodstained fork where it sat on the counter next to the sink.

"I was going to guess, based on the shattered plate I

found this morning, that last night went about as well as I could expect after what he did," Regina said, tearing off a piece of her own pastry. "But you seem quite cozy."

I hung my head in my hands, thinking over everything that had happened in the last twenty-four hours. I shook my head to try to clear it of everything running through me. "I feel like I'm losing my mind," I whispered, turning a grimace to Regina. "What's wrong with me?"

"Why does anything have to be wrong with you, *reinita*?" she asked, tilting her head to the side and reaching across the island to pat my hand with hers.

"He put a gun to my head, and I let him fuck me. He put a gun to my head, and I smiled at him and acted like everything was okay! And then he leaves and I remember who I'm supposed to be. I remember who I was. My family is probably terrified that something happened to me, and I'm sitting here drinking orange juice."

"You're surviving, *mi reina*," Joaquin said. "The strongest people adapt when life throws them a curveball. You've done that."

I shook my head. "I'm barely holding on to the girl I used to be."

"So don't," Regina said. "Why would you want to be that girl? Were you happy?" She paused when I didn't answer, too afraid to give voice to the answer that pulsed through my veins.

I hadn't known what it was to be happy until I'd met Rafael. I hadn't known what it was to feel *anything*. Now I had a lifetime of emotions tearing me apart every second of the day, but there was no complacency with him in my life. Never a dull moment, never an instance where I didn't feel *something*. And I didn't know how to cope with it.

"What is so bad about embracing the woman we all see

clawing to escape the cage you've put her in?" Regina asked, reaching over to the sink and grasping the bloodied fork in her grip. "This is the woman you are meant to be," she said, tossing it onto the counter so that I had no choice but to stare down at the red stain. "You are meant to be the woman who bleeds the man who does her wrong. You are meant to be the woman who challenges him to be better and to do better for you. But more than anything?" Regina asked as tears built in her eyes. "You are meant to be whoever the fuck you want to be. Your family doesn't get to make that choice for you. Rafael doesn't get to make that choice for you. So be the woman who stabs Rafael Ibarra with a fork and doesn't fear the consequences. Be the woman who looks the devil in the eye and says 'fuck you.'" She sniffed back her tears, wiping her face as she dropped her apron on the counter. "Be the woman I wasn't strong enough to be."

She fled the kitchen, leaving me staring at that fork for what felt like hours. "You'll never be that girl again," Joaquin said, murmuring his agreement with everything I'd already come to realize. He stayed silent at my side after that, watching over me as I worked through the dueling sides to my personality. I would never leave Rafael. He'd made that painfully clear, and the Isa I'd once been had no place in his life. She couldn't survive in his world.

But the little demon who wanted to dance with the devil in the moonlight would thrive there.

*R*egina had composed herself before Rafael emerged from his office in the middle of the afternoon. His face was drawn and serious as he met my eye and nodded, something hanging over his head. I had to hope it didn't concern my family, because I wanted that phone call. Even if it did terrify me to talk to them. Even if I still had no clue what I would say to explain my absence. I didn't want to lie, but the truth seemed so far-fetched and too painful to admit.

I'd fallen in love with my captor.

Rafael guided me to our bedroom, sitting in the chair beside the bed and leaving me to curl my legs underneath me on the mattress. He dialed my mother's phone number for me, handing me the phone as I swallowed back my nerves. I took it with trembling hands, holding it up to my ear as it rang. There was a brief moment where I wondered if she would answer. If I'd be saved from having to decide what to tell her by her undoubtedly hectic schedule with two of her daughters missing.

"Hello?" My mother's voice sounded weak, as if she hadn't been able to sleep since I'd gone missing. Since I'd stopped returning phone calls and hadn't come home with Chloe as planned.

"Hi, Mom," I whispered, my voice catching as I tried to sniffle back the sadness surging inside me. I knew deep in my heart that the first moments of this phone call would be the last time my mother thought of me as her good girl. They'd be the last seconds of my life where I did what my parents asked of me, and losing that piece of myself felt like tearing part of my soul away.

I'd been the obedient daughter for so many years. I'd done what was expected of me without fail. Shedding those expectations was like a splintering of my soul.

"Isa?" she asked, her voice trembling as a sob caught the breath in her lungs. She'd already had to watch her daughters die once. Reliving that possibility thirteen years later seemed like a cruel twist of fate.

"It's me," I agreed, my voice hesitant as Rafael reached out a hand and wiped the tears off my face. He studied me as if he couldn't relate, and I expected he couldn't. His father had been a cruel man and his mother died when he was young.

When was the last time Rafael cared about someone other than himself, before me? Was that part of why he clung to me so tightly?

"Oh my God, Isa," she sobbed, bringing more tears to my eyes. *Ten days.* Ten days had passed with me missing in another country, after Chloe returned home with horror stories about the kind of man I'd spent my time sinning with. "Waban!" she called, my father's name echoing so loudly over the phone that I had to draw it away from my ear. "It's Isa!"

"Isa?" My father's voice said as my mom put me on speaker. "Baby girl?"

"Hi," I said with a sniffle.

"Are you okay? Honey, where are you?" my mom asked. "The embassy said that they spoke with you and you chose to stay in Spain. But Chloe said not to believe them."

I cast a look toward Rafael, reprimanding him for making it look like no crime was ever committed. "The embassy was right. I chose to stay," I agreed, hating the lie as it rolled off my tongue.

But I couldn't ever change the reality that I was never coming home, at least not for anything longer than a visit. My family needed to believe I was happy in my new life.

It was the best gift I'd ever be able to give them. The peace of believing their daughter was safe.

"Why would you do that? And why wouldn't you call?" my mom asked, her voice raising an octave as she tried to come to terms with what I'd done.

"I didn't know what to say," I admitted. That part felt like the truth, because I still didn't know what I could say to them to explain the drastic change in my life. I didn't think anyone could ever understand what pulsed between Rafael and me.

Not when I didn't even understand it myself.

"Just come home, Isa," my dad said, his voice cracking with the words. "We can make sense out of all of this once you're home."

"I'm not coming home, Dad. I need to get settled into my life here. I'll come visit when I can," I said.

"Isabel! You will get your ass on a plane right now and come home!" he snapped. "Your life is here. Your family is here."

Rafael's face darkened with anger as my father raised his voice to me, and I knew I had to do what I could to diffuse the situation before he got involved. Still, the words caught in my throat. "Rafael is my family now," I said, swallowing back bile at the harshness of my words. "I've never felt this way about anyone." Whether I loved Rafael or not, he brought out all the parts of me I'd thought long dead.

"I don't understand," she said. "You've been gone for less than three weeks, Isa. It isn't like you to act so rashly."

"Please try to give me the benefit of the doubt. I don't make impulsive decisions, so trust that I made this one in the same way. I made the choice very carefully," I whispered, watching Rafael's posture relax slightly. "Is Grandmother there?" I asked.

"She's at the center. She can't bear to be here knowing you're gone," my mother said, trailing off as she struggled to find what else she could say.

"Mom!" a voice so similar to mine said in the background as I heard the front door close.

"We're in here, honey!" my mom called back to my sister.

"Odina's home?" I asked, my face dropping in my dejection.

"She came home shortly after you left for Ibiza. She seems...better," my mom said hesitantly. "Isa, please just come home. We can figure this out."

"Maybe this is for the best. Maybe without me there to get in the way, you can mend your relationship with her," I said, trying to fight back the hurt. But I'd always been in Odina's way. I'd always been a reminder to her of the day she died. "Everything happens for a reason, right?" I asked, trying to keep back the bitterness I felt at knowing that Odina had swept in the moment I was gone. That she'd moved to claim our family as hers alone with me gone.

I glared at Rafael, wondering if she'd somehow known I wouldn't be coming home. His face was a careful mask, designed to keep his secrets away from me.

"Isa, that's not fair," my mom said.

"Life's not fair," I said back, smiling despite the harsh words. "I'll call you soon. I love you," I said, ending the call with a stab to the phone screen. In my frustration, I hadn't even waited for them to say goodbye.

Maybe Rafael was my penance for what I'd done. The price I'd have to pay to make amends with Odina.

I'd gladly pay it.

But first, I needed to know why she'd thought it safe to come home.

*I*sa's suspicious eyes landed on mine the moment she ended the call. The knowing glare in them only served to make my cock hard, to drive me further toward the edge of my own restlessness. In just a few moments, I'd have to leave her.

In just a few moments, I'd have no choice but to get in my helicopter and head for the plane I kept on the mainland. Pavel's eldest son had shown his face in Rome, and my allies there had been all too willing to share that information with my contacts. He could disappear at the drop of a hat, and I wouldn't even have time to fuck my wife one last time before I left if I wanted the best chance possible of catching him.

"You made the right choice, telling them what you did," I said, attempting to soothe the wars waging in her eyes.

She tossed my phone to the surface of the bed, cocking her head to the side as she stared at me. She stood slowly, unfolding her limbs carefully until her feet touched the floor between us. She gathered the hem of her dress in her hands, carefully tugging it further up her legs while I watched her pink panties peek out between her thighs.

Placing one knee in the chair beside me, she maneuvered herself up until she straddled my lap and stared down at me with her hair falling in a curtain around her. Other men might have described *mi reina* as an angel in that moment, with the sun shining on the right side of her face.

Those men didn't know shit about Isa.

Darkness swirled in her green eyes, vengeance dancing in a tempting play of edge against the sweet lines of her face. No one would ever suspect the demon that hid inside her when they looked at her. No one would think her capable of the things I knew I would push her to do at my side.

She touched a finger to my jawline, dragging her nail over the stubble on my face and moving it down to my throat. My hands grasped her around the waist as I pulled her down into my lap more firmly, desperate to feel the heat of her pussy against my cock.

She accommodated me with a mischievous smirk as she wrapped her hand around the front of my throat. She leaned her weight into it, pressing against my Adam's apple as she glared down at me. The feeling of her delicate hand against one of the most vulnerable parts of my body should have brought out all my defense mechanisms.

Instead, my cock twitched between us, seeking the warmth of her tight sheathe as she leaned forward and touched her forehead to mine while she squeezed my throat.

"Did Odina know I wouldn't be coming home?" she asked, her voice steady and strong despite the conversation that might have broken her only a few days prior.

But Isa had already been broken, and she wasn't one to stay down. "I'm not certain," I admitted. "You'd have to ask

Hugo. He's the one who dealt with her after they drugged you."

"And what exactly did he do to my sister?" Isa asked, leaning forward to brush her lips against mine gently.

"He told her to shut her fucking mouth as far as I know," I said with a deep chuckle when she squeezed her hand tighter. "She agreed, so long as you were hurt in the end. I think she'll be disappointed, don't you?" I murmured the words against her mouth, darting out my tongue to lick the seam of her lips playfully. "You might have been hurt, but here you are with your hand on the devil's throat."

"And you had nothing else to do with her?" Isa asked, staring at me intently. I suddenly understood the darkness swirling her vision.

Jealousy. Possession.

Mi reina wondered if her sister might have played with her favorite toy before she'd had the chance.

I chuckled, the vibrations of my laughter shaking her palm at my throat. "Is that what you're worried about, Princesa? That I touched your sister?"

"It wouldn't be the first time Odina fucked my boyfriend," she snarled. I slid my hand up her body, wrapping my own hand around her throat to match her grip on me. She gasped against the touch, her hips grinding down on me involuntarily as she accepted the violence of my hold. I unfolded myself from the chair slowly, setting her on her feet with my grip on her neck until she backed up the few steps to the bed.

I laid her out across it on her back, straddling her hips as I came down on top of her and reversed the positions. She squirmed, releasing my throat to pretend to be as gentle as a kitten beneath me.

We both knew she was more of a lioness, ready and

waiting to claw my eyes out if I admitted to having been with her twin before her. "I've never touched Odina, much to her dismay," I said, watching as Isa's nostrils flared.

"Why not? She looks just like me, so why wouldn't you want to take her if she was willing?" she asked as I tipped her head back with my grip at the base of her jaw.

Leaning in to run my lips over the delicate skin of the side of her neck, I murmured the truth Isa hadn't ever come to accept. "I don't fuck underage girls, but even if she'd been eighteen, I wouldn't have touched her. Because she's not you."

She pushed up against my hand despite the way it must have further restricted her breathing. With her lungs emptying of air with every second that she challenged me, she growled her frustration in my ear when I bit down on the sensitive skin of her neck.

Even with all the physical evidence of my possession on her body, I still felt the desperate need to have her marked. The bite mark on her shoulder could be hidden, but the bruise I left on her neck as I sucked her flesh between my teeth would be a far greater task to conceal from the world.

With my absence looming, it was all that offered me any comfort.

"Would you like to know that your brother tried to seduce me?" Isa asked, her voice dropping lower as she relaxed back into the bed and stopped challenging my grip on her.

"Fortunately for me, I do not have a brother. Because if I found out he'd laid a single hand on you, I would kill him. Is that what you want to hear, *mi reina*? That I understand just how bloodthirsty you feel right now?"

"You're always bloodthirsty, you psychotic ass," she said, drawing a smile to my lips. I leaned back to stare at her, watching as she touched her hands to my forearm and dug her nails into the skin where my shirt sleeve was rolled up. The feeling of her nails sinking into my flesh, and marking me in the way I had her, appealed to me on the most instinctual level. "I don't really think I should be judging my bad behavior using you as a guideline."

"Why not?" I murmured, leaning in to touch my lips to hers. With her eyes holding mine steadily, she nipped my bottom lip playfully, before her little pink tongue soothed the wound she'd left. "Why is being bloodthirsty a bad thing when your sister helped drug you so you could be raped? She wanted me to hurt you. To kill you or break you so severely that you were out of her way and her life. She deserves your ire."

"I don't think you're in any place to judge Odina for her sins against me when you don't know what I did to her first," she said, her voice dropping low as the seriousness of the conversation chased away the playful bits of her that had come out to play in the moments after her phone call with her parents.

Her exhaustion had made her moods tumultuous, unpredictable even. I never knew when she would cry or when she'd stab me with a fucking fork. As much as I hated to be away from her, the sleep she would get without me to wake her up in all hours of the night would be a benefit for Isa. "So tell me, then I can understand," I said, leaning my weight back onto her hips as I sat up straight. I released my grip on her throat, staring down and waiting for the confession that would finally make me understand all the pieces of what made her, *her.*

She smirked, shaking her head at me. There were only two things she denied me, and both were just words. The confession of her love and the reality of her secret.

I didn't know which one grated on my nerves more.

She propped one of her elbows up beneath her, leaning closer to my space as she touched the opposite hand to my cheek delicately. Teasing me with what she knew I wanted to know, I understood with a sudden clarity that she would never willingly give me the answers I sought.

I'd have to force them from her another way, and my mind spun with the possibilities of how I could do just that.

"I don't want to be weak," she said instead of responding to my inquiry, touching her nose to the side of mine and teasing my face with a gentle caress as she mimicked what I did to her so often when I wanted something from her.

"And you think you will be if you tell me the truth?" I asked, narrowing my eyes into a glare.

"No," she scoffed. "I think I *am* weak because I have no defense against you or anyone else. Regina told me I should embrace who I'm becoming. You said something similar. I want to learn how to defend myself."

"So you can stab me more?" I asked with a chuckle. "I don't think so."

"So I can stab people who might want to harm me. You sent me away when that man showed his face in Ibiza, so I'm inclined to believe there are people who would hurt me. I don't want to be helpless," she pleaded.

I stared down at her, rage rattling the cages of my soul as I contemplated what she was saying without actually voicing the words.

Isa didn't trust me to keep her safe.

"I won't ever let anyone touch you, Princesa," I murmured. As much as I loved that the Queen was coming to the surface more and more, I couldn't deny the fact that she would be more difficult to contain. That she'd be more of a struggle for me and I would need to fight her to remind her of her place.

The place where she was mine.

"You put a gun to my head," she snapped, raising her eyebrow at me as if she dared me to contradict her. "You can't protect me when you're part of what I need to protect myself from."

"Ah, but you're my wife now," I said, anger leaking into my voice as I dropped it low and reached out a hand to cup her around the back of the neck. "I have everything I want in my arms. I have no desire to die, and if I killed you, I would have to follow you into the pits of Hell."

"So romantic," she hissed sarcastically. "You're fucked in the head, *El Diablo*. Regardless of whether you want to kill me or not, I want to know how to get away from a man if he wants to hurt me. I should think you would want that too, since I'm not sure you'd appreciate someone else touching your favorite toy."

"I forbid it," I growled, watching as her eyes went wide with the extreme reaction. Every word she spoke was a nail in the coffin, another insult to my ability to protect my *fucking wife*. "Joaquin is there to keep you safe when I am not, and there are emergency procedures in place to make sure you're protected at all costs." I released her, lowering myself off the bed and standing next to it. Even as I despised the distance between us in the moments before I left her, the inevitable reality of the conversation was undeniable.

Isa would always push back against being dependent on me, and her desire to protect herself was only a consequence of that shift in her life. Her independence no longer mattered, because as the wife of *El Diablo*, her only responsibility was to keep me happy.

To take what I gave her when I needed to fuck my frustrations out on her body so that I wouldn't murder those who disappointed me. To calm the nightmare inside me so I could function without burning the world to the ground in a rage.

"You forbid it?" she asked, raising her eyebrow at me as she flared her nostrils and sat up straight. There was something in those words that felt like a challenge, as if she wanted me to understand that the order had been a very grave mistake.

"Yes. I forbid it. I will not teach you to fight. If I discover anyone else has disobeyed me in this, I don't think either of you will like the consequences," I said pointedly, touching my hand to her shoulder. My thumb dragged over the spot where she would have a brand if I hadn't taken kindness on her, reminding her exactly what was at stake if she disobeyed her husband.

She glared at me, shrugging off my hand on her shoulder before standing in the tiny space between me and the bed. "I hope you like fucking your hand then, since I *forbid* you from touching me."

She moved to step away, rounding the foot of the bed to make for the terrace. I grabbed her around the back of her neck, holding her still with the weight of my hand as my thumb and forefinger dug into the flesh there. Stepping up behind her, I touched my face to her hair while she trembled with her fury. "It's cute you think you can deny me anything, *mi reina*," I murmured. "I know how much you love my hands on you. How much you love to feel my cock moving inside you." I bent my head forward, gathering her thick hair in my hands and curling it around her right shoulder.

"I hate you," she warned.

Touching my lips to the side I'd bared for my assault, I

trailed gentle lips up and down her neck. At odds with the harshness of the words that would follow, I kept my touch feather soft and enjoyed the way her skin pebbled with goosebumps as her desire rose. "Would you still hate me if I threw you on the bed and buried my cock in your throat?"

"I'd bite it off," she growled, and I believed it of her in those moments.

"I guess it's fortunate that my pussy doesn't have teeth then," I laughed darkly, reaching around her body to hike her dress up her legs. She shoved at my hand, forcing me to gather both of them in my grip and hold them behind her back. One of my hands was strong enough to restrain her as she struggled against my invading touch, pushing her ass back into me when I cupped her through her panties.

"Let go of me," she said, her voice coming out more breathy than she wanted as I kicked her legs apart and stroked her through the fabric of her underwear.

"You do not get to deny me what's mine," I growled the warning, sliding my fingers up to slip them into her panties.

My phone rang in my pocket—the reminder that my time with Isa had come to an end, and I needed to get my ass to the helicopter. I ignored it, stroking my fingers over her clit as she dropped her head forward in her attempt to deny the desire flooding her body. "Your body belongs to me, Princesa, and I will fuck it whenever I please. We will not be one of those couples that deny one another access to our body because of a disagreement. You're pissed at me? Then bleed me while you ride my cock," I said, shoving two fingers inside her while she trembled in my grip. When her pussy clenched around me and her orgasm approached, I pulled my fingers free and out of her panties.

She gasped her shock, her horror that I would stop with her so close to the edge as I sucked the taste of her off my fingers. With my cock as hard as steel in my pants, I released her as she spun to glare at me. Cupping her face in my hands, I kissed her gently despite her desperate attempts to shift the embrace into something carnal.

When I stepped back from her and moved to the closet, she stood gaping after me as I tossed the bag Regina kept packed for me onto the bed. "Where are you going?" she asked.

"I have to go to Rome to kill a man," I said, watching the way she winced at the harsh reminder of who and what I was. "It's part of protecting you, even if you don't think I'm capable," I grunted.

"That's not what I said!" she yelled, her legs squirming as she stood in place.

"It is exactly what you said, Princesa," I argued, ignoring her neediness even though it killed something inside me to walk away from her when she wanted my cock.

It would do Isa good to spend a couple of days thinking about just how badly she missed it. I pointed to the corner of the room and the cameras that were tucked away discreetly. Her eyes narrowed on them as she swallowed, undoubtedly thinking about all the homemade movies I had of the two of us when she'd been too wrapped up to remember they were there. "If you touch my pussy while I'm gone, I'll know. You don't get off unless it's with me," I ordered, hauling the bag up into my hand.

"And what if I do?" she asked, crossing her arms over her chest.

"You don't want to find out," I growled, turning on my heel and leaving her with that to consider. I couldn't shake the sinking feeling that Isa would disobey me while I was gone just to spite me.

Rebellious women were a pain in my ass.

♟♟♟♟♟

J walked down the narrow streets of Rome with my hands tucked into my suit pocket. With the cobblestone roads and the stunning buildings to either side of me, I enjoyed the dim lighting as the sun went down.

Rome was a unique beauty, a remarkable city that I knew Isa would have loved to visit if given the opportunity. With her love of history, there was no way she could do anything other than admire the home of the Roman Empire. Even with my anger at her, I couldn't deny the desperate desire to show her everything the city had to offer.

One day, I'd be able to take her to the cities of my allies and show her the world. One day, I'd be able to trust that she wouldn't stroll off into the night and try to escape the clutches of the devil who held her captive.

I pulled the phone out of my pocket, glancing at the screen as I dialed Regina's number. It rang a few times before she finally answered, putting me out of my misery. "The devil's house," she said. "Would you like your balls roasted or fried?"

"I take it Isa is taking my absence well?" I asked, my lips tipping up despite the snarky response from my housekeeper.

"She is doing as a true Queen does," Regina replied as dishes clanged together. Given the hour, I suspected she must be cleaning up after dinner.

I already felt the need to go home to be with *mi princesa,* but having Regina's cooking rubbed in my face and knowing I couldn't eat it only worsened my bad mood. "And what does a true Queen do?" I asked, humoring the woman as I made my way through the area of the city where Leonid had last been seen by my allies.

"She plots her revenge," Regina said, a smile tinting her voice. A male snicker came from the background, the familiar voice of Joaquin as he found Regina's response particularly humorous.

"And how is she plotting revenge?" I asked, knowing very well I wouldn't get an answer. Isa hadn't been with me for long, but she'd already turned Regina against me. Women stuck together, and I wished I could say that Joaquin or Alejandro would take my side over Isa's. But they wouldn't either.

"We both know I wouldn't tell you that even if I knew," Regina said. "But I don't. She's been quiet. Stuck in her own head. Should I expect more bloody cutlery when you come home?"

"I'll try to keep her isolated to the bedroom when she bleeds me from now on," I said dryly. Her concern for my wellbeing was touching, and I found my hand drifting up to touch the wound where Isa had stabbed me.

I hated the scars of my brands on some level, detested the man who had given them to me when I'd been a child. But the marks from Isa were an entirely different story, a compulsion that reminded me that she owned me just as much as I owned her.

If she marked me when we returned home, I would love every second of it. I'd wear her scars with pride just as I wore her name on my skin. "Keep her out of trouble," I reminded Regina.

"Would you like to speak to her?" Regina asked, and I shook my head before I realized she couldn't see me. "Not just yet. I'll talk to her tomorrow."

"Smart choice," Regina agreed. "You should give her a chance to miss you."

"Fat fucking chance!" Isa yelled in the background,

making Regina bark out a sharp laugh. I hung up the phone with a groan. My wife would be the death of me.

And I'd love every second of it.

I stood with my back against the wall, kicking up a leg to settle in and wait for the hours to pass. At some point, Leonid would emerge from the bar where he'd chosen to settle for the night to drink his problems away.

Only a foolish man got drunk, particularly in a territory that wasn't his own, but the Kuznetsov family thought themselves above all their rivals. They believed they were the toughest and most powerful family because of their history.

The Russians had been at the front of organized crime alongside the Italians and the Irish for many years. But as crimes modernized and new alliances formed without cultural and familial allegiances, new powers rose.

Old powers would fall. Until all that remained would be one power.

Mine.

I spent most of the night plotting ways to kill him. So much so that my dreams were filled with blood and gore. By the time I woke up the next morning, I hated myself for the violent turn in my sleep.

I didn't want to be like Rafael. I didn't want violence to consume me just because I was dominated by the presence of a devil. I would only be letting him win if I allowed him to change who I was.

But there was something brutal inside me. A part of me that longed to find justice where there was none.

I'd been thrown into a river without consequence. I'd watched time and time again as the crimes against my people went ignored. I'd been lied to. I'd been stripped of all my choices. I'd been drugged and kidnapped.

My entire life was a series of paying for other people's crimes. Just once, it would be nice to be the one committing them.

It would be bliss to earn the punishment myself.

It all simmered within me, feeling like I sat on the edge of a reckoning. As if the part of me that seemed to come to the surface after Rafael's introduction to my life had always been there, and I guessed it had.

The darkness had always been a part of me. I'd always been more at home in it than I had the sunshine.

The bed seemed foreign without Rafael's presence. Without his heat at my back and his hand cupping my breast in his massive grip while he slept, it felt like just another empty bed. A piece of furniture. I should have felt freer with him gone; instead I just felt alone.

I stretched my arms above my head languidly, pushing the button on the nightstand to draw the curtains open. I'd gone to bed with pajamas on for the first time since coming to Rafael's island, since he insisted on me sleeping naked with him.

But at some point in the past couple of weeks with him, I'd gotten more comfortable in my own skin. I couldn't stand the coarseness of even the satins and best cottons against my skin while I slept, especially not against my core that throbbed with need after his bullshit the afternoon before.

My eyes went to the cameras as I debated challenging him and his authority over me by touching myself, but I pursed my lips and got out of bed instead.

I'd wait until the night to torment him. To distract him from the real rebellion.

Hopefully, he'd never see that one coming.

I sat out on the daybed with a book beside me after eating one of Regina's pregnancy-inducing breakfasts. If there was any benefit to Rafe's absence, it was that I wouldn't be getting knocked up while he was gone.

We'd had unprotected sex far too often for my comfort,

and I touched a hand to my stomach cautiously before shaking it off. I looked over at Joaquin, pursing my lips as I considered how to ask him for what I wanted from him. "Do you still think girls like me don't need to learn kickboxing?" I asked.

He dragged a hand over his face. "That's really none of my business. I suggest you take it up with your husband, *mi reina*," he said, clearly uncomfortable with the suggestion. It seemed like maybe Rafe had been verbal about his interest in keeping me protected like I was made of glass.

I wasn't, and I was sick of being treated like it.

"I did. He forbade it," I said with a shrug.

"As expected. You could get hurt kickboxing," Joaquin said in reprimand. "Let's not forget that it's only a matter of time before you're pregnant and need to think about those things."

"Well, I wasn't actually asking for kickboxing lessons. Just for him to teach me how to defend myself a little in case of emergency."

He hung his head, pinching his nose between his thumb and finger in aggravation. "You suggested that Rafael can't keep you safe. No wonder he tore out of here like there was a fire up his ass," he laughed. "You insulted the devil's manhood and lived to tell about it. Congratulations, *mi reina*. I think that might be a first."

I stuck my tongue out at him, not even bothering to argue the fact that I hadn't insulted him. Men were stupid and impractical and apparently their egos were more important than common sense. "What do *you* think?" I stressed, looking to get his opinion rather than just Rafael speaking through his mouth like the puppet master he liked to pretend to be.

"I think I like my tongue inside my mouth, so I'm not about to speak out against Rafael," he said.

"So you disagree. You think I should be able to protect myself just in case, because that's the sane thing! Why wouldn't he want me to be safe?" I asked, raising an eyebrow at him.

"It might have something to do with the fact that you've already stabbed him once. Just a thought," Joaquin argued, but he twisted his lips to the side and came to stand directly next to the daybed. His eyes drifted over to the house in the distance where I'd seen the brothers emerge on the day I first spotted them, and my heart clenched in my chest at the reminder of my friend's betrayal.

Well, I supposed he'd never really been my friend in the end.

"He's not coping well, Isa," Joaquin said, wrapping his hand around the post that held up the canopy on the daybed. "He misses you."

"He has no right to miss me when he lied to me the entire time I knew him," I snapped, crossing my arms over my chest in defiance. It felt childish even as I did it, but I couldn't control the bitterness I felt at the very mention of Hugo. All the while he'd pretended to be so outraged over my sister's betrayal and the fact that she'd broken my trust in such a profound way, he'd been lying to me like an asshole.

Using me for a job.

"So did I," Joaquin pointed out, perching on the edge of the daybed. "You have to understand that Hugo, Gabriel, and I had no say in what happened with you. Rafael summoned us to Chicago because there was a security issue he needed us to handle for him in the long term. We didn't even know you existed until we were already on the plane."

"Is that supposed to make me feel better?" I asked, glaring at him as my throat stung with the tears of betrayal. I wanted to hate them. I wanted to cling to the fact that they'd all hurt me, because I needed to rage against *something*.

Rafe was the appropriate object for my anger, but the feelings I had for him complicated that. He'd betrayed my trust before I'd ever even met him, and yet I couldn't hold onto the anger I should have felt with him for that.

"What would you have had us do, Isa?" Joaquin asked, glaring at me as he pushed me to admit the truth. I knew it down to my bones, even if I didn't want to acknowledge it.

They'd been just as trapped by the circumstances of Rafael's plan as I had been. They'd been sent to a strange city to watch over a girl they didn't know all because of his twisted obsession with me. "You could have told me the truth," I said.

"What would that have accomplished? You would have fought. You'd have tried to find a way out of it and only put your family at risk in the process. This way gave you time. I'd hoped that his interest in you would fade after he left Chicago and he didn't have to live with the knowledge that you existed in the very same city as him, but he never wavered. So we all waited. We kept you safe. It was all we could do."

"I don't know that it makes much of a difference," I sighed, curling my knees into my chest. "I'm here. I'm not going anywhere, but I have no interest in trusting the people who hurt me."

"Just talk to him, Isa," Joaquin pleaded. "Let him explain his side of things. If you can do that, then in the rare moments when Rafael is off the island and we have the opportunity, I'll take you to a clearing nearby and teach you some very *basic* moves to protect yourself."

"What about Rafael? Won't he punish you if he finds out?" I asked, staring up at him in shock.

"He'll punish both of us *when* he finds out, so you need to be certain you're ready to deal with whatever that might look like. I can handle the pain. Can you?" Joaquin asked, standing and holding out a hand for me to take.

It was so similar to the night that Rafael had asked me to go to bed with him, the first moment I'd accepted that the devil would be mine for even just a moment, that my heart caught in my throat. But the need to do something just because I wanted to was tangible, and despite knowing the potential consequences, I accepted Joaquin's hand and let him pull me to my feet.

He released me as soon as I stood, turning on his heel and making for the clearing between Rafael's yard and the village in the distance. Following at his back with my heart in my throat, I couldn't decide what I dreaded more.

Looking Hugo in the eye, or whatever punishment Rafael would decide on when he learned the truth. Joaquin's words, the *when* and not *if*, struck me as truth. I couldn't imagine anything happened on the island without his knowledge.

I dragged my feet as we walked, feeling like I was closer to marching to my death than going to have a conversation with a friend. My heart pumped in my throat, tears burning it like acid as I fought to keep them back.

The house the brothers lived in was beautiful. A yellow building that was well-kept and had flowers growing in planters on each of the windows. It blended in with the rest of the houses in the village that wasn't really a village, just a small town that reminded me of Dalt Vila in Ibiza Town.

Small. Old fashioned. But there were touches of luxury everywhere I looked.

Joaquin pushed open the front door, leading the way inside as I glanced over my shoulder at the people watching me with whispering lips. They gathered, the soft murmurs of *reina* echoing through the space between us until Joaquin closed the door and separated us from them. "They'll get used to you," he said in an attempt to reassure me, guiding me toward the back of the house. Gabriel and Hugo both sat at a patio set on the terrace, a pitcher of sangria in the center despite the early hour.

Joaquin cleared his throat to get their attention, and the brothers spun to face him. Hugo's eyes widened briefly before he vaulted to his feet when he saw me. "Isa," he said, moving toward me as if he might hug me.

I held up both hands and clenched my eyes closed, warning him off as best I could without words. I didn't think my voice would work.

I suddenly couldn't bear to speak any of the thoughts that had been in my head since I'd learned the truth. I didn't think anything could soothe the wound his deception had left.

He waited, watching me cautiously with his hands clenched into tight fists at his side. "Why?" I asked, even though I already knew the answer. "Why did you have to make me care about you? Was that part of your job?" I asked finally.

He shook his head, scrubbing his hands down his face. "No. I needed to be your friend and we needed to watch you. That's all."

"Then why?" I whispered. "What was the point?"

"You care about me because you have a huge heart. Because you don't give your love often, but when you do? You give it *all*. Just like me," he sighed, moving forward to take my hands in his despite my resistance. "And I love you.

You're my best friend, Isa. I didn't want this for you. Please believe me," he begged. He didn't move to touch me more than the contact at my hands, where I had no doubt that he would have once hugged me and held me.

His fear of Rafael was too strong, even with him absent.

"How can you say that? You don't lie to people you love," I accused.

"I lied to you about why I was in Chicago, but the friendship we built was real. You're a part of me. You're a part of all of us now. We knew you before you were Señora Ibarra, and we'll always remember that girl," Hugo said.

"But the woman she's growing to be is a force to be reckoned with, and we very much look forward to watching that journey," Gabriel said from the table. Hugo pulled on my hands, drawing me over and sitting me in one of the seats as I cried.

"It's okay to cry," Hugo said, wiping some of the tears away from my eyes.

"I don't know who I am anymore," I admitted, watching as his face twisted. I knew he'd understand better than anyone, because he'd known me before Rafael.

"You're *mi reina*. You're exactly who you have to be to survive *El Diablo*," Hugo said, taking a seat next to me.

I didn't let people in often. I didn't accept that I needed others, because I knew in the end other people only ever hurt me.

They used. They took.

But sometimes, they were worth loving despite all that. Sometimes they were worth forgiving, even in the tiniest sliver of my heart.

I just had to hope I didn't get burned a second time, because I wouldn't survive the ashes again.

It had been far too long since I'd stalked through the streets of a city that wasn't my own. Since I'd moved through the night like the darkness was mine to claim. There was no bodyguard at my back, no one to protect me if something went wrong.

It wouldn't, because no one could defeat the devil when the sun went down.

Leonid stumbled through Rome blindly and half drunk, entirely unaware of the nightmare who trailed at his heels and prepared to kill him slowly.

To make him suffer for the sins of his father.

The apartment he stepped up to would have been a secure fortress that few could compete with when trying to gain access. But such things didn't matter for men like me.

His men were all half drunk on their own arrogance and vodka, letting me slip inside the building as if I belonged. I followed him up the stairs at a slower pace, allowing Leonid to guide me to the space that would be the last he ever saw.

I would sear the memory of it into his eyes long after they stopped seeing, letting the reminder of his passing haunt him in death. He fumbled with the keys he pulled from his pocket, scraping the doorknob with his unsteady hands.

Stepping up behind him, I took the keys from his loose grip. "Here, let me help you," I said, feigning kindness. Turning the key inside the lock, I twisted the knob and pushed the door open as Leonid's stunned gaze came to rest on the side of my face.

Just as he moved to shout, I shoved him inside the apartment with a rough hand at the back of his head. He tumbled to the floor in his drunken state, tripping over his legs until he fell in a puddle of awkward limbs. I closed the door behind me and turned the lock, my eyes landing on the woman tied to a chair at the dining room table. She squirmed and screamed into the duct tape covering her mouth, drawing a disgruntled sigh from my lungs as I turned my stare back to Leonid.

The duct tape proved convenient as I grabbed the roll off the table and tore off a piece with my teeth. "Help!" Leonid finally yelled as I moved toward him. Sighing, I drew the gun from my pants and readied myself for the stampede of security that would follow his pathetic attempt at salvation.

The door blew off the hinges as his men came charging in blindly. My gun kicked back in my hand as the first shot struck the lead man between the eyes. He dropped to the floor like a sack of meat, leaving the two others behind him vulnerable as I shot them in rapid succession.

Three shots, three men. With them dead and no longer my concern, I turned my attention back to Leonid where he cowered with his back to the wall. He hadn't bothered to stand, only holding out two hands as if he thought he could reason with *El Diablo*. But there was no absolution from the Devil.

Only an eternity of suffering.

I grabbed the bodies one by one, dragging them inside the apartment so I could close the door. I didn't expect any more of Leonid or Pavel's men to come so quickly, but only a fool would leave himself entirely vulnerable. Even though the door didn't latch, it would still buy me an invaluable moment of time if someone did manage to come and try to interfere with my fun.

"Ibarra," Leonid rasped out. "What are you doing in Rome?"

"I should think that's obvious," I warned. "I have never appreciated your father's fondness for games and small talk, Leonid. I won't start with you."

"What do you want?" he asked with a grimace. "You've already killed my men. Surely that's enough retaliation for whatever you think my father did to you."

"Not hardly. Your father won't miss your men in the slightest. He will, however, miss you," I said with a dark smile. I turned my attention to the girl tied up at the table, tearing the duct tape off her mouth and untying her quickly. She moved to stretch her limbs, staring up at me hopefully as I dropped a wad of cash from my pocket onto the table. "Get out of Rome for a while," I ordered, nodding my head to the door and dismissing her as I turned my attention back to Leonid. He'd started attempting to shift his way closer to the door when he thought me distracted, to the armed men and the weapons he could use to defend himself.

It shocked me to think that Pavel's son wouldn't always carry his piece on him, but his offspring had never been the brightest bunch. They were often too reliant on the allegiance of men who could easily be bought or swayed with a threat to the people they cared about.

I trusted no one more than myself.

The woman stood on shaky legs, the bruises on her skin a deep purple as she blinked her swollen eyes up at me. "Thank you," she murmured when I didn't give her my attention.

As much as I would have liked to say she was a unique case, Pavel and his sons left a trail of women just like her wherever they went. She was just another victim in their string of rapes and trafficking, and sadly she was one of the luckier ones.

She'd walk away alive and free.

She scurried for the door when I kept my eyes on Leonid and closed the distance between us. Squatting down in front of him, I stared him in the eye and silently dared him to say something to contradict everything I already knew. He was as big a piece of shit as his father. As my father had been.

"Did you rape her?" I asked, tilting my head to the side as I studied him. He clenched his jaw, not saying the words we both knew were true. Even if he hadn't yet, he would have had I not come to kill him. "Or did I take away your new toy before you got a chance to break her in?"

"I fucked her last night," he spat, snarling in my face. "But you can't rape a whore like that. You should have heard her scream for me."

Patting my knees, I rose to stand over him. My eyes fell to his suit clad legs, the memory of his father's knee cap snapping filling my head with a sudden burst of pleasure. "It's fortunate for you that I have a wife to get home to," I said. "Otherwise I might be inclined to call in some of my friends who enjoy fucking men like you in the ass."

"*Wife?*" he huffed a laugh. "Fucking Christ almighty, you married that American cunt? My father was right. You really *have* gone soft."

I slammed my foot down on his kneecap, crushing it in

the same way I had his father's not long ago. He screamed his pain, clutching at it as I twisted it back and forth and ground the shattered bones into dust. *"Fuck!"*

"I'm not soft for you," I said, leaning forward to pat his cheek harshly and turning back to the kitchen. Grabbing the entire butcher block of knives, I went back to where he sobbed against the wall in his pain. "You see, I'm not a fan of men talking about my wife," I said, setting the block on the floor behind me. With a steak knife in my hand, I cut through the fabric of his shirt to reveal pale white skin beneath. Covered in the tattoos of the Bratva, his torso heaved with exertion as he moved to strike me.

I grabbed his hand as he lifted it, pulling until I twisted him to lie flat against the floor. Pulling his arm out to the side and pinning it beneath him, I stabbed through the flesh with the steak knife until it held steady in the floorboards. He yelled his pain, raising his other arm to hit me and fight me off as I grabbed another steak knife and repeated the process on the other hand.

He whimpered as he tried to lift the knives out of the wood floor, his flesh sliding along the knife until he dropped back down in agony. Ripping the shirt off his torso, I grabbed the filet knife from the butcher block and pressed the tip to his chest while he tried to sink into the floor to get away. The tattoo over his heart was the unique mark that the Kuznetsovs wore to signify their impeccable genetics. To show that they alone were the heirs to the specific line of the Bratva that Pavel ran in Siberia.

I sank the point of the knife into his skin, gliding it through his flesh as I carved around the edges of his tattoo. "Fucking stop!" he screamed as the blade sank deeper beneath his ink and flayed the skin off his chest. I peeled it back, the skin tearing off the muscle and blood red flesh until the patch hung limply in my hand with the black ink of the Tundra Wolf and stars glimmering underneath the red stain. I tossed it to the side, listening to the wet sound as it stuck to the floor. "You're insane," he mumbled, his breathing harsh as I touched his face with blood-soaked fingers and laughed.

"You have no idea," I chuckled, dragging the tip of the knife down his sternum and leaving a trail of blood in my wake. The devil inside me craved the blood and the scent of fear and pain in the air.

I couldn't wait until I could share that part of myself with Isa. For the little demon inside her to admit that she craved the bloodshed and death just as much as I did.

"I used to think I'd get bored eventually," I sighed. "After a lifetime of violence, how could I not?" I asked, pressing the knife through the skin of his chest carefully. I pushed it deeper, making slow and careful glides with the knife to get through the chest wall until I felt the familiar press of bone against the tip, sliding straight down along the sternum. I set the knife on his stomach to slip eight fingers in the cut I'd made on his chest, pulling the flesh apart to reveal the breastbone. He stared up at me in horror, his eyes fluttering closed as the unimaginable pain of having his chest cavity opened while he looked on settled over him. "But that day has never come."

I used the tip of the chef's knife to crack open his breast bone, pleased he still breathed as I reached inside his chest cavity and wrapped my fingers around his beating heart. Isa was the love of my life, my heart, and Pavel had nearly cost me that. With his life in my hands, I pulled his free until he blinked up at his own heart in the moments before his death. Opening his mouth, I shoved the bloody organ between his teeth and trapped the last breath in his body.

It protruded from his face, a mouth full of his own heart as it pumped the remaining blood within it all over his face and neck. I dragged my fingers through it, drawing on the floor beside his body.

One down.

Four to go. I stood, washing my hands in the sink in the kitchen. Making my way back toward the door to the apartment, I pulled it open and strode into the hallway after closing it behind me. Pulling my phone out of my pocket, I dialed Pavel's number and chuckled when it went to voicemail as expected. "Are all your sons morons like their father? Or was that only Leonid?" I asked, ending the call and turning to wander down the streets of Rome.

I smiled at the old woman I passed sitting on her steps, making my way back to my gracious host's house.

Massimo Farrante was one of the few men I trusted to keep me safe until I could return to Isa, but he and I had business to discuss before I could leave Rome.

Tomorrow would be soon enough.

By the time I'd finished my business and made my way to the room set aside for me for the night, exhaustion made my limbs heavy. I wanted to go home to Isa, but getting some sleep first would do me wonders. My conversation with Massimo would continue into the next day, working to help him find a solution to his own woman problems without crossing the line. Men like us walked a careful line, and if we didn't take the time to evaluate our actions, we may cross into the forbidden zone of those we condemned.

I flipped open the screen on my laptop despite my

fatigue, wanting to watch *mi reina* sleep for a few moments to settle the violence rattling in my bones. Not having her to fuck the remaining adrenaline out of my system was torture, and I resolved to taking her with me whenever I could do it safely.

As I brought up the camera feed and my eyes settled on her face, there was no denying the restlessness of her body. Despite the late hour, she was wide awake in the center of the bed. Suspicion took me, and I rewound the feed slowly, watching with a tightening jaw as I realized what Isa had done.

I kept rewinding until the moment she'd shrugged the sheets off her body and spread her legs. Baring herself to the camera, she was entirely naked as she slid her hand between her thighs and played with her pussy. With her eyes on the camera, there was no denying that she'd chosen to defy me intentionally.

She didn't try to hide the rebellion, instead using it to torture me as her fingers worked her clit knowingly with an arrogant smirk on her face. Her fingers slid lower, gliding inside her pussy and pumping slowly.

I dropped my hand to my cock, grasping it tightly and mimicking the speed of her fingers as I stroked myself. Isa bit her lip on the camera as if she could see me touching myself, taking pleasure in driving me further into my rage and desire for her.

I'd explicitly forbidden her from touching herself, and she'd decided that my greedy little pussy needed attention that I wasn't there to give.

Her back arched as she moved those naughty fingers back to her clit, circling it with an increasing rhythm as my hand stroked my cock faster. As I imagined her beneath me and begging for my cum while I pounded inside her. She reached up a free hand, pinching her nipple like I might and shattering into an orgasm while I watched her chest heave and her thighs tighten around her hand.

I pumped my cock until I came on my stomach, promising myself the revenge I'd take on her ass when I went home the next day.

She'd be lucky if she could walk by the time I was done with her.

*H*ugo watched from the sidelines as Joaquin centered himself in the small clearing on the opposite end of the hillside. The village and Rafe's house were tucked away on the opposite side and we were off the beaten path that the people from the town walked or drove to get to the church where we'd gotten married.

The sea was visible in the distance through the trees, but for the most part we were tucked away safely. I still hadn't been brave enough to take Regina up on her offer to take me through the village and introduce me to the people who called the island home. I hadn't yet forgiven them for allowing Rafe to do as he pleased with me and not daring to intervene.

Even if I knew it was illogical to expect such a thing.

With leggings and a tank top to cover my skin, I stared at Joaquin as he stripped off his sneakers.

"Rafe is going to murder you when he finds out, and he *will* find out," Hugo scolded his older brother. "Have you lost your damn mind?"

"He won't murder me. Isa won't allow it," Joaquin said

with a brittle smile that said just how little he believed that to be true.

Hugo only rolled his eyes. "Okay, so he won't kill you. He'll just beat the fucking shit out of you. What could have been worth this?"

Joaquin winked at me, refusing to tell Hugo the truth that I'd promised to speak to him only in return for this very moment. "We just have to make it count while we have time," he said, nodding at me.

I agreed silently, hoping that my distraction the night before would keep Rafael focused on *other* rebellions. Maybe he'd be so focused on punishing me for touching myself that he'd overlook the more serious transgression that he would hate with every fiber of his being.

Exhaustion already made my limbs feel heavy with the exertion of the day.

When Joaquin said he meant to make the day count, I hadn't realized he meant to work me until I couldn't walk. But the feedback he gave me would be valuable if it ever came to a point where I needed to protect myself. I was small, and most men were massive compared to me, especially the men that seemed to surround Rafael.

The man who he'd seen outside *Moon* in Ibiza hadn't been small either, though Rafael towered over him.

Using my size to my advantage was in my best interest. Playing on the expectations that I would be nothing but a tiny girl with no ability or interest in fighting. Jabs to the dick, the heel of my palm into the end of a person's nose and thrusting up, and the side of my hand to the edge of a man's neck.

All the ways I could take a man to his knees long enough to escape. What I would do from there, I didn't know. But I guessed the hope was that someone would be there to help me after that was done.

"Gouge out his eyes if you can," Joaquin said, taking my hand in his grip. Hugo flinched every time Joaquin touched me, as if the point would work against him every single time he did it. He bent two fingers at the middle knuckle, tucking them together and guiding them to the right side of his nose. "Strike with all the force you have, and you'll blind them. Temporary or permanent, that will give you a huge advantage through the rest of the fight and will probably give you the opportunity to get away. Objects are even better. If you can puncture the eye itself, you'll stand a chance at killing them."

I twisted my body back, pulling my hand away and practicing the spacing between my fingers. "One eye at a time?" I asked, trying to spread my fingers wide enough that I could take out both at once.

"You'll get more force that way," he said, pushing them back together. I jabbed at his face, stopping just short of his eye. He blinked back at me, looking far too trusting as he looked to the sun in the sky. "We should get you back before Regina sends out a search party."

"Okay," I agreed. Even though I wanted to keep going, my body ached with the tiredness from the day. I didn't have an active lifestyle in Chicago, and I hadn't done much to change that since coming to Spain. We turned and our way back for the house, walking through the clearing as I thought over the reality of the last twenty-four hours.

Rafe was gone from the island. He wasn't in my way, and Joaquin had shown he was willing to defy Rafael in some ways.

Yet I hadn't once asked him to take me off the island or to help me escape. I should have wanted my freedom more than anything, but I didn't. He'd taken my choices and left me with no other option but to do what he wanted. But there was something amazing about not being responsible for once.

There was something addictive about having someone else make the hard choices for me, and that terrified me.

Because if I liked it, it was never going to stop.

How long could it really go on before Rafael crossed a line?

Hadn't he already?

ılılış

$\mathcal{M}$y bones hurt. It didn't seem like it should be possible for a person's bones to hurt, but mine throbbed under my skin. The muscles clenched and contracted as I shifted my body in the bathtub of our bedroom to try to soothe my sore limbs. Regina didn't expect Rafael home until the next day, given the nature of his business in Rome, apparently, but I needed to be able to move by the time he returned.

If I couldn't walk, he would know I'd done *something* wrong. He'd know that there was a secret I kept, and I knew the moment he started asking questions would be when he got the answers I so desperately wanted to keep from him for as long as possible.

If I had to be punished, I wanted to get more than one lesson out of it first.

I sighed, leaning my back against the tub fully and letting the water glide over my skin. It had long since cooled down from the scorching hot that I'd filled it with, but I couldn't bring myself to move.

I didn't know if I could get out on my own, and the

thought brought a chuckle to my lips. Maybe I'd just stay in the bathtub until Rafe came home and discovered me as a pruned mess.

I moved slowly, forcing myself to sit up first and wincing at the pain that pulled through my stomach muscles. "Are you feeling alright, Princesa?" Rafael asked suddenly, standing in the doorway that was open to the bedroom. I hadn't even heard it open, so absorbed in my own pain.

"Rafe," I gasped, turning my head to look at him in shock. All the bravado I'd felt in his absence was nothing but a fleeting memory the moment I was hit with the over-whelming reality of him again.

Despite the pain in my body, I forced myself to move as naturally as I could. To not allow my stiff joints to show just how sore I was. "I'm just feeling a little queasy," I lied. The random moment of nausea I'd had the day before hadn't returned since, proving to be nothing more than a case of being too tired.

It seemed ridiculous when I didn't *do* much, but the emotional weight of all that had happened put me in a constant feeling of needing to sleep. Rafe walked forward, leaning toward me and touching his lips to mine briefly as his fingers tested the water. "It's cold," he observed.

"It is," I admitted. "I was just being lazy and didn't want to get out."

He smiled, the dark grin making my own falter. "I want to show you something," he said, holding out a hand for me. I swallowed before placing mine in his, letting him pull me to standing. He wrapped a towel around me, drying me off and picking out pants for me to wear while I stared at him in my own nerves.

Did he know?

He held out underwear for me, and I placed my hands

on his shoulders before stepping into them and letting him pull them up my legs to cover my body. I knew something was very wrong, because there was no world in which I wouldn't have thought Rafael would want to fuck me the moment he came home.

Unless he'd had another woman to entertain him in his absence. My old insecurities plagued me as he helped me pull a sports bra over my head.

"What's wrong, *mi reina*?" he asked, his fingers tracing the seam of my pussy through my panties. "Did you do something that you shouldn't have while I was gone?"

I swallowed, letting him help me into the jeans he held out. "I think we both already know the answer to that."

He hummed, pulling a shirt over my head and leaving me to stare at him in annoyance. "Well you clearly don't need your husband's cock," he mused. "So I'm not sure why you seem disappointed that I'm dressing you." Socks and shoes followed, driving home the point that we would be leaving the house.

I suddenly wondered if I'd be returning.

"Where are you taking me?" I asked when he took my hand and guided me out of the bedroom. Regina smiled as if nothing was wrong as we made our way past her and into the SUV in the front driveway. There probably *was* nothing wrong in her world.

She wasn't the one who'd defied the devil and felt like he was leading her to her funeral.

⚜

*R*afael pulled up to a stable with barn hands working through the open aisle in the center. He helped me out of the car while I stared at him in confusion, letting him guide me to the massive gate across the front of the open barn doors.

"You have horses?" I asked, turning to look up at him as he pulled the gate open and stepped into the barn. A tan horse was cross tied in the aisle, looking clean and pristine with an orchid halter on its face.

"I do," Rafael admitted, stepping up to one of the open stall doors. A massive ebony horse poked its head out, turning his strong neck to face Rafe and leaning into his body. Rafe accommodated the affectionate touch, stroking his face with a gentleness I'd only ever seen him use with me before. "This is Valerio," he said.

Rafe walked to the table at the head of the barn, grabbing a cube and hand feeding it to the massive horse who took it from him carefully with massive, flat teeth. I didn't move to them despite the horse's beauty, too distracted by the tan horse in the aisle. The horse's warm brown eyes studied me cautiously as it tossed its head twice. "That's Challen," Rafael said. "*Shining Moon.*"

"Shouldn't he be white to be a shining moon?" I laughed, stepping forward cautiously.

Rafael hummed his amusement. "Perhaps, but you were always my shining moon in the night. It seemed fitting since he's yours."

"Mine?" I asked, wincing when he took my hand in his and held it out for the horse to smell. The whiskers of his nose tickled the back of my hand as he scented me, his nose twitching against my skin. "But I don't know the first thing about horses."

"I've had him for over a year, so he's well trained. He'll be a good horse to teach you anything you want to know." Rafe released my hand, letting me move closer to the horse that studied me as uncertainly as I did him. I touched my palm to the top of his face, stroking over the short hair there and chuckling when he raised his head into the touch and his nose brushed against my stomach. His nose twitched there, tickling me through my shirt gently. Rafael went into the room off to the side, emerging with a fabric pad that he tossed onto the horse's back. He secured it beneath his body, pulling it tight. Challen nudged me with his nose, his eyes glimmering as Rafe disappeared again and came back with a leather and rope halter. He attached reins to it, tossing them over Challen's neck before unfastening the one from his face and taking it off.

He moved me to stand beside Challen's shoulder, placing the halter in my hands and helping me to guide it on over his nose. Once it was secured around his jaw, he pulled the reins free from his shoulders and placed them in my hands. I stood there, holding the fucking horse with no clue what to do, while Rafe moved and grabbed a helmet from the tack room. He put it on my head while I stared at him in horror.

"You can't possibly think I'm about to ride a horse," I protested. "Shouldn't there be a saddle or something at least?"

"I have always thought the best way to learn to ride is bareback. You can feel the horse's movement better, and there's just something about the connection it creates that you can't achieve with the barrier of a saddle," he explained, stepping out toward the back entrance of the barn. He motioned for me to follow, and I hesitantly guided Challen to turn. He followed at my side, his footsteps so close to mine making me nervous.

I backed away, giving him more slack in the reins but he just moved closer to me once again until his shoulder almost brushed against mine. "You sound like a man complaining about condoms," I said to Rafe with a swallow.

"And what would you know of that, *mi reina?*" He laughed, stopping just outside the barn. When Challen and I caught up to him, he took the reins from my hands and tossed them over his neck. The horse stood still as Rafe moved me to line up with his back. He bent down slightly, putting his hands out and cupping them. "Left foot in my hand. I'll give you a leg up. You get your body on his back and pull your right leg to the other side."

"Oh for fuck's sake," I groaned. "That sounds way too coordinated for me. You realize I trip over my own feet right?"

He raised an eyebrow at me without answering, leaving no doubt that we wouldn't be going until I tried. Putting my foot in his hand, I shrieked when he flung me up onto Challen's back. The poor thing must have hated me as I struggled to maneuver my aching body onto him and swing my leg around, but he didn't so much as take a single step. "See? Not so bad."

"Are they always so tall?" I asked dumbly, knowing the answer to the question as I gathered the reins in my hand.

"Challen's a pony, *mi reina,*" he chuckled. "He's small for a horse."

"Well I'm glad for that," I mumbled, touching the short multicolored mane that stood up straight on his neck with a chess board design of black and white cut into it.

"He's a Norwegian Fjord. That's a typical style for the mane," he said, smirking as if he could hear my thoughts. He took my foot in his hands, tilting it harshly as my sore muscles protested the change in position. "Always keep your heels down. It helps your seat and will keep you on the horse."

"Smart. Remind me about the potential of falling, because I see *that* being totally helpful." I swallowed as he touched my spine, guiding me to straighten it beneath his touch.

"We're just going to go for a walk today," he teased. "Maybe we'll do some trotting. I want you nice and sore by the end of the day." I swallowed again, the reality of already being sore feeling like a condemnation as I tried to shove off the physical signs of it. Maybe the riding would give me an excuse for it and I wouldn't have to worry about hiding it any longer.

"Why do you want me sore?" I asked nervously as he clucked at my side. Challen walked forward, keeping pace with Rafael as I fought to sit still through the intensity of the movement beneath me.

"I told you there would be consequences for playing with my pussy while I was gone, Princesa. You did it anyway, so now I am going to take it out on this pretty little ass of yours before I fuck it." I fought back the heat that built in my core, the driving force making me ache in an entirely new way.

The friction of Challen's movement between my thighs wasn't a good combination when met with Rafael's filthy words. Even touching myself the night before hadn't been enough to curb the insatiable desire Rafael caused.

I'd been needy and greedy for him minutes after finding my orgasm, needing him inside me to ever feel truly complete. He'd been my first, and he'd ruined me for all pleasure that didn't involve him.

He'd broken me. Totally and completely, and I didn't think I could even make myself regret it.

"Keep your heels down!" I shouted, watching Isa tentatively walk Challen around the ring for the tenth time. She was gentle with her hands as if she worried she would hurt him by using them to steer him, but I hadn't given her a bit for that reason.

Not that Challen needed one. The stubborn pony was much more likely to refuse to trot than he was to take off with her. She fixed her legs, tilting her feet in the way I'd shown her. The position was uncomfortable to adjust to, particularly without stirrups, but she understood the basics at least. I stepped in front of them as they came closer, watching Challen gladly stop. Isa reached down to touch his neck. "You ready to trot?" I asked.

"Nope," she said. I laughed, moving to her side and taking her foot in my hand. "When you want him to go faster, apply *light* pressure with your heels. Not a kick or anything like that, just give him a little squeeze with your calf. When you want him to slow down, sit heavy and squeeze with your thighs."

"Isn't that confusing?" she asked.

"Not for him," I said with a smirk, clucking at Challen as I pressed her calf into his side. He walked off at a quicker pace than before, making Isa tense up. "Relax," I urged her, clucking again. The horse glared at me, but picked up the trot regardless.

Isa's tense body bounced on his back, and I winced along with the poor horse. "Sit. Keep your ass on his back." She sat deeper into the motion, moving with him instead of tensing up and fighting the motion. "Now post," I instructed.

"I have no idea what you're talking about," she hissed at me, but there was a smile in her voice that hadn't been there before.

"Use your thighs to lift your ass off him. Up. Down. Up. Down." I instructed. She looked at me like I'd lost my mind, glancing down at the lack of stirrups. "You can do it."

Heaving a sigh, she finally tried and managed to lift herself up and lower herself down carefully, but her face was pained as she did it. It seemed I had underestimated just how much Isa needed to work on her core muscle groups. "Okay," I said, letting her off the hook. I walked up as Challen slowed to a walk and took the reins from Isa's hand to guide them back to the dismount area. "Swing your leg over and I'll help you down." She did as I said, letting me guide her body down Challen's side slowly until her feet hit the ground and she gave a tiny whimper.

The pain shouldn't have been so immediate, and suspicion filled me and left me wondering why Isa seemed so miserable.

I took Challen back to the barn, handing him off to Esteban and taking Isa's hand in mine. I guided her into the spotless tack room that was nicer than the kitchen in the house Isa grew up in. Stripping the helmet off her head, I hung it on one of the hooks and kicked the tack room door closed behind us.

Isa spun to face it, swallowing down her nerves as she squirmed where she stood. I moved closer to her, forcing her to back up until her ass connected with the edge of the table in the center of the room. "What are you doing?" she whispered, staring up at me as I cupped her face in my hand. Running fingers over the skin of her cheekbone and my thumb beneath the spot in her eye, I leaned into her space and kissed her softly.

Tracing the seam of her lips with my tongue, I groaned the moment she opened for me and accepted me inside despite her anxiety. Her fear built as I enjoyed the taste of her on my tongue. I'd been gone for a day, and already I felt pathetic with how much I'd missed her in such a short timeframe.

Mi reina was part of me. Printed on my very soul in a way that I couldn't escape.

I pulled back from her mouth, kissing along her cheek as I slid my hand into her hair and tugged her head back so sharply she gasped in pain. "I don't appreciate knowing you disobey me while I'm gone, *wife*," I murmured. She shuddered in my grip as I released her and stepped back just enough to turn her to face the table. Reaching around to the front of her pelvis, I unbuttoned her jeans and slid down the fly, jerking the fabric down her thighs harshly.

"What are you doing?" she repeated, her gaze straying to the window on the door. Isa still didn't understand that no one would dare to look at her. But even if they did, I didn't care that they saw her with my cock buried balls deep in her ass. She was mine to fuck, mine to use.

Mine to do whatever the fuck I pleased with.

"Bend over the table," I ordered, pressing a hand between her shoulder blades until she laid flat.

"Rafe," she protested, earning a warning swat from my hand as I smacked the tight globe of her ass. She jolted against the table, laying her torso against it until the side of her face rested against the back of her hand.

"You're going to hold *very* fucking still, Isa," I said, stepping away to quietly pull one of the riding crops off the wall while she couldn't see me. "If you move, I'll tie you up. Do *not* fucking test me."

She nodded her head even though she didn't know what was coming, the fear in her so unlike my rebellious wife that suspicion continued to rise in me. The reaction was extreme, because she had to know that I would use sex to punish her for playing with my pussy while I was gone.

I slid her shirt up until it caught on her bra, baring her lower back to me so I could trail the riding crop down her spine. She jolted when the foreign object touched her, trying desperately to see behind her to know what it was. Pulling it back and stepping to the side, I cracked it against the flesh of her ass.

She cried out, a whimper following as the sting of the initial blow faded into a trail of fire across her ass cheeks. "Rafe, please," she begged. I hit her again, leaving a second strip parallel to the first one. Her skin flushed such a pretty red in the wake of the blows, and I chuckled as she rose up onto her toes to try to escape the strike she knew was coming.

"You shouldn't have played with my pussy," I argued, crossing the next strike across the first two. She whimpered, rising up to her hands and trying to escape the pain of further punishment. I clutched her to my chest and grabbed a lead rope off the wall, wrapping it around her wrists while she fought to get free.

Eventually subduing the woman so desperate to escape her punishment, I pressed her forward until she laid against the table once more. I hit her across the ass and the tops of her thighs with five quick strikes of the riding crop against her flesh, getting harder with every whimper she released.

I knew Isa well enough to know that when I put my fingers between her legs, my hand would come away soaked with her. I hit the top of her ass one last time, tossing the crop to the side and slipping two fingers into her drenched pussy. She moaned in spite of the pain that lit her ass on fire and the defiance I saw in her green gaze as she turned her face back to glare at me.

Using my other hand, I pulled the bottle of lube I'd grabbed from the bedroom when Isa had been in the tub out of my pocket and released my cock from my jeans. Spreading lube all over it, I pulled my fingers free of Isa's pussy and moved them to her ass. Pressing a finger into the tight bud of flesh, she hissed and tried to wiggle her way away from me. "Don't you fucking dare!" she growled, the warning echoing in the small tack room while I chuckled.

I added a second finger, spreading her open just enough to take my cock without tearing her. I wanted to hurt her, wanted her to feel the sting of me gliding through her tender flesh.

I wanted her to feel the sting of my hips smacking against the marks on her ass.

"It isn't like my pussy needs this cock," I argued, pulling my fingers free and lining my length up. I pressed inside her slowly, letting her body open for me as she forced herself to relax into the intrusion. Usually when I took her ass, I played with her pussy to add pleasure to the unique pain.

I refused to do that this time around, leaving her to squirm beneath me as she took inch after inch in her ass. She whimpered when my hips touched the red marks from the crop, and I grabbed her by the rope that tied her hands together behind her back. Using it to hold her steady, I set a slow but harsh rhythm inside her.

Fucking her. Using her to get off.

Our reunion should have been in our bed with me making love to her. Instead it was in a tack room with her whipped and tied up.

Either one worked for me, so Isa had only punished herself in the end. "Rafael, please," she begged.

"Do you even know what you're asking me for? Do you want me to stop?" I asked, not waiting for the response before I fucked her harder. Taking her in harsher strokes that made her cry out with each glide of my cock inside her. "Well?"

"I don't know!" she screamed, the sound accompanied by a harsh cry that soothed the rough edges of my anger. Taking pity on her, I drove myself toward my release, working her over until I came inside her with a grunt. Pulling back from her, I untied her hands as I zipped myself into my jeans.

She straightened her body, turning to face me with a wince. Dropping my hands to her jeans, I moved to help her pull them back up. "You hit me!" she accused, swatting my hands away as she worked her pants up and over her tender ass.

"You liked it," I reminded her with a smirk. "You wouldn't even be that mad if I'd gotten you off."

"Maybe I should do it myself," she snarled. "Since I don't need your cock." Unable to fight back my amusement, I grinned at her. Guiding her toward the bathroom off the tack room so we could clean up before heading back to the house, I couldn't resist the laughter that caught in my throat.

"Princesa, if you want me to spank your ass some more all you have to do is ask."

♟♟♟♟♟

She got out of the car with a huff, slamming the door and making her way into the house as quickly as her sore ass would allow. The fabric of her jeans must have hurt her skin with every move despite the under-wear she wore beneath them, but she did her best to not let me see the physical pain that was a consequence of her defiance.

I was sure the swelling in my greedy little pussy didn't help matters since I'd left her neglected and desperate for my cock. Once her anger abated, she'd have a more difficult time keeping me from seeing the symptoms of that. I'd gladly give her what she needed, but only after she admitted she wanted me.

After she gave me the words she so often kept from me.

I followed behind her, striding into the front doors of the house. Aaron met me at the door, stepping into my path with a solemn expression written on his face. I turned my gaze to watch as Isa settled herself in the breakfast nook, perching carefully with her eyes on the chess set on the small table that was so rarely used. She winced with pain as her ass hit the wood, but refused to give up and go to bed.

She'd need aftercare when she stopped being so stub-born. "*Joaquín y su esposa se fueron al bosque,*" Aaron said, gathering my attention as the words struck me in the chest. *Joaquin and your wife went into the woods.*

"*Qué hicieron ellos?*" I asked. *What did they do?*

"*No lo sé*, Señor Ibarra," he admitted. "I did not follow them."

"Thank you, Aaron," I said, dismissing one of the younger men who worked security around the house. I turned my attention back to Isa, watching as she studied the chess board thoughtfully. When her eyes came back to mine, she froze solid with her hand in mid-air. Her breath hitched and she swallowed, and I knew without a doubt.

Mi princesa was hiding something.

Rage boiled my blood, but I turned my back on her to walk toward my office. I kept my steps as light as I could as I turned on the gas fireplace in the corner and brought it roaring to life, grabbing the three irons out of the cupboard where I kept them and chucking the ends into the flames.

I watched the fire dance over the irons, staring at the very different marks for a moment before I turned and stormed past where Isa still sat dumbstruck and slid out the back doors. "Rafe!" she called out, a commotion coming from inside as I hurried across the yard.

Joaquin stood in the clearing where the pyre would burn if I had any patience for delivering his mark another day, but given his latest betrayal involved my wife, I wasn't certain he would live to receive it. He stood still, waiting for my wrath to fall upon him as I approached. When he was within reach, my fist connected with his jaw so hard that he stumbled and nearly fell to the ground.

"Rafe!" Isa called again as she hurried out the back doors of the house and tried to follow me. Her aching body slowed her down, giving me a few precious moments with Joaquin before I would have to remind her what happened when she defended other men.

I would put him in the ground and never regret a moment of it if she *dared* to interfere.

"Did you touch my wife?" I asked, jabbing him in the nose. Blood sprayed my knuckles, but still he didn't fight back.

"Yes," he said. "I touched her." The raging fury inside me cooled to an ice I had never felt before, a cold and sharp thing that no longer cared if he suffered.

I just wanted him dead.

"Rafe! It's not what you think," Isa said, stumbling into the clearing. She stepped up to me, taking my hand in her grip despite Joaquin's blood on it. She gasped for breath, but when I looked at her I felt nothing but the shards of a betrayal that went far deeper than I could have ever imagined. "He taught me to fight," she wheezed. "That's all."

"So you did not *fuck* the man I left to keep you safe?" I asked, tilting my head to the side as she stared up at me in fear. Whether that fear was for herself or Joaquin, I couldn't know. I didn't think I wanted to know, because the unfortunate reality for *mi reina* was that she *should* very much be afraid for what the consequences of her betrayal would be.

"No!" she gasped. "How could you think that? It's only ever been you," she said, soothing some of the sharp edges, but my anger still pulsed within me.

She'd defied me with another man.

"Do you want to?" I asked, lashing out with my other hand and catching her around the throat. "Would you like me to bend you over so he can fuck your pretty little ass just like I do?"

"Rafael, stop it!" she yelled as I did just that, bending her over in front of me. Joaquin didn't move, didn't so much as twitch or glance down at the obscene position that put her jean clad ass in the air. "I don't want anyone but you. You're my husband," she whimpered.

Hearing those words from her, I knew without a doubt

they were a manipulation. A reminder that I should be gentle with her, that I should be a good husband to my *wife*. But she hadn't married a good man. She'd married a man who put a gun to her head to claim her. She'd married a man who would kill anyone who thought to take away what was mine.

"You did something I explicitly forbade," I reminded her. "Did you think there would not be consequences for that?"

"The consequences should be mine to pay. It was my decision," she begged, her face leaning forward toward the ground. I released her, stepping back and putting distance between us as I glared over at Joaquin.

"I'll meet you in my office," I ordered him. He nodded, glancing to Isa unsurely but left us in peace so that I could deal with my rebellious woman. She stood up straight, staring me in the face as Joaquin entered the house and disappeared behind me. Her bottom lip trembled, but she glared at me all the same.

"If you'd have just taught me yourself, this wouldn't have happened," she said, jutting her chin up. "You want to leave me vulnerable, but you like it when I challenge you. How am I supposed to make sense of what is tolerable and what isn't when you give me so many mixed signals?"

"I will give you a hint, *Princesa*," I growled. "If it involves another man, you do *not* disobey me. I do not care if I've forbidden you from looking at him or speaking to him, you do what you're fucking told."

She swallowed. "Don't punish him for what I asked him to do. Punish me instead. It was my choice."

"Did he or did he not know that I would disapprove when he agreed to it? Because as much as you may like to think Joaquin or Hugo or Gabriel are your friends, they are *my* men. They answer to me alone. He stood here and waited for his penance because he knew it would come. He betrayed my trust anyway, so he'll pay the price." I turned, stalking toward the house and expecting Isa to follow. She didn't, standing still in the clearing and glaring at me instead. "Come here," I ordered, watching as she ground her teeth together but forced her feet to move.

She strode past me, walking quickly to make her way into the house before me. When she thought to sidetrack to the bedroom, I caught her hand in my harsh grip and squeezed it in warning as I dragged her toward my office and the brands waiting there. I shoved her toward the sofa, sitting her down with a glare before turning my attention to Joaquin where he knelt on the floor shirtless.

He kept his head bowed, submissive despite the tension in his body. "Don't do something you'll regret," he murmured to me, darting his eyes off to the side to glance at Isa where she sat with her hands curled around the cushion.

"What I do with my wife is none of your concern," I reminded him, stripping off my t-shirt and grabbing the glove from the cabinet by the fireplace. I slid it onto my hand, grabbing the brand for his mark from the fire and eyeing the red-hot iron. He didn't flinch as I touched it to his chest, adding a fourth tally to his sins against me. His failures.

It was a miracle I allowed him to live, because if he reached seven?

He'd be exiled from *El Infierno*. He'd leave behind the only true home he'd ever known and become someone else's problem.

No matter who might miss him.

"Get out." I tossed the iron back to the fire, turning my attention away from him. He stood, gathering up his shirt and retreating from the office without another word. Isa stayed where I'd left her on the sofa, watching me warily as I turned furious eyes to her. "Do you know what happens when a man reaches seven failures on my island?" I asked her, stepping over to the sofa. My hot gloved hand touched the back of it and burned the leather as I leaned into her space. Glaring down at her wide stare, I used my other hand to grasp her around the jaw and force her to hold my gaze when she wanted to escape it.

"No," she whispered.

"If the sins are small? I send him away. If they're more problematic than that, I kill him," I said, feeling the motion in her throat as she worked to swallow. "Would you like to be responsible for Joaquin's death?"

"So if I want to leave, all I have to do is defy you seven times?" she snarled, challenging me as she leaned closer into my space despite the fear making her tremble.

"No, *mi reina*. You are the only person who is a prisoner here. You have no rights like freedom. Not when you're mine," I said, standing tall and backing away from her. I grabbed one of the brands out of the fire, studying the shape at the end intently. Isa watched me with a trembling lip, wincing when I held out my left forearm and stared at the part of the tattoo that matched the brand perfectly.

She watched in horror as I pressed the end to my skin, searing the flesh on my arm with gritted teeth. When I pulled it back and set it back in the flames, Isa stared down at the red skin in shock.

The words *mi reina* stood out more in red amongst the sea of black tattoo ink on my forearm. That would only be more true when the wound healed and the skin raised.

Just like Isa's.

"*T*attoos can be covered up or removed, unfortunately. But a brand is forever, *mi reina,*" he said. His skin burned in an angry red color as he turned toward his desk and swept everything on top onto the floor. "Come here," he ordered, raising a brow at me when I refused to move. "*Now,*" he growled.

I shook my head, flinching back into the sofa as he approached. "Don't!" I yelled out the moment his hand wrapped around my wrist and he pulled me up to stand. The few steps to the desk felt like a lifetime, an eternity passing before he brought me to stand next to the same surface where he'd tattooed me instead of branding me.

Somehow it felt like we'd always been meant to end up right back here.

He tore the shirt off my head while I struggled, my bra following, and then he tore my pants and underwear down my legs, pulling them off my feet along with my boots. He lifted me onto the desk while I struggled against the harshness of his grip, depositing me on the edge. The cool wood stung the marks on my ass, drawing a pained gasp from my lips that I somehow knew would be nothing compared to the pain that was to come. "I will never forgive you for this."

"You will," he said with a condescending laugh. "You would forgive me for anything, Princesa. Because this is what it is to love a man like me." He pressed a hand to my chest, easing me onto my back on the desk. I glared up at him, waiting until he turned to go back for the branding iron in the fire. The moment his back was turned, I scrambled off the desk and for the other side of the office.

As futile as it would probably be, I couldn't just lie back and take it.

"Get over here so I can fuck you while I mark you as mine permanently," he warned, dropping his hands to his jeans and undoing them to pull himself free. He stroked his ungloved hand over his cock, the already hard flesh offering resistance to his hand. "Did I not warn you what would happen the next time you disobeyed me? You knew what was at stake, and you did it anyway. Now come and accept your penance."

I shook my head at him, wincing when he closed the distance between us with the speed of the devil, grasping me around the neck and maneuvering me back to the desk. He laid me down on top of it with more force, my back aching as it hit the surface with a sharp thump. He moved back to grab the last branding iron quickly, holding it in his gloved hand as he used his other one to spread my legs and insert himself between my thighs.

I glared up at him, wincing when he shoved inside me with one brutal thrust. I was still wet from his display in the barn, but my pussy clenched around him with the lack of preparation. He leaned forward over the edge of the desk to meet my eyes as he grabbed my arm and pulled it down next to my body. I squirmed beneath him as he brought the iron close to my skin. The heat was unbearable, even without it touching me. "Hold still," he warned.

"Don't," I begged with tears streaming down my face suddenly. He wouldn't back out a second time. He wouldn't show me mercy, because the devil didn't have any. "Rafe."

He moved inside me, gliding through tender tissue to pull back and press deep once more. When I was filled with him, he lined up the iron and pressed it to my skin. The skin sizzled as I screamed, my entire being narrowing down on the excruciating pain as I tried to get away, but Rafe only held me tighter.

Nothing else existed as I burned, my breaths coming in fast pants as my head went fuzzy and consciousness slipped away. "Shhh," Rafe soothed, drawing the brand away finally and tossing it into the fire. He shifted me higher up on the desk, laying his weight over mine and cupping my face in his hands as he moved between my legs.

Full awareness returned slowly, his face gentle as I blinked up at him. My arm started to numb as he stroked my face, laying his mouth against mine to coax me into an affectionate kiss. As if the mark on my skin took away the mark on his soul that I'd left by disobeying him. "It hurts," I whimpered, though I was grateful for the steady numbing as my nerve endings died.

He touched my fingers to the burned flesh on his arm, the red mess still hot to the touch as he moved his cock inside me. "Will you forget that you're mine now?" he asked, kissing me lightly as his eyes held mine. With slow and easy thrusts, he made love to me while he soothed the pain he'd caused, morphing it with pleasure as the initial agony faded.

"I never did," I protested with a whisper, wrapping my legs around his hips to pull him deeper. He grabbed my arm carefully, lifting it so I had no choice but to stare at the words *seared* into my skin.

The angry red flesh looked like the devil himself. *El Diablo* owned me.

He always had.

"My wife does not disobey me, and men do not think to touch what is mine without my permission." He thrust into me, slipping a hand between our bodies to touch my clit as he dropped his lips to my breast and drew a nipple into his mouth. He nipped it sharply, drawing a moan from me as my orgasm built higher and higher. "Now anyone who looks at you will be reminded of what happens to men who touch what is mine," he growled, bringing his lips back to mine as his fingers worked my clit harder.

I came suddenly, his mouth swallowing my screams as he pushed deep and rode out his own climax inside me. I was too exhausted to move as he pulled out and gathered me in his arms to move us to the sofa. I fell asleep with his hands in my hair, his fingers running through the strands as he stared down at me like I mattered.

Like I was everything.

I slept the rest of the day after Rafe wrapped a bandage around my brand and put ointment on the marks on my ass from the riding crop. I slept through the night and late into the next morning, with him watching over me. By the time he forced me to get out of bed, it was already past noon. After a quick lunch with Regina, he took my hand and guided me to his office.

Nothing good ever happened in his office.

He sat me down in one of the chairs in front of the very

same desk he'd branded me on. The same one he'd tattooed me on. Taking the one next to me, he wordlessly grabbed the folder off the surface and handed it to me.

The weight of his stare felt ominous. He'd been oddly quiet all morning, brooding over something, and yet still attentive to me physically and the fact that I needed his intimacy in the wake of all that he'd done to me the day before. I needed to know he loved me, because his actions weren't those of a man in love.

But of a man obsessed with something he owned.

I glanced down at the folder as I took it from his hands, pulling the cover open and staring down at the gruesome photo in front of me. A man sat in an office chair, his head tilted to the side and a hole in the side of his head where blood trickled out. I closed the folder immediately, looking up at Rafael in confusion.

"Why are you showing me this?" I asked, handing it back to him.

"That—" he paused, leaning forward to rest his elbows on his knees as he set the folder on the desk "—is the officer who filed your accident report after you nearly drowned."

"You killed him?" I asked, swallowing back bile. "Why?"

"That photo is from a week after your accident," he answered, reaching forward to touch his fingers to the bandage that covered my arm. He didn't touch the spot where the brand itself was, but the area around it stung with the pressure of his hand. "They called it a suicide, but I think we both know it wasn't."

"I don't know what you're talking about," I said, pushing to stand up. His hands came down on my knees, shoving me back into my chair while he glared at me.

"I've been very patient with you," he said. I snorted. "I've been patient with you about this, but enough is enough, Isa."

"What difference does it fucking make what happened? It was over a decade ago," I said, shaking my head.

"Your sister wronged you in a way that I take very seriously. I am your fucking husband," he growled. "It is my job to keep you safe and to kill the people who would put you in harm's way. Should I just kill Odina instead? Would that be simpler for you?"

"No!" I yelled, glaring at him. "You're being ridiculous."

"And you are stalling," he said, picking up his cellphone. "All it would take is one phone call, Princesa. One call to end her life, and I wouldn't even have to leave your side to pull the trigger. We both know she deserves it after what she did to you."

I glared at the phone in his hand, unable to voice the secret that plagued me. I already knew how Rafael would react. I'd heard it all before. *It wasn't your fault.*

But it was, and nothing would ever change that.

"This isn't about what Odina did. This is about you wanting *everything.* You have some fucking nerve. You branded me! You do not get to bring me in here and make more demands. Why can't I just have one thing that's mine?" I growled, slapping the phone out of his hand. He left it where it fell, reaching forward to run his thumb over my bottom lip.

"Because you're mine. Every single part of you is mine. Whatever happened made you who you are, and it made you *fucking leave me* even though you're so fucking in love with me you can't see straight," he accused, dragging my bottom lip to the side as I gaped up at him. "This has power over you. It has power over us, and I will do whatever it takes to understand fucking *why*," he warned, standing from his seat to grab his phone off the floor.

"Fuck you," I snarled as he bent to grab it. Kicking his hand away, I stood and grabbed his chin between my fingers. He tilted his head up to mine, possession swirling in his gaze as he studied me standing in front of him. "Leave it alone, Rafael."

He moved suddenly, snatching the phone in his grip and entering in his passcode while he kept his eyes on mine. He stood, extending his limbs as I moved for the phone and wrapping me up in his arm to clutch my back against his body and hold me still. I stomped on his foot, wishing I had heels to stab him with.

He grunted as he dialed a number, lifting the phone to his ear behind me as I swallowed back the urge to vomit.

Tears streamed down my face, pulling from the darkest part of me as he spoke. "Why does Odina hate you so badly, Isa?" he asked before speaking into the phone in Spanish as my lungs heaved. Desperation like I'd never known made me want to keep my secret safely tucked away, but I couldn't let her die for me.

I already had once.

"Because I killed her!" I yelled, my lungs heaving with the weight of the confession as it tore free from my soul. "It was my fault," I sobbed, leaning forward against his arm to try to get free. He released me, letting me fall to the floor at his feet as his mouth dropped open and he moved around my body to stare down at me.

I dropped my gaze to the floor, unable to look him in the eye, and I knew when I finally did...

He would never look at me the same.

I ended the call, watching as Isa huddled in on herself. Whatever I'd expected to come from her when she finally had no choice but to tell me the truth, *that* hadn't been it. I tossed my phone onto the sofa, dropping to my knees in front of Isa and grasping her chin with a gentle finger. She darted her eyes away, refusing to look at me as I leaned in and touched my forehead to hers.

"I'm sure that's not true," I murmured, raising my hand to stroke the skin under her eye as I willed her to give me her stare. I'd rather she rage against me for forcing the truth from her than this desolate inversion of herself. "You were just a child. Whatever happened can't change that."

"She never would have been in that river if it hadn't been for me," she whispered, her eyes finally meeting mine as she subtly shook her head.

"Tell me," I prodded, hoping that the answers would come easier now that her guilt was out there for me to see. With me already knowing the worst of it, hopefully the pieces could come together.

"There was a man," she whispered, a sob catching in her

throat. "Mom was talking to a friend we bumped into on our walk, and he came up to us while we were playing. He said —" She paused, sniffling and turning her head away from mine. I forced her eyes back to mine with a stern grip on her chin, holding her steady as she drew in a deep breath. "He said there were kittens stuck in the bushes next to the water. He asked if we would help him get them out safely because there were too many for him. Odina didn't want to go. She begged me and said there was something scary about him."

"But you went with him anyway," I said, realization dawning.

She nodded. "He said that I had kind eyes, and that he knew I would help when he saw me. Odina followed us because she didn't want to leave me alone. We bent into the bushes and looked for the kittens, but we couldn't find them. When I crawled out to tell him, he grabbed my jacket with both hands."

"And he threw you in the river," I finished for her, watching as she nodded slowly. "Did he say why?"

"Not to me," Isa said. "Odina said that she screamed when she saw him throw me, and he mumbled something about the bitch not deserving two daughters before he threw her in after me."

"Does your mother have any enemies who would want to hurt you?" I asked, furrowing my brow as she shook her head. "That's why Odina hates you? Because you made a mistake as a child?"

"Partially," Isa admitted. She bit her bottom lip, closing her eyes before she continued on. "We were both in the water by the time Mom realized we weren't where she'd left us. It all happened so quickly. The current pulled me into the barbed wire," she said, her hand drifting down to absently brush against the scar on her thigh. "But it kept pulling Odina down river. We were too far apart, and she knew she wouldn't be able to get to us both in time." Isa swallowed back tears, exhaling as her eyes opened. "She had to make an impossible choice. She could only save one of us, because there just wasn't enough time."

I stared at Isa as my lips pursed together. I couldn't begin to imagine the pain of choosing which child would live and which would die. "She chose me," Isa whispered, her voice cracking with the words. "I lost consciousness before she pulled me out, but Odina said she remembers watching our mother swim for me. She remembers that moment where her own mother left her to drown, and it *haunts* her, Rafael."

"How did she survive?" I asked, moving to sit in the chair and drawing her into my lap. I knew she needed my assurance in the wake of her confession, but I needed all the answers first. I needed to understand.

"She stopped fighting the current apparently. She just gave up. A man pulled her out a couple of minutes after me, but she was already gone. They brought her back, but the sister I knew died that day. My parents already lost one daughter because of my bad choices, and now they've lost me too. *That* is why I had to go home even though I fell in love with you," she whispered, looking up at me as she said the words for the first time. "I owe them that to make up for what I did."

She curled into me, seeking the reassurance that I would still love her despite what must have felt like a horrible revelation to her. She couldn't see that she'd only been a child. That the only person who was responsible for what had happened was the man who threw her into the river in the first place.

"Did you tell the police about the man?" I asked, needing the verbal confirmation.

"Of course. If you've seen the police report, then you must have already known this," she mumbled.

"There's no mention of any of this on the report, *mi reina*. According to that report, you and Odina simply fell into the river when your mother wasn't looking. The man never existed," I said, cupping her face in my hand as she stared down at me, dumbfounded.

"But I told the officer about him. I don't understand."

"It would seem that the man who threw you into the river had friends in high places. I'll find him now that I know the truth. I promise he'll suffer for what he's done," I told her, leaning forward to touch my lips to hers.

She returned my kiss, sinking further into my embrace as a bittersweet smile took over. "Because that's your job as my husband?"

"Exactly," I murmured against her mouth. Soothing the wounds of her confession and the pain that came along with it.

I'd spend the rest of the day reassuring her that *nothing* could make me stop loving her.

♟♟♟♟

*W*ith Isa occupied in the kitchen the next morning, with Regina teaching her to make *ensaimada* to distract Isa from the insecure way she'd acted since her confession, I retreated to my office. Grabbing the phone off my desk, I texted Ryker to update him with the confirmation that Isa had been pushed into that river.

I wanted a fucking name.

Alejandro stepped into the office, taking advantage of one of the first moments I'd had without Isa in my arms since our conversation the afternoon before. "What do you want?" I asked, moving behind my desk as he met my eyes.

"Is she okay?" Alejandro asked tentatively. "She seems...off."

"She told me about the accident finally. She's apparently feeling a little vulnerable after that. I think that's to be expected, given she blames herself for what happened," I said, stopping from telling him more. I suspected Isa wouldn't be happy to have another man know the intimate details of her life and what she thought was her greatest shame.

Even if it shouldn't have been.

He caught on quickly, clearing his throat before moving on with business. He dropped a photo on my desk, Pavel's second son's face staring up from the blurry capture from a security camera. "Maxim was spotted in Barcelona."

"And what was Pavel's new heir doing in Spain?" I asked, my lips tipping up into a smile.

"He paid a visit to your Uncle, who called to let you know this morning, but you were busy with *Reina*," he said. I studied him as I thought over my options. As much as I hated to admit it, Isa was in no place for me to leave her again so soon, but allowing Maxim to stroll into my country without consequence couldn't be tolerated either. "What will you do?"

"Tell Regina to pack a bag for Isa. We'll leave tonight," I said.

"You're taking her with you?" Alejandro asked, raising an eyebrow. "You really think that's wise."

"I think I put two trackers in her body. If she tries to get away, she won't get far." I shrugged, smirking at him as I picked my phone up off the desk and texted Joaquin to get himself and a team ready. "Get the boat ready."

He nodded, retreating from the room as I stared out the door and into the hallway. Isa might have been vulnerable following the admission and thought herself a killer, but the timing would never be perfect to push her to become the Queen she was always meant to be.

We'd know if she could handle the devil she'd married in a matter of hours.

It was late evening by the time Rafael's yacht docked. I'd spent the trip lounging in the sun next to the dip pool. The cushioned platform was covered with pillows and the perfect place to curl up with a book and a chess board, relaxing with the warmth of the sun on my skin. Rafael sat in a chair next to the lounge bed I occupied, his face buried in his phone as he worked frantically to make arrangements for whatever was so urgent we had to leave *El Infierno* immediately. Every now and then he'd glance up and smirk at me studying chess strategy so I could eventually beat him.

He was quiet about the reason for the trip, but despite the sinking dread I felt that something was about to go down, I couldn't seem to focus on that sense of premonition within me.

I was off the island for the first time. I could have the opportunity to escape, and I didn't know what to do with that. I couldn't imagine my life without Rafael, but I also didn't want to insinuate that everything he'd done was okay.

None of it was. But even if I left him, I could never go

home. Not when it was the first place he would look, so where would I even go? There was also the minor detail where I'd admitted I loved him. In the heat of the moment, it had seemed like the appropriate thing to do, but I couldn't help but feel like I'd signed my soul to the devil with those words.

Like he would use them against me, and manipulate me into becoming whatever it was he thought his wife should be. Like he'd own the last pieces of me.

I didn't want to give them to him.

He shoved his phone into his pocket, somehow looking relaxed and comfortable in his suit despite the heat. He shrugged on his jacket as he stood and the boat came to a halt at the dock, reaching out a hand to help me out of the lounge. "Leave your book," he said. "We'll sleep on the yacht tonight." I unfolded my limbs carefully so I wouldn't flash the crew my underwear, letting Rafe pull me to stand. The back of the yellow wrap dress was longer than the front, where it was cut perfectly to reveal the scar on my thigh.

With my tattoo and brand open to view, I felt like I had more scars and marks on my skin than I knew what to do with. The faint outline of Rafe's teeth still graced my shoulder, and it was fortunate that no one could see the pink welts on my ass from when he'd whipped me with the riding crop. Regina had all but forced jewelry on me as she helped me dress, a mix of moonstones and turquoise necklaces and bracelets layered on my neck and the left arm that was free of tattoos.

I'd never worn jewelry—not because I didn't like it, but because we hadn't had the money to waste on such things. The metal against my skin felt itchy and uncomfortable just because I wasn't used to it. Rafe brought me through the cabin and down the steps to the lower level at the back, and we stepped onto the boat dock. Two men stood at the other end on land, greeting Rafael with hesitant smiles.

"Who are they?" I asked, grasping him around the elbow and leaning into his side more. Aside from the people he couldn't avoid introducing me to, Rafe seemed content to keep me entirely isolated.

"My cousins," he said, turning a soft look down to me as I stumbled.

"Your cousins?" I hissed. "And you didn't think to tell me you were taking me to meet your family?"

"I knew you'd stress out. Now you have approximately ten seconds of freaking out before it's over and done with." The casual tone to his voice set my nerves even more on edge as we closed the distance between us. "Isa, these are my cousins, Sebastian and Thiago," he said. "This is Isa. *My wife.*" They widened their eyes briefly, before nodding with bright smiles that seemed so different than the darkness that always clung to Rafe like a cloak.

"It's a pleasure to meet you," Sebastian said, stepping in and kissing my cheek. Rafe growled at my side, deterring Thiago from doing the same.

"You too," I said, feeling awkward under the tension of Rafe warning off his own cousins from touching me. But given what he'd done when I defied him with Joaquin, I wasn't willing to push the boundaries and call him out on his bullshit publicly.

"Father is inside," Thiago said, turning on his heel. Sebastian followed as Rafe guided me up the path to the house a little ways up the hill.

"Where are we?" I whispered as we walked.

"Just outside of Barcelona," Rafe returned, patting my arm gently.

"Maybe I should stay on the boat," I said as we

approached the grand villa. "I don't want to be in the way." Rafael only chuckled as he led me in the back doors of the house, guiding me to a man who sat in the open living room. He stood from the couch, unfolding himself to stand tall and formidable.

None of Rafe's family looked like him, his appearance clearly taken entirely from his mother's side. "Rafael," his uncle greeted, moving forward to clap him on the shoulder before his eyes fell to me. They were filled with curious suspicion as he studied me, only turning his attention away when Rafe cleared his throat. "Uncle."

"Maxim came to tell me that you need to be put down like the rabid dog you are before you ruin the family's reputation. He said a woman has turned you into a lunatic." He raised his brows as his gaze fell to mine. He sat in the chair, motioning for Rafe to follow as he guided me to a loveseat. "So, some of what he said was true. There *is* a woman."

"That woman is my *wife*, Uncle," Rafael warned, his voice dropping low and his glare menacing as his hand tightened on my thigh. I swallowed past the lump in my throat, feeling the tension rising in the room as his cousins hovered at the edges with tight faces.

RAFAEL

*y uncle's gaze fell to the rings on Isa's finger as I unbuttoned the jacket of my suit and stripped it off. I hung it over the arm of the couch, rolling my sleeves up as his eyes followed the motion. Revealing the ink on my arm and *mi reina's* brand on my skin, he raised a brow at me before a smile tipped his lips up hesitantly.

"Should I be insulted that we were not invited to the wedding?" he asked, and my cousins heaved a breath of relief before they took their respective seats in the comfortable chairs next to his.

"He never bothered to invite me, so I would think not," Isa said, smiling sardonically in her attempt to ease what remained of the tension. I huffed a quiet laugh at her side as my Uncle's face twisted in confusion. When she met his stare with a blank one of her own, he barked out a loud laugh and shook his head.

"I think I like her," Sebastian said, grinning at me. Given the way he'd kissed her cheek in greeting, it was brave to make such a statement. Cousin or not, I would cut his tongue out before I ever let him near Isa.

"I think perhaps you should refrain from such comments," Thiago warned, grinning at me knowingly as he chuckled. "Else Rafael might feed you to the pigs."

"Tell me," my uncle said, leaning forward onto his knees as his eyes held Isa's. She didn't blink or balk in the face of all that attention, even though she must have suspected that my family would be in a similar career path as I. "If he did not invite you to your own wedding, how did you come to be my new niece?"

"He put a gun to my head," Isa said, shrugging as if it was inconsequential even though we both knew it was not. Of all the things I'd done to her, I suspected my threat to kill her if she refused to be my wife was among the worst for *mi princesa*. Her inability to kill me to gain her freedom meant she had expected me to love her enough to let her live. To let her be free.

A good man would have, but I wasn't a man at all.

My uncle Andrés laughed, assuming she was kidding. When Isa met him with a deadpan stare, he tilted his head to the side and nodded as his gaze landed on me. "You always were an asshole, but this takes it to new levels, *sobrino*."

"She could have avoided it if she'd just said 'I do' on her own, but *mi reina* is as stubborn as a bull," I laughed, flinching back when Isa slapped my bare arm with a gasp.

"You're one to talk, *El Diablo*," she said, her tone mocking. "You are the most stubborn man I have ever met."

My cousins watched the smile consume my face with shock, their eyes landing on the pinkening skin of my bare arm where Isa slapped me. "Do you see what I have to put up with? She pretends to be so innocent, in the meantime she stabbed me with cutlery."

"How can you expect your woman to love you if you treat

her this way? Wives must be treated with gentleness and affection," Sebastian said, staring at Isa as if he could compel her to see the reason in his words.

"Spoken like a man who has never had a passionate woman in his bed," my uncle laughed. "I hardly think Rafael's marriage is any of our business."

"*Mi reina* loves me just fine," I said, leaning back and grasping her chin to turn her to face me. She met my eyes with an unamused look, leaning back in her own chair and crossing her legs delicately. Her scar gleamed in the light, and while I still hated everything it represented and the fact that someone had dared to hurt her, it was the mark of a survivor. The mark of a woman who had lived and adapted to whatever life threw at her.

If she could survive the devil in her bed, she could survive anything.

"Tell me about Pavel," Andrés said, his face turning serious. "Why is he gunning for you?"

"Aside from the fact that Rafael is planning a coup?" Thiago snorted.

"He disrespected me by inserting himself when he was not wanted. He nearly cost me Isa," I said, glancing over at her as I realized I'd never introduced her to my uncle as anything but my wife.

It was the most important label anyway.

"So you killed his eldest son." Andrés nodded, as if he understood the consequence. He would have done anything for his wife, and the prospect of someone taking her from him would be enough that he would do the same. Spending my summers with my uncle and cousins had shown me what love was supposed to look like. It had made me realize just how twisted my parents' marriage was. While I'd decided that love wasn't for me, I couldn't help but admire the love they shared.

Even if I'd thought I would never have it for myself.

"Should we be discussing murder so openly in front of the woman?" Thiago asked with a laugh. "Mother doesn't like it."

"I have no secrets from Isa. She knows exactly who and what I am," I answered, dropping my hand onto her thigh. She might not have known exactly what I was doing when I'd left her, but a murderer was a murderer.

I'd spare her the details of what it was to hold a beating heart in my hand, but that was as far as my secrets went for now. We'd find out exactly what she could handle soon enough.

"So as far as you're concerned, has his penance been paid? Will his other sons be left to live their lives in peace until the time comes to remove Pavel from power?" Andrés asked, his voice trailing as he said the words. He already knew the answer to them.

There was nothing I would not do for Isa, even erase an entire lineage from existence.

"They were already set to die. But Maxim coming here solidified that," I returned. Isa stilled at my side, the confirmation that more murder was coming bringing all her more traditional sensibilities to the surface. I'd break her of them once and for all soon enough. She would not live a conventional life, and death would be a part of her future.

"How do you want to proceed?" my uncle asked. "Would you like to leave Isa with us while you and your men handle him?"

"No," I said, turning my eyes to Sebastian. He grinned back at me, always testing me and pushing the limits of what I would tolerate. We'd grown up together, almost exactly the same age, and been competitive on the best of days.

My wife was not a competition he wanted to test me on.

"Isa will come with me," I said. "We'll have dealt with Maxim by the end of the day." I stood, holding out a hand for Isa and helping her to her feet. She looked confused, baffled as to what part she might play in the murder of a man.

She didn't yet know she would be the one holding the knife.

ılı.ls.

*I*sa stared out the window of the car as we drove through Barcelona in the night. Her eyes worked to absorb all the details, memorizing everything she saw. I wished desperately that I could give her the kind of honeymoon she deserved, an exploration of all the history Europe had to offer that she would adore.

But until the conflict with Pavel was resolved, I could only afford short excursions off *El Infierno*. We could only venture so far without risking Pavel's anger. While I was confident in my men, I would not risk her for anything.

"I'll bring you back to see the city as soon as it's safe, *mi reina*," I assured her, squeezing her thigh until she turned her attention to me.

"Will it ever be safe?" she whispered. "It seems like your life is dangerous by nature. How do I know I won't be trapped on the island for the rest of my life?"

"Your happiness matters to me. I'll give you whatever I can so long as it is safe for me to do so." I parked the car on the side of the street up the road from the restaurant where Maxim wined and dined his conquest for the night. She had no way of knowing that we would save her from what was likely to be a miserable fate, and she'd probably be traumatized by watching him be snatched off the street.

Where Leonid was nothing but a creep and showed his colors at every opportunity, Maxim was far better at hiding the darkness within him. He wore a mask, much like I had done when I seduced Isa.

I just didn't do it regularly or sell the women off when I was finished with them.

I guided Isa out of the car, the sound of her heels clicking against the pavement as we moved to lean against the Mercedes we'd borrowed from my uncle. Watching Maxim through the window, we knew he was entirely unaware of the devil lurking outside the restaurant. Waiting for him to step outside. Joaquin emerged from the backseat, resting his ass against the hood of the car on Isa's other side as he watched and waited.

In the event something went wrong, he was under strict orders to get Isa to safety immediately. But nothing would go wrong.

Not with the van filled with my men waiting directly in front of the restaurant.

"Why am I here?" Isa asked, her voice barely a whisper. "Wouldn't it have been better to leave me at home?"

I ignored the way it felt to have her refer to the island as home, the distinction something I wasn't certain she was ready to face herself. "You're here because this is a part of me, and you cannot love part of me without loving the devil too," I said, turning my attention away from the restaurant. I leaned in and kissed her softly, melding our mouths in the same way our souls felt combined. I only pulled back when Joaquin cleared his throat, forcing me to turn my attention back to where Maxim and his date stood from their table.

He helped her into her coat, playing the role of the gentleman so efficiently that I would have believed it if I hadn't seen the evidence of what would follow.

Of what always followed his dates.

They stepped out of the restaurant, the woman giggling drunkenly at his side, far too lost to the alcohol he'd plied her with to understand what was coming. With Isa's hand held tight in mine, I guided her into the center of the sidewalk until we stood directly in Maxim's path. "Hello, Maxim. Welcome to Spain," I said, tilting my head at him with a dark smirk.

He stopped short, his eyes going wide for a moment before he released his hold on his date and moved to reach for his gun.

The gun that was already gone, clutched in the hand of the shadow who moved without ever being seen. Joaquin tossed me the weapon, melding back into the shadows next to the car as he watched and waited for Maxim's next move.

The bag came down over the top of his head as two of the men jumped out of the van, grasping him around the shoulders and prying him away from the woman who stumbled away in terror. Isa was quick to move to her, touching her arms gently and rubbing them with a soothing touch. "Let's get you a cab," she murmured softly, guiding the woman to the side of the street. Entirely uncaring about the people who watched her from inside the restaurant, she accepted the Euros I held out to her and helped the drunken woman into the back of a cab while the driver stared at her baffled.

Isa trusted me to protect her from any repercussions that might come from her being recognized, of being left to deal with the innocent in the situation while my men secured Maxim into the back of the van.

Once the woman was on her way home, Isa returned to the car and lowered herself into the passenger seat as Joaquin held the door open for her.

I smiled, knowing I'd made the right choice.

Mi reina was ready.

The drive back to his uncle's house felt like a dream, like a nightmare made real. The reality of what I'd done settled over me with the heaviness of everything I knew I should have been.

I'd watched him abduct a man off the street, and instead of being outraged or trying to stop it, I'd put the witness in a cab and sent her home. I'd been far more concerned for her than for the man that Rafael was sure to kill shortly.

I should have felt appalled by my actions. There should have been that moment of realization when I came to understand just how far I'd fallen from the girl who did as she was told and who did what she had to do to keep her parents content.

What would they think of me now?

"You're quiet," Rafe observed as he turned up the driveway. We followed behind the van with Maxim in it, watching the back doors to be certain that nothing had gone wrong.

"What would you like me to say?" I asked, fiddling with my hands as I tried to find the words to explain the mess of emotions swirling inside me. "I just don't understand how this is my life right now. I should be getting ready to go to college and study my ass off, not sitting in a car with you while we drive to a murder site."

"This is your life, because you fell in love with the devil," he said with a casual tone as he passed the house and continued further up the hill. The van pulled over to a stop beside a shed as we followed, watching as his men wrestled Maxim out of the back of the van. With the sack still placed over his head, they guided him into the shed. Rafael climbed out of the car, moving around to open my door and pull me out. He kept my hand in his, and I glanced back to the safety of the house.

His cousin said their mother didn't like to know the details, but it seemed Rafe had a different opinion of how our marriage would proceed.

I didn't know how I felt about that.

"You know, the books always say that kidnappers only cover your head if they intend to let you go. That it's when they don't blindfold you or wear a mask that you have to worry they'll kill you. We both know you plan to kill him, so why the sack over his head?" I asked, tilting my head to the side. I was struck with the sudden and harsh reality of the question. With the kind of detached carelessness that came from discussing the methods behind a man's death rather than the fact that it shouldn't happen at all.

"It's disorienting, but it will also make him think I plan to release him alive. If he thinks there's a chance, he'll be much more likely to offer me valuable information in exchange for his life," Rafe murmured, pulling a hair tie from his pocket and securing my hair into a low ponytail at the back of my head. "But I don't expect him to have much of value to give me that I do not already know from my Russian contact."

He took my hand, guiding me into the shed as I swallowed back my fear of what I might see. Could I really watch him kill a man and accept that? My stomach churned with nausea, my breathing coming in ragged breaths that felt like they pulled from my soul rather than my lungs.

The shed door was open as we approached, Maxim hung from a hook in the ceiling in the center of the shed. With his arms extended up over his head, he was shirtless with only his pants hanging around his hips. I immediately had the distinct impression that he might have been nude if not for my presence, but Rafael wouldn't want me to look at another man's cock.

That was just fine for me. It would have been like seeing a four-year-old's stick figures after a *Van Gogh*. I'd already seen the pinnacle of beauty.

Nothing else could ever compare.

Racks hung from the walls, all sorts of tools I didn't recognize covering them and hanging along the edges. The hood had been pulled off Maxim's face before they strung him up, and his pale blue gaze landed on me as he struggled against the rope wrapped around his wrists. With a groan for the tension in his shoulders, he snarled at me and turned his attention to Rafael just as he released my hand and moved to the wall. He studied the various tools in thought as I watched.

"How nice of you to bring me a snack, Devil," Maxim said, his voice strained despite the bravado. His stare fell back on me, and I suddenly wished I had more clothes on. The yellow wrap dress felt too feminine to be in a shed filled with torture devices. It felt too revealing to have a murder victim leering at me.

Rafe chose a bat off the wall, turning suddenly and swinging it with all his might until it connected with Maxim's stomach with a loud crack of bone. Maxim groaned as he swung back and forth in the room, the chains clanking above his head. Rafe swung the bat again, striking the back of Maxim's shoulder. I watched as it dislocated, the arm slipping out of the shoulder joint as he screamed.

"That's *my* fucking snack," Rafael warned, his voice deeper and more menacing. The devil played at the surface of his face, his multicolored eyes gleaming joyfully as he tortured his enemy. I swallowed back the bile in my throat, trying to remind myself that I didn't know what the other man was capable of. He could have been a murderer for all I knew.

But so was Rafael.

The lines of right and wrong were so blurred for him that all I could do was imagine *him* being the one hanging from the rafters while an enemy tortured him. "I can't do this," I whispered, drawing Rafe's eyes to me.

He closed the distance between us, reaching up a hand to cup the back of my neck gently. He traced soothing circles against the skin there, working to calm me as his forehead touched mine and those glowing eyes danced right before my face. "You can," he said, reassuring me. "Do you want to be a pawn in the games of men?" He paused, his hand moving to wrap around the front of my throat. "Or do you want to be *mi reina?*"

Staring up at him, I swallowed as I bit my lip. Indecision warred within me. For all his pushing, this was the moment where Rafael gave me the choice. He let me decide this one thing about my future, and I was so tired of being a pawn in the games other people played.

I wanted to be a fucking Queen.

I shoved down the impulse to run, nodding against his face slightly. When he was certain I was stable enough, he tossed the bat to the table at the edge of the shed and grabbed a loop of barbed wire off the wall. My heart stuttered as he unwound it, wrapping the length around Maxim's stomach three times. "Grab the wire cutters," he ordered, drawing me into his game. I nodded, moving to the wall and grabbing them off the hook where they hung. I paused just before I reached him, hesitating for only a moment and then cutting the wire in the place Rafe indicated. He grabbed the tail of the wire in his hands, ignoring the way the barbs tore the skin of his palms open and pulled it tight until they dug into the skin of Maxim's stomach.

My hand involuntarily drifted down to the scar on my thigh, feeling more vulnerable with the reminder of the pain that had torn my leg open as a girl. Broken ribs and dislocated shoulder were a pain I didn't know. They were a pain I would hopefully never understand. The barbed wire was something I understood.

Rafael picked up the bat again, slamming it into the wire wrapped around Maxim's stomach until the barbs sunk deep and his skin turned an angry red as blood trickled out from the wounds. His eyes met mine as I forced back my horror and then he disappeared around the back of Maxim's body. "Usually I don't like my victims to be this subdued. It's much more entertaining when they *fight*," he grunted, the sound of the bat striking against bone resonated through the shed. "But I don't think my Isa is quite ready for that."

"Fuck you," Maxim groaned, jerking against the restraints with his good arm when Rafael dropped the bat onto the table. He pulled a long hunting knife off the table slowly, gripping it so the blade itself faced out. He walked around Maxim's body, dragging the edge of the knife through his flesh and leaving a bloody trail in a line around his stomach. As he stepped around to the front of Maxim, he glared up at the man who slumped forward.

"Should I tell my wife how you like to sell children into sexual slavery?" Rafael asked, tearing down the doubt I had regarding my involvement in his crime. "How you like to have your men impregnate women so you can tear the babies from their arms while they scream?" I reached down to touch my stomach, my fingers curling into the soft flesh. To the child that would be inevitable given Rafe's determination to get me pregnant. To think of someone taking that away from me was unimaginable, even if I hadn't thought I wanted children.

I'd kill anyone who tried.

Rafael turned back to me, something dancing behind his eyes that I was certain I wouldn't come to enjoy. "Show me your darkness, *mi reina,*" he murmured, echoing the words he'd given me when he gave me the chance to take my freedom back. The chance to stab him in the heart and walk away from the life of death and destruction he offered me. He came to stand behind me. His blood-soaked hands stretched around me, wrapping me in his embrace as he lifted my hand to wrap around the hilt of the knife.

With my breath caught in my lungs, Rafael's blood from the barbed wire covered my skin. He lifted my other hand, wrapping it around the hilt and covering me with his massive grip. The man hanging in front of me eyed the knife, dragging his eyes up to look at me as he barked out a sharp laugh. "You let your *cunt* of a wife do your wet work now, *El Diablo?*" he asked, wheezing as he tried to breathe through the pain of near dismemberment. His stomach sagged as if the skin was only one cut away from splitting in two.

I shook my head as Rafe took the first step forward, bringing me closer and closer to the man he wanted me to kill. "I'm not you," I whispered.

"You're right," Rafael murmured in my ear as we came to a stop. One of his men who had been lurking at the door to the shed positioned a metal chair beneath Maxim's body as Rafe nodded, another working to lower the restraints until he dropped into the chair with a thud. With him sitting in the chair in front of me, Rafael shuffled me forward a few more steps as Joaquin stepped up behind Maxim's chair and drew his arms up over his head. Restraining him while Rafe guided my hands to line the blade up to the left of Maxim's chest and parallel to the ground. "You're my Queen."

He helped me slide the knife forward slowly, the tip popping through the resistance of his skin as Maxim groaned. A vision of Rafael's eyes stared back at me, framed in a little girl's round face as I thought about all the children he'd torn from their mothers. My hands slid forward slowly, sinking through flesh as Maxim gaped up at me in shock and held my gaze. I hit bone, his rib blocking the way as Rafael shifted me lower and helped me glide between his ribs.

Maxim's eyes went slack as I drove forward, slowly puncturing his heart with the knife. I watched as the life bled from his eyes, his head dropping forward as his final breath wheezed out of his lungs.

I dropped my grip on the handle, stumbling back into Rafe's body as he drew me into his arms and held my head against his chest. "There's *mi reina*," he murmured softly, swaying back and forth with me in his grip as I gripped his shirt in my blood-soaked hands and wept.

For the girl I'd been. For the girl who would never exist again.

El Diablo had been reborn in flames. *Mi Reina* had been reborn in water.

But our love was born in blood.

RAFAEL

*I*sa was silent as I guided her into the Mercedes, taking the driveway down to the docks. I gave her the little bit of time I knew she needed to process, knowing full well that I would push her and pull her out of the shell of her mind the moment we were on board. I guided her out of the Mercedes, taking her into the yacht wordlessly. The bedroom cabin called my name, and I hurried her inside it.

She didn't so much as glance around the sleek white lines of the master cabin as I guided her through it and into the luxury bathroom. The black and white marble of the bathroom was stunning as I turned on the shower, helping a quiet Isa out of her blood-stained dress. "I killed him," she whispered as I untied the knot on the wrap. It fell away from her torso, revealing the smooth contours of her body in the white lace I'd set out for her before leaving *El Infierno*. I pushed the straps off her shoulders, letting the fabric pool at her feet. With the most intimate parts of her concealed in the innocence of white and the black heeled sandals on her feet, she'd have been stunning with those things alone.

But the blood drying on her hands called to the devil

inside me, wanting to see her bathed in it. I touched a hand to the white of her bra, leaving a red mark on the fabric. "You did," I agreed. While it might have started with me taking her along for the journey, pressing the knife against Maxim's heart, the end had been all Isa.

She alone had dealt the killing strike.

She shivered as I wrapped a hand around her back, unclasping her bra and drawing it off of her. She stood as I knelt at her feet and pulled the heels off her one by one, gliding my hands up her thighs and leaving a trail of red until I grasped her underwear in my grip and tugged them down her thighs. She stared down at me blankly, lost to the reality of what she'd done.

Retreating further into her shell with every moment that passed.

I stood and made quick work of stripping off my suit and shoes until I was as naked as Isa. Guiding her into the shower, I let the water work to pull her back to the moment. I stood in front of her, taking her hands in mine and working to wash the blood from her skin even though I liked it there.

She watched the water run red as it flowed toward the drain, and it was only after my hands were free of blood that I grasped her chin and tilted her face up to mine. I leaned forward, teasing her lips with mine as I compelled her to come back to me. To accept who she was, because I sure as fuck did.

If she could love the devil, then she could love the queen who completed him.

She opened for me, letting me sweep inside and consume her with my kiss. I washed her body and her hair when I took breaks from kissing her, and then I pulled her out of the shower and dried her body. After I dried myself off, I lifted her into my arms and took her back to the bedroom, laying her out beneath me as I leaned into her space and rested my weight on my elbows.

She stared into my eyes, her unique stare feeling heavy. "You turned me into a monster," she whispered. "I should be begging you to let me go. I should want to get away from you, even if only to save myself."

I slid a hand into the side of her wet hair, running my thumb over her cheekbone as I smiled down at her. "You let me inside you," I murmured. "I took your innocence, and I corrupted you. I complicated you and made you mine. You think you can ever be free of me after all of that?" I asked, leaning forward to kiss her softly as the last pieces of the girl she'd been shattered beneath me while I watched. "I own your soul, *mi reina,* and you gave it to me willingly."

I positioned my hips between her legs to get her to spread wider for me, gliding inside her slowly and watching her face ignite with pleasure as I filled her. She moaned lightly, biting her lip and drawing my attention to it. When my cock hit her cervix, she wrapped her legs around me and pulled me closer. Wrapping me up in her arms, she accepted the truth of my possession.

She was mine fully in that moment, in a way she hadn't been before. She danced with the devil in the moonlight, lifting her hips to meet mine as I made love to her with slow, hard thrusts inside her. "I love you, *mi reina,"* I murmured, watching as her eyes lit with the confession the moment she felt it.

The moment she felt the truth to the words and understood that I meant more, because words would never be enough for what connected us.

Her teeth sank into her bottom lip, her face softening as she considered the words. "I love you too, my devil," she whispered, stretching her head up to capture my mouth with hers. I leaned into her, giving her more of my weight as my thrusts turned harsher. Taking her hard and deep as she moaned into my mouth. Her nails raked down my back, scratching my skin as I bit her lip in return.

She came, crying out her orgasm against my mouth as I rode her through it, watching as she came down from the high. As she settled and stared up at me while I moved inside her, I rolled to my back and kept us connected. She rose up on me, riding me slowly as my own orgasm loomed on the horizon.

Watching my wife, my queen, roll her hips on my cock while her breasts bounced with the motion, I determined there'd never been a sexier sight. That when I died, *that* would be the image that stuck in my head. Her face looking down at me from beneath the curtain of wet hair, her hands pressed to my chest and knowing that only moments before they'd been soaked in the blood of my enemy.

She was everything.

I came inside her with a muffled groan as she leaned forward and took my mouth with hers, working me through my climax as her pussy contracted around me with her second orgasm and milked the cum from my balls.

She collapsed against my chest, her body heaving with exertion. She'd sleep the entire way home, but first we'd need to get out of bed and say goodbye to my family.

Then we'd go home, with Isa my willing wife for the first time, and not my captive.

*I*sa chatted with my aunt in the kitchen while my cousins, uncle, and I discussed what she'd done with Maxim. They strongly disagreed with my insistence on involving her in the violence, but there was no denying that it had been exactly what she'd needed to understand me better.

To connect the two halves of the man she'd married.

I had no regrets, not even watching my uncle's frustrated face when he couldn't force me to see reason. Would I bring Isa along every time I needed to kill someone?

Of course not. But now I knew she was capable of protecting herself. Of protecting our children when they came. She would do whatever it took to save them.

"I've got to get Isa home," I said, glancing at the clock to see the late hour. She needed sleep, and it was already well past midnight. I looked over at the kitchen island where she'd been sitting and talking to Martina to find her gone. With a furrow to my brow, I stood and made my way over to my aunt. "Where's Isa?" I asked.

"She went to the bathroom a few minutes ago," she said, pointing her finger down the hall. I followed her gaze, moving around the corner. I saw Isa immediately.

She stood in the hallway, a picture frame in her hand that she'd pulled off the wall. I furrowed my brow, stepping up behind her as she blinked at it with something like shock on her face.

"Do you know this man?" she asked, her voice barely a whisper as she pointed to the only man in the photo. He stood with my mother and I, one of the only portraits of us as a family before her death.

After his death, I'd gotten rid of all the evidence of him

from my home. I wanted *nothing* to do with Miguel Ibarra. I never wanted to look at his face again.

So why did Isa look as if she'd seen a ghost?

"That's my father," I admitted, taking the photo from her hands. I stared down at my mother's hesitant smile, at the signs of the abuse she'd already begun to suffer at my father's hands as his sanity faded away and he was lost to the intense paranoia that consumed him. He'd never been a good man or husband, but there was bad and then there was worse.

"Your father?" she whimpered.

I hung it back on the wall, turning back to Isa when I realized she hadn't moved except to stare up at the picture as her cheeks grew wet with sudden tears.

"Princesa?" I asked, catching her chin with a delicate finger and forcing her to look at me. "What's wrong?"

There was a pause as she stared at me, blinking back the tears that consumed her. Her breathing turned ragged, as if she was caught in a waking nightmare.

"That's him," she whispered. "That's the man who threw me in the river."

*R*afael & Isa's story continues in Until Retribution Burns. Coming April 30th!

>>Pre-Order Now.

*F*all in love with a Bellandi? You can find Matteo, Ryker, and Enzo's stories in Adelaide's Bellandi Crime Syndicate series.

>>Start with Bloodied Hands.

ALSO BY ADELAIDE FORREST